The Stars and Stripes Between Us

a novel by
Audrey Rivero

AMONOUX

ISBN: 978-1-951803-09-4

Proofreading by Jenn Jarrett (jennjarrettedits.com)

"If you want the truth to stand clear
before you, never be for or against.
The struggle between "for" and "against"
is the mind's worst disease."
~Jianzhi Sengcan, c. 700 C.E.

"To dialogue."
~ Nate

For my parents, who taught me to think.

Chapter 1

Nathan Campbell, of course, was late.

He blew into the MIT ice rink like a gust of wind, flecks of snow in his rainbow hair, the bright glint of mischief in his eyes.

"Where the fuck have you been?" Tiffany snapped as she tightened the straps of her hockey pants. "We're about to go on."

He grinned, slinging his messenger bag into the molded plastic seats and digging into his much larger, much bulkier sack of equipment. "Nowhere."

Leo snickered. "Who is it this time, *Romeo*?"

"I don't know what you're talking about," Nate said with a coy wave, his other hand pulling out skates, pads, socks, gloves and throwing them into a tangled heap on the ground.

Tiffany scowled. "Well, hurry up. The other team is already on the ice."

She shot them one last glower before toddling through the open rink door and gliding out to join the rest of their players.

"I didn't realize we'd suddenly joined the Bruins," Nate said, yanking on his gear at top speed.

"You know Tiff," Leo drawled, lounging back on his elbows as if he, in all his long-limbed, dark-skinned, muscled glory, didn't need anything so pedestrian as warming up. "Can't take anything lightly, even a club sport." Leo adjusted his posture and Nate tried *not* to think about the shape of his roommate, even under all those

1

layers. "So how's Ross?"

Nate huffed in exasperation. "Totally disinterested. Dude walked *right* by me without so much as a lifted eyebrow. And he was in his *gym shorts* too." His voice trailed off into a pleading whine.

Leo chuckled, pushing to his feet. With the added inches of his ice skates, he looked positively gargantuan.

"You don't even know if he's into guys."

Nate winked. "Can't lose if you don't play, right?"

That deep, rumbling laugh boomed out of Leo, making the air around them feel like velvet. "Ever the optimist."

"Why shouldn't I be? I get the best of all worlds."

Leo shook his head, still laughing. "Well, you know he'll be at the crew party on Saturday."

"Urg." Nate dragged his helmet out of the chaos of his gear bag, trailing a scrap of hockey tape. "I was hoping to avoid that particular mess. You know who's hosting it, right?"

Leo patted Nate's shoulder. "What are a few drunk Republicans in the face of true love? Now let's go before Tiff eats our livers for breakfast."

There was a delicious release in stepping from the thick rubber padding around the rink onto the ice. Nate always thought it was the closest thing humans came to flying: that slick, weightless drifting on sharpened blades and the crisp, controlled crackle of stopping. Admittedly, he wasn't very good. He'd played a few years in middle school before theater started sucking up all his time. Two years ago, when their little squad of wide-eyed first years decided to join the queer community's club team—jokingly nicknamed the Gay Neutrals—he'd thought the muscle memory would come right back.

He'd been wrong.

At first, their whole team had been an utter disaster. With five players moving at top speed with almost no ability to stop, mayhem was never far away. More than once, Nate had been at the bottom of a pile-on simply because none of them were able to change course fast enough. But now, two seasons after that first game, Nate felt powerful and controlled on the ice.

He did a lap, grinning to himself.

If only he could be so put together in the *rest* of his life.

The referee whistled, and Nate, at a signal from Tiff, drifted to the midline. He was a fair starter, not their best, but the team liked to save Tiff for later. Besides, after the second bloody nose, the refs had given them a stern warning to tone her down.

Smiling behind the cage of his helmet, Nate tapped his stick on the ice and looked up, a witty taunt already on the tip of his tongue.

But when he saw the face in front of him, all words blew out of his brain like morning fog.

"Ready for a butt kicking?" sneered the most beautiful girl Nate had ever seen.

He had no response.

She was dazzling, with smooth chestnut skin and gold-flecked brown eyes. Her smile was wide and white and rimmed in full lips. He glimpsed a jet-black braid twining over one shoulder, shimmering like oil in the sun.

Hot damn, he thought, fighting to keep his mouth from falling open.

Thankfully, there wasn't enough time for her to notice him gawking at her. The referee's sharp whistle pierced his blissful little bubble, the puck fell between them, and she was off.

"Wake up, Nate!" Tiff shouted, zooming past him.

He shook his head, diving into the game with renewed determination.

The girl had the puck and was weaving between bodies with a dancer's grace. Nate came up behind her, using his stick for balance as he swerved to avoid one of their defensive players. His team's goalie, an ex-girlfriend of Tiff's, was shifting to block, but Nate could see the mystery woman from behind, see the way her hips were swinging right even as she feinted left.

"Watch it!" Nate called.

Too late.

The puck hit the left post with an echoing, metallic *clink* and ricocheted into the net, followed by the harsh grating of the buzzer.

She swung around, flashing a smug smile.

"Nice try," she said, and her voice was throaty and dense and *wonderful*.

Nate couldn't help but laugh. "Oh, it's on."

The game continued as most club sports do. There were a few crashes, a handful of people spontaneously falling over, and the two scores chasing each other higher. But to Nate, who had never been very sporty in the first place, the hockey rink had narrowed to the girl and her smile, to the dizzy orbiting of interested young people.

Tiffany made the next goal, Leo stole a pass, and then the mystery woman was back, evading Nate as if she could read his mind.

"Too slow," she taunted, taking another shot.

It missed.

"Am I distracting you?" Nate called.

"You wish!"

After the first period, Tiffany took charge and began to offer advice on which players to target. Nate was only half paying attention. He could feel the girl's eyes on his helmet, her curiosity on his back. And for a moment he wasn't thinking about Ross and his gorgeous calves and the fact that he was probably straight, dammit. This was Nate's show, the game he'd excelled at since before he even knew what it was.

Flirting.

4

The second period escalated quickly. Tiffany knocked over a tall, angry-looking member of the other team, who quickly retaliated after the face-off, barreling forward and scoring a goal himself. Nate ducked in, accepted a pass from Leo, and dove down the rink, plunging into the opposing team's territory.

She was at his side in a heartbeat.

"Can't get enough of me, can you?" Nate panted, pumping his elbows for momentum.

"Don't flatter yourself." She laughed, swerving toward him.

He ducked, spun, shot.

The buzzer sounded.

"Booyah," he said, pumping a fist.

The girl snorted. "What are you, a ninja turtle?"

He wanted to call after her, tell her that he'd never heard anyone make a joke about his *absolute favorite childhood show*. But she was already headed to the bench to get water as the second period ended.

"Leo," Nate said, swerving up to the break area, "what team are we—?"

"Careful with that one," Tiffany cut in, sweeping into the circle. "He keeps trying to check me." She jerked her chin at the leader of the other team, a dark-haired boy with thick eyebrows and what looked like a perpetual frown.

Leo laughed. "Maybe that's because you tried to trip him with your stick."

"Who, me?" Tiff did her best to look innocent. "Look, we've got this. Just keep our lead up for another twenty minutes—"

"And we'll solve world peace and win a million dollars," Leo said, feigning excitement.

Tiff punched his arm.

"And you," she said, rounding on Nate. "Your friend over

5

there seems great at sneaking in shots. Keep an eye on her, ok?"

"My pleasure," Nate said, one eye obediently on his target as she lifted her helmet to scratch her hairline, revealing a smooth, elegant neck.

As the third period started, Nate was aware of little else besides that black braid, swinging like a metronome. The buzzer sounded a few times, but he hardly cared if they were winning or losing. No, the score in his head was one of jeers and comebacks, a far more interesting tally.

"You play like my *abuela*," she said.

"Your *abuela* sounds like a badass," Nate called back, passing to Leo who immediately scored.

And then, seconds later after scoring herself: "Too bad there's no treatment for sucking."

"C'mon, that's just lazy," Nate said and was delighted to hear her laugh.

They were tied with two minutes to spare and Tiff was getting angry.

"Focus, everyone. We can do this!"

"Your teammate is a bit serious, isn't she?" the girl said as she and Nate bent in on either side of the referee holding the puck in the air.

"Don't worry. This is her having fun," Nate said.

"I'd hate to see her mad."

"Me too."

And then they were crashing together, her hip-checking him into the wall to steal the puck and sprint down the rink.

The clock counted down.

"GO!" Tiff screamed.

Nate was behind the beautiful player, Leo on his left, but she was fast, weaving through their defense, taking aim. The goalie shifted, but she passed to the angry one, who shot...

The puck flew in, thumping softly against the net.

Leo straightened, glancing back just in time to see the clock run to zero.

"That's the game," he said.

"Dammit." They both heard Tiffany mutter as she joined them in the circle, throwing her hand in the middle of their huddle and all but spitting out their "*No fear, we're queer!*" chant.

But Nate didn't care. He was grinning, buoyed by what felt like a game well played indeed. Sliding in line behind Leo to shake hands with their opponents, he watched the other team skate past him, waiting for his chance.

"Tell your *abuela* I did her proud," Nate said when she reached him, her hair fraying out of its braid, sweat dripping down her mahogany skin.

She only had time to laugh before moving on to shake their goalie's hand.

Leo looked over his shoulder, eyebrow arched. "Feeling spiritual there, bro?"

"Hmmm?" Nate said, watching her drift to the edge of the rink, surrounded by teammates. What would she look like under all that bulky gear?

Leo cleared his throat. "You do know who we just played, right?"

"Whoever they were, they were good."

And gorgeous, he thought to himself, toying with pick-up lines. *So, I guess we've already broken the ice, eh?*

"Those are the CCCs."

Nate didn't answer, eyes still following the other team as they filed off the ice.

Leo grabbed his shoulder and spun him around, looking like a

7

teacher trying to explain something to a particularly slow student.

"The Conservative Catholics on Campus?"

It took a moment for those words to burrow through Nate's excitement.

"*What?*"

"Bunch of fucking white supremacists," Tiffany said, barely bothering to keep her voice down as she followed them into the stands. "Too bad their hockey skills aren't as garbage as their ideas."

"Well," Nate said, glancing at the team shedding layers further down the rubber-coated walkway. "Shit."

Leo's smile twisted into a half-pitying, half-amused expression, as if to say, *better luck next time*.

But Nate only shrugged, his mind already shifting gears.

Whatever.

Like most of his crushes, it had been nothing but a brief amusement, a bit of passing fun. In fact, the vast majority of his dating life was like that, the prolonged act of falling from one bed into the next. It had occurred to him, once or twice, to worry if his constant bumping around in the dark had a cost, if he was becoming jaded or exhausted or romantically ADD. Or worse, if his exuberant physicality was hurting the rest of the bisexual community, many of whom weren't nearly as excitable and didn't appreciate being slut-shamed because of randy assholes like him.

But those concerns never lingered long.

After all, he had Ross to worry about and plenty more after him. Really, there was a whole *world* of people that Nate could fall in love with, people who cared about justice and freedom and the safety of children. People who didn't hide terrible beliefs behind beautiful faces.

No, this mystery woman might be a terrific hockey player, but she sure as hell wasn't right for him.

Chapter 2

Marina Salinas was trying to hold onto the bliss of their victory, not to mention a damn fun game. But as always, the temporary high was washing down the shower drain with her sweat. Changing out of her hockey clothes and stepping into the shower felt counterintuitively overwhelming, like dismantling the buffer that, for one euphoric hour, had kept the tidal wave of her world at bay. Back in her apartment she was again surrounded by chores, homework, applications, schedules, to-do lists. Even standing there, savoring the steam and heat and water pounding her shoulders, made her worry that she was wasting precious seconds of productivity.

She sighed, bracing against the wall and forcing herself to take deep breaths, to focus on the blue inlay pattern of the tiles.

Finally, when she couldn't stand the silence anymore, she turned off the tap.

Patting herself dry, Marina thought of the team they'd played. The Gay somethings. Normals? She'd long grown used to the unnatural hair colors and piercings that seemed so prevalent at MIT, but every so often it struck her how far she was from Virginia. And, even more shocking, how little she seemed to notice anymore. Had she actually been *interested* in that guy with the technicolor faux-hawk and scoundrel smile? An 18-year-old Marina would have been horrified by the idea of dating someone on a team named the Gay *anythings*, but it was amazing how much three years could change a person.

Maybe Jordan was right.

She needed a distraction.

Wrapping her bathrobe around herself, Marina stepped out into the combined dining and living area of their little two-bedroom apartment. The lights of Harvard Square flashed and arced in the far window, a display she used to call dizzying. When they'd found this place, Marina had protested that it was too small, too noisy, too far from campus. But Jordan had fallen in love with the historical brick building and Marina conceded, grudgingly, that some distance from school might be good for her.

As usual, Marina emerged from the bathroom to find Jordan and her boyfriend tangled together on the couch, their noses touching.

"You do have a room, you know," Marina said warmly as she padded around their kitchen table.

"And you have clothes," Ben shot back, pointedly not looking at her short bathrobe.

"Oh please. It covers the basics."

"That's the spirit of purity," Ben said, voice dripping with sarcasm as Jordan unknotted herself and rose to hand Marina a package.

"Arrived this morning. Sorry I forgot to give it to you before the game."

Marina took the thick envelope, trying to hide the slight quiver in her hands. It was the application packet her professor had told her about, for a fully funded science writing summer program at Stanford. Marina hadn't even wanted to write in for the *application*. She had a perfectly good internship at the Media Lab which would funnel her into a top tier master's program and a stable biomedical engineering job. How could she entertain the idea of risking her education—not to mention her heaping pile of debt—on something as precarious as a career in *journalism*? And on top of all that, the notion of her fitting into California culture was more ridiculous than her interest in the guy from the rink.

But Professor Rankin had insisted.

"Thanks," Marina said, thinking that she'd make sure her advisor saw the packet before recycling the paper.

"Good game, by the way," Jordan said with a small smile. "I was cheering for you."

"Their team captain is an absolute trash pile of a human," Ben inserted, rising to linger protectively behind Jordan.

"Ben!" Jordan said reproachfully, her soft voice as loud as it ever got.

"What? Didn't you hear what she called us? It's only fair."

"Doesn't that mean you're stooping to their level?" Marina asked, toweling off her hair in her bedroom doorway.

"No, it means I'm playing by their rules." Ben straightened, his thick, black eyebrows pulling together. "Besides, I'm not taking any shit from their type this year. It's ridiculous how much the school bends over backwards to protect *their* stupid feelings while ignoring our right to free speech."

"Ben..." Jordan said, face pinched with concern.

"It's happening on college campuses everywhere, and I won't stand for it. Not this year. I'm going to do something, you'll see."

Jordan touched his arm. "I know you will. Can I have a minute with Marina?"

Ben shrugged, unfazed by Jordan's dismissal. It was familiar ground between them, him getting hotheaded about some issue or another and pacing their apartment as he ranted, her listening and nodding and, at the right moment, calming him down. Marina often wondered what Ben would be like if he hadn't met the two of them

11

during the Catholic social for freshmen, expressing his outrage over coed housing and gender-neutral bathrooms and finding a sympathetic ear in Jordan.

A lot angrier, probably.

Jordan shook her head as the door to her bedroom shut with a louder-than-normal *thunk*. "Don't mind him. He's just bracing for another semester."

Marina understood. Ben, like the two of them, wore a crucifix proudly on his chest, not always an easy thing around Boston. Marina was used to the double takes, the stares, the surprised *are-you-really-wearing-that* raised eyebrows that made her feel like she was wearing a red A and not a sign of God.

Shifting the towel to dry the other side of her head, Marina leaned against the doorframe. "So did you really want to talk to me? Or did you just want a break from your boyfriend?"

"I heard that!" Ben called from behind the closed door.

Jordan smiled and it made her delicate face seem almost elfin. "I wanted to talk about that guy. Remember? The one I mentioned?"

Marina swallowed the explosive *not again* that threatened to burst out of her. She knew Jordan was just being nice, but she didn't have *time* for a new relationship, not with her coursework and volunteering and the internship application to think about.

She forced herself to look interested, inviting Jordan to continue.

"Well, it turns out he'll be at Ben's house party tomorrow. He's on the crew team with one of their roommates."

Marina rubbed the ends of her hair, stalling.

"Come on," Jordan wheedled. "You missed the last one, and even *you* don't want to do homework on a Saturday night."

"It's not about wanting—"

"This guy's perfect for you. He's tall, cute, Christian. His hair's a normal color."

Marina chuckled. "Sounds like a unicorn."

"Hey, I found one, didn't I? They do exist." Jordan looked up through her eyelashes in that pleading, puppy-dog way that even her professors couldn't resist.

Half-Vietnamese and half-Malaysian, Jordan was petite with straight black hair, a slender frame, and cherubic cheeks. It had been a delightful surprise for Marina, when moving from Virginia to their tiny shared dorm room, to meet this tiny, warm, quiet person who joined her for church on Sundays and didn't listen to loud music. And in the intervening years, Jordan had become far more than just a roommate. She'd become one of Marina's closest friends and confidantes.

Which had the unfortunate side effect that Jordan knew exactly how to get Marina to do what she wanted.

"Please?" Jordan begged.

Marina huffed. "You know I can't say no to you."

Jordan clapped her hands. "Perfect. You can help me set up. I think he'll be there early, so maybe you can get some time to talk before the drinking games start."

Marina rolled her eyes. *Drinking games*? She felt like it had been years since she'd been to a party with *drinking games*.

"Ok, so what's this guy's name?"

Jordan smirked knowingly. "Gonna Facebook stalk him?"

"Maybe."

"It's Austin Scali. Check out his climbing pictures. They're really something."

"I can still hear you!" Ben called, and they both burst out laughing.

But as Marina clicked her door shut, she felt a thrum of something she couldn't quite describe. Was it envy? Loneliness? Or

13

maybe just that undertow of stress that seemed to vibrate like a tuning fork in her ribcage, constant and relentless. There was so much to *do* and agreeing to attend a party, even on a Saturday night, felt wasteful, even negligent.

"Don't forget to have fun," her *mamá* had said on their last phone call. But how could Marina have *fun* when her parents had sacrificed so much to bring her to America and were paying to send her here and working double shifts to make sure she didn't have to? Every wasted second felt like dollars down the shower drain, like little stones added to the pile she'd carry for years. College was too expensive, too important to just *have fun*.

She started her favorite Spotify playlist to tune out the low murmurs and giggles coming from Jordan's room — the couple was waiting for marriage for the big event, but there was a lot of ground the Bible wasn't specific on. Brushing her hair, Marina decided she'd make an appearance, for Jordan's sake. She'd be a good friend, accrue a little social time to tell her parents about on Sunday, and then come home to get a healthy full night's sleep.

Chapter 3

Nate spread his arms, grinning at his two roommates.

"Too much?"

Leo, who was reclining with his hands folded behind his head, watching *Dark* for the second time, frowned.

"I'm not sure it conveys the right message."

"What?" Nate said, looking down at his graphic-T. "I love this one."

Which was an understatement. This shirt, a gift from his mom last Christmas, was his absolute favorite. It was a simple black background with the words *I came, I saw, I made it awkward* written in rainbows with a cat stretching against the last letter. Nate saved it in the back of his closet for special occasions, privately dubbing it "lucky" in his mind. And, with his frustrated affection for Ross growing more desperate by the day, Nate had decided he needed all the luck he could get.

Leo snorted, eyes sliding back to the TV. "I sure hope he gets your sense of humor."

"If not, I'll just have to retrain him," Nate said. "Besides, who doesn't love cats?"

"I don't," Tiffany said, not looking up from her laptop.

"You monster!"

She huffed. "You wouldn't like them either if your grandma

had seven and they'd all bitten you." Tiff's fingers flew over the keyboard, blue light flashing in her enormous reading glasses.

"What are you working on?" Nate said, bending around to look at the screen. It was a crowded Twitter feed, filled with exclamation points and GIFs.

"Taking down some local news anchor who thinks he can make jokes about *women's work* like we're still in the fifties." She hit enter with a flourish. "Let's see how he feels under *that* salt dump."

Nate met Leo's gaze over her head. Though neither of them spoke, they both knew what this meant.

Something was wrong.

When Nate had first met Tiffany, he'd thought of her as a machine. On the surface, Tiff was one-woman army against bigots and internet trolls and the uninformed masses. She was always first to correct assumptions or language in their study groups, among their other queer friends, and had even, on several notable occasions, confronted their political science professors outright during class. She was the founder and main contributor of the student-run news blog, The Dyke Digest, and attended or planned every protest, march, and rally that Nate had ever heard of. To the outside world, she was a hardened warrior, made of steel.

But after living with her, Nate and Leo had come to realize that she wasn't made of steel at all. No, Tiff was what Leo liked to call a cream puff. All that thorny rage had been weaponized to protect something soft and tender, ghosts from her past that she rarely spoke about. And the more vocal she became about social issues, the more those ghosts were haunting her.

Knowing she wouldn't tell them until she was ready, Nate grabbed his coat with feigned nonchalance.

"Well," he said, shrugging it on, "it sounds like you've got *thrilling* Saturday plans, but I'd really love some company for this shindig. Any takers?"

"Not me," Tiff said, flicking her gaze up and then right back to her task. "I deal with enough assholes online. I don't need to party with them."

"Oh c'mon. It's a crew thing! There'll be tons of people there. You'll hardly notice a few far-right idiots in the crowd."

She kept her eyes on the screen. "No thank you."

Nate shifted his attention to Leo, smiling hopefully.

"Eh," Leo said, shoving to his feet and stretching languidly, "I've got nothing better to do. Could be exciting to see some drunk Nazis."

Tiff made a noise of disapproval, but Nate slapped his friend on the shoulder.

"Thanks, man."

Leo waved off Nate's gratitude. "Hey, I'm always down for free booze. Let me get my coat."

Leo disappeared into his room, humming under his breath.

Nate waited, rocking on his heels, buttoning and then unbuttoning his jacket. The wind howled outside, and Tiff was quiet, still typing away, and he felt the overpowering urge to pull out his phone, check his Facebook feed, *move*. Was it nerves? Or just his regular twitchy impatience? He tried to convince himself that there was nothing to worry about, no pressure on this evening, just a bit of fun.

It didn't work.

Worry filled his undistracted mind, already anticipating the rejection. Or worse. Ross had seemed sweet and put-together in their Urban Planning and Development classes, but what did that really mean? Nate had dated enough jerks—of all genders—to wonder. What if Ross was the kind of guy who didn't call back? Or spread

17

nasty rumors? What if Nate realized he wasn't all that interested when things got hot and he had to endure yet another anticlimactic sexual romp that left him feeling cheap and even lonelier than before?

Was it even worth going out into the cold to chase down a stupid fantasy?

But at that moment, Leo reemerged, wrapping a thick scarf around his neck. "Ready?"

Nate grinned, pulling his hat over his ears. "Always."

Chapter 4

Marina had often wondered how Ben had found such a beautiful house to live in. The two-and-a-half-story, four-bedroom, free-standing home was all elegant paneling and hardwood floors, modern appliances fitting elegantly into an old-world feel. It was clean and bright, with furniture that was the perfect blend of manly and comfortable. The walls were decorated with colorful posters of faraway places: Paris, Shanghai, Moscow, Delhi. Even the clutter was luxurious. The side tables and built-in shelves were festooned with trinkets the various inhabitants had brought back from their travels or hometowns, treated with the carelessness of children's toys. As if a souvenir bought in London was little more than a relic to be left behind, an *I was here* signature or funny joke.

To Marina, who had stepped onto her first airplane since infancy for the MIT interview, it seemed obscenely lush.

But then, that was Benjamin Sharps.

"You morons are gonna be drunk before anyone gets here," Ben was accusing from the far corner of the dining room, surrounded by his housemates and gesticulating with a water bottle as Marina and Jordan set out bowls of chips, M&M's, pretzels, and ice.

"We're pregaming, Ben," Austin shot back. "You know, games? Fun?"

"I have plenty of fun without compromising my brain cells, thank you very much."

Jordan giggled, already tipsy after one cider. Marina could see the night unfolding before her like reverse déjà vu: Ben getting more and more energized as he debated politics and shouted jibes across the room. Jordan passing out on his bed upstairs after a handful of drinks, probably no more than three.

And her standing awkwardly among strangers, wishing she was home.

Oh joy, Marina thought, already looking forward to the comfort of her bed and her laptop and a few episodes of *Friends*.

"Eh, I've got brain cells to spare," Austin joked, tapping his Solo cup against the mug his rowing friend had chosen to drink out of. Ross? Marina couldn't remember. If she was being honest, they both looked the same. Tall, broad, with half-zip sweaters and khaki pants. Either one of them could have walked right out of an L.L.Bean catalogue.

"Cute, isn't he?" Jordan muttered under her breath as the boys continued to bicker.

"Sure," Marina said with loving exasperation, holding up the string of lights so Jordan could pin them to the ceiling. "He's fine."

"Ben says he's part of a Big Brother program with the local community. And he's an Eagle Scout."

"Yeah, I saw the picture on Instagram." Marina adjusted, helping Jordan move the chair she was standing on further down the wall. "He seems nice."

From across the room came a guffaw. Ben's voice rose louder to continue the impression he was doing of a student he'd faced off with last semester, debating about gun statistics. Marina had already heard the story twice.

"I can't wait to see who Ben butts heads with this year, huh?" she muttered sarcastically as Jordan clambered back onto the chair.

Jordan didn't take the bait.

"Marina Salinas, you can*not* just hole yourself up in your room this whole semester. God didn't make us to be alone, you know." Jordan's voice was muffled as she stretched both arms as high as they'd go, reaching for a hook under the molding that had been installed long before any of the current housemates had lived here. "You've got to at least *try* dating before you give up on it."

Marina felt her shoulders hunching in defense without her instruction. She wanted to tell Jordan she didn't have *time,* that there were more important things to do than waste her evenings on dates with unsuitable partners who probably wouldn't last longer than a New Year's resolution. She wanted to say that just because *Jordan*'s boyfriend had practically fallen into her lap didn't mean it was so easy for the rest of them, that Marina and Boston didn't match, that even the so-called Christian boys around here didn't have the faintest resemblance to anyone she'd want to spend her *life* with. MIT had been a great education, but she'd already come to terms with the fact that this wasn't the place for her to find a husband.

However, she knew from experience that those arguments would fall on deaf ears. So Marina shrugged, forcing a smile as she helped her friend down.

"If I go talk to him, will you leave me alone?" she said in a low voice as they went over to where Ben was holding court.

Jordan winked. "Maybe."

Then Ben was throwing out an arm and pulling Jordan tight against his side, still waving the water bottle around with his other hand. "So apparently, for this social commentary class I'm taking, I have to start a blog."

"You mean like that Dyke one everyone's always going on about?" Ross asked, lounging against the table.

Ben smiled mischievously. "Something like that. But I'm thinking of putting this girl to the test, right?"

Austin groaned. "Oh man, what are you gonna do now?"

"Well, I'm gonna call my website Red Nation, if that gives

21

you any hint."

The two other boys half-laughed, half-sighed.

"Let the fireworks begin," Austin said, shaking his head.

Ben's eyes narrowed. "I was *going* to ask if you would help me start it."

Ross lifted his hands, glancing left and right in a facsimile of being cornered. "Not me, dude. I don't deal with any of that political shit."

Ben rounded on Austin. "And you?"

Austin shrugged, taking a swig of his beer. "Possibly."

Jordan threw Marina a *see-what-I-mean* look and Marina pulled up one side of her mouth, hoping it looked like a smile. But the truth was that the spitfire energy that drew quiet Jordan to loud-mouthed Ben wasn't really her thing. The idea of Austin writing long, charged think-pieces about things she already agreed with didn't quite get her engines going.

Then again, she wasn't sure what did.

As Austin and Ben began to discuss the various topics they might post about, Marina forced herself to look at Austin with an evaluating eye. He was handsome, sure. And, judging from the way he responded to Ben's ideas, intelligent. Jordan said he was studying some kind of engineering, so they'd have lots to talk about. And he was a man of faith, allegedly—she could see no sign of a cross. So why did she feel so… blah? Why did the idea of going on a date with him feel about as exciting as going to the dentist? Marina didn't really believe in love as a concept, not the way the songs and movies liked to portray it. To her, love was the dull and unglamorous act of compromise, of choosing a person day in and day out, of sacrificing for family and duty and all the things that kept a real life afloat. Love wasn't this uncontrolled magic that people liked to make it out to be. It was a choice, logical and rational.

So, if he was such a rational choice, she had to give it a shot. Didn't she?

Austin was telling a story about a girl he'd dated last semester who honestly believed math was racist. Marina leaned in, expressing disbelief with the others, *participating* as her mother might say.

"I guess you could argue that people always think Asians are good at math?" Jordan said over Ben's indignant snort.

"But you *are* good at math, babe."

Jordan ducked her head, trying to hide her proud smile.

"Sounds like quite a character," Marina said, taking a small step forward to join the circle.

Austin's eyes fell on her. The way they brightened with interest told Marina that she wasn't the only one who'd been prepped for the evening.

"She was," he said. "Nice girl, but super into all that gender nonsense."

Marina tilted her head, raising her eyebrows to invite him to continue. "Gender nonsense?"

"You know, that stuff about people being *non-binary*."

"That's total horse crap," Ben cut in, ignoring Jordan's *shut up and let them talk* glare. "There's no such thing as non-binary."

Austin shrugged. "I mean, whatever, people can live their lives. But she kept wanting me to call her friend *they* and stop saying *guys* when I walked in the room. It was exhausting."

"But it's totally hypocritical," Ben raged, apparently not noticing Jordan's attempt to poke him in the stomach. "Anyone who so much as *questions* global warming is branded some kind of 'science denier,' and then *they* try to argue that there are more than two genders? That gender is just a social construct? Ridiculous."

"I don't know," Marina inserted, heading off one of Ben's tirades. "Maybe there really are people who aren't one gender or the

23

other. I mean, we can't read their minds. And lots of folks feel strongly about this, right? They're lobbying to get the school to teach it in my biology classes. So it can't just be made up."

"It's a political ploy," Ben said.

Jordan elbowed him in the ribs, hard.

"Or a cry for attention," Austin said over Ben's surprised *oomph*, gaze focused on Marina. "I mean, this whole movement sure seems like a fad that people are jumping on. I know there have always been people who weren't comfortable with conventional gender roles or sexualities, but there are so many these days. I hear the population of people who identify as transgender has doubled. There's no way it's all real."

Marina pursed her lips. "I wouldn't be so sure. People used to write off postpartum depression as female hysteria. Look how wrong we were about that."

"Don't even get me started on depression," Ben muttered, guarding his stomach with his water bottle.

"I'm just saying," Marina went on. "I'm open to hearing why a person thinks they're between genders. Or neither, I guess."

Austin's eyebrows pulled together, thoughtful. Ross was watching them, wide eyes bouncing back and forth like he was following a tennis match.

"So you believe they're right?" Austin said after a pause.

Marina's mouth curved up in a challenging smile, as if Austin was meeting her on the hockey rink and not for a relaxing back-to-school party. "Right about what?"

"The fact that people can be born in the wrong body?"

"I mean, it's obvious some individuals think so. And I respect that. But the question is, what do we about it? How can we help them?"

Austin folded his arms. "Help them?"

24

"Of course. They're people, just like us. And, just like us, they deserve whatever treatment will result in the best outcome."

"So you're in favor of transitioning kids?" Austin's tone made it very clear how he felt. "Or using puberty blockers?"

"I didn't say that. But I'm not entirely against it either. I think there's a lot of research to be done."

"Hmm," Austin said, tossing back the rest of his beer.

There was a moment of dense silence. Marina could feel Ben's gaze on her, Jordan's worry, Ross's amusement. But she was watching Austin, wondering why it felt so good to push back. Only a handful of years ago, she'd have been agreeing with him, laughing with Ben, letting herself get swept along by the jeers and jokes that were so normal back in rural Virginia.

What was happening to her?

Just then, as if to rescue her, the doorbell rang.

"Coming!" Ben called.

Austin stepped aside to let his roommate through, watching Marina with an inscrutable expression. She met his gaze without blinking, eyes flinty, arms folded to mirror his posture.

"It appears I need another drink," he said without looking at his cup. "Can I get you one?"

"Yes, thank you," Marina answered, ignoring Jordan's completely unsubtle grin. "I'll take a cider."

Austin dipped his chin, exchanged a look with Ross, and left.

As Jordan hooked an arm through hers and dragged her into the living room to make way for the newcomers, Marina tried to rally some excitement for his return, to convince herself this would be fun, maybe even fateful.

But secretly, she felt like it was going to be a long night.

Chapter 5

Nate was trapped in a conversation about baseballs.

Leo and some Indian kid had started, as a joke, to debate the various effects that ball construction could have on score. This had devolved into a full-on argument about how the recent uptick in home runs had been a direct result of computerized factories that made the margin of error significantly smaller and led to more perfectly sized and weighted baseballs. They disagreed vehemently, it turned out, about whether or not there should be an official push to revert to the previous standards, therefore making baseball more "interesting," or if the factories should continue to improve their precision in an effort to keep the game as fair as possible.

Fucking nerds, Nate thought, swirling his beer and watching Leo gesture emphatically to make some point about ball spin.

He'd tried, on more than one drunk occasion, to make things work with Leo. There was a myriad of reasons it was a stupid idea: they lived together, Nate was too pale and un-muscled to be Leo's type, their friendship was too important. But when Nate stumbled home after particularly bad rejections, it was Leo's warmth he was drawn to, Leo's voice that comforted, Leo's friendship that sustained him. He knew it wasn't really *that* kind of affection, for either of them. But sometimes it was difficult to determine the boundary between lust and friendship, especially when Nate had stepped over

27

that line more times than he cared to count.

Dammit, where's Ross? Nate thought, rolling onto his toes to scan the crowd. He usually appreciated his six-three vantage point, but in this crowd of rowers he could barely see the entrance, much less individual faces.

"But you can't argue that it's *worse* to have more regulated balls," the Indian kid was saying with fervor.

"Sure I can," Leo said, leaning in. "It's objectively worse for the game to have more home runs."

"Everyone loves home runs!"

"Because they're rare. If they become less rare, then they aren't as fun, the scoring goes up, and the audience is bored."

Like me, Nate thought, finishing his drink.

The guy threw his hands up. "But it's only fair that all balls should be the same."

"Too bad evolution didn't get that memo," Nate muttered.

The other student looked at him blankly. Leo snorted into his beer.

"I need more alcohol," Nate said louder, pointing to his cup and ducking out before he had to explain the joke.

As he wove through a crowd of sorority girls and sports bros, Nate found himself wondering why he was even there. Ross was gorgeous, sure, but right for him? Probably not. Like everyone else at this party, Ross wore a pea coat and probably vacationed at Cape Cod. Nate had fucked *enough* of those in high school to satisfy him for a lifetime. So why was he barking up this stupid tree again? To please his parents? To feel wholesome?

Was he just bored?

There was a line at the fridge, so Nate waited, playing with the neck of his bottle as he scanned the tops of heads, looking for a particularly dark one.

His gaze snagged on sleek black hair at a much lower altitude than he was expecting.

Hockey girl.

She was squeezing her way into the kitchen, only a few feet away from Nate, brandishing an empty bottle of her own.

Before he could stop himself, he was calling out to her.

"Hey!"

He froze.

Why did I do that?

But she was already stopping, turning to him with the surprised openness of someone caught off-guard. And Nate found himself breathless, the air knocked out of him by the power of those gold-flecked eyes. Without consciously deciding to, he began to wonder what those wide lips might taste like, how the skin of her neck would feel under his mouth. What he could say to end the night with answers to those questions...

Don't be stupid. She's a bigot, he told himself firmly.

But a smile was spreading over her features, cautious and tired but dazzlingly bright. He found himself wanting, no, *needing* to make her laugh, to drive that slightly weary look away.

"Hey, it's the ninja-turtle," she said, tossing her empty beer into the overflowing recycling bin and stepping around the tiny kitchen table to move closer to him. "Still sore about losing?"

"I'll recover," Nate said with a grin, folding his arms in his best imitation of Leo. "Didn't expect to see you here."

She tilted her head, hair tumbling to one side in a glorious fan. "Oh?"

He pointed to the cross on her chest, hanging from an elegant gold chain over the modestly high V of her shirt.

"Aren't you supposed to be like sober for life or something?"

She laughed. "I'm Catholic, not Mormon."

"Can't say I know the difference."

"There's a great musical to explain it." The crowd around the fridge had thinned and she was reaching inside. She withdrew two ciders, fingers expertly wrapped around the necks of the bottles. "Want one?"

Nate's nod turned into an expression of surprise as she used the countertop to pop off the cap.

"You're unexpected," Nate said, accepting the bottle.

She cocked one hip, leaning it against the kitchen counter in a way that was altogether too distracting. "And what did you expect?"

"Fire and brimstone?"

"I'm saving that for later."

"Oh, so there's a later now?"

She smirked. "I think that's up to you, isn't it?"

Nate waved a dismissive hand. "*Psht*, that's just patriarchal nonsense. Who decided men have to make the first move anyway? I never agreed to that."

She was shifting positions, half-sitting on the counter as if she intended to stay for the conversation.

For some reason, the thought made Nate ridiculously happy.

"I think women tend to find it more romantic," she said.

"Sure, women who've been socially indoctrinated to believe that men should be in control."

One of her eyebrows arched. "You think it's all societal indoctrination? What about biology?"

"Gender roles are a construct. There's nothing biological about them."

A laugh burst out of her, but it wasn't mocking. It was surprised, a sort of *I can't believe you said that* sound.

"Funny, we were just talking about this earlier. You really believe there's no such thing as biological gender?"

30

"Of course."

"But what about evolution? What about the way chimpanzees behave?" Her tone, to Nate's surprise, was politely interested, as if she really wanted to hear the answer and wasn't just waiting for the opportunity to strike. Nate shrugged again, half-anticipating, half-dreading the inevitable explosive terminus this conversation was leading to.

At least it'll make it easy.

"Well, obviously there are *physical* differentiators between sexes. I mean, genitalia and all that."

"So you acknowledge there's a difference," she cut in, but not aggressively. More to clarify.

"Sure, but *gender* is an internal thing. It's different than sex. We're born with a natal sex, but gender is something that's taught to us. Which means you can be born with a sex that doesn't match your preferred gender."

"But that defeats your argument, right? If, say, you're born with female parts but a male gender, then that's because the male gender has different behaviors and this theoretical person adopts those, behaving like a man."

Nate shook his head. "It doesn't have to be that binary. There's plenty of evidence that those behaviors aren't hardwired, that the roles of 'men' and 'women' are constructed by the society they exist in. Therefore, theoretically, our ideas about gender should be a lot more fluid than we've historically allowed."

"If that's true, then how can you explain the organic deviation of interests in really equal places, like Sweden? Or the raw personality differences that have been repeatedly shown with big data aggregates?"

"Those people have probably absorbed enough from their surroundings to still be internalizing their given roles."

31

"You don't think there's any kind of natural inclination?" she asked, and Nate had the strange sensation of the noisy kitchen falling away, the rest of the world blurring until all he could see was her face, her eyes, her question hanging in the air between them. "For example, that men tend to naturally be more interested in engineering and women more naturally interested in healthcare and teaching?"

"No."

Her lips quirked. "The data don't agree with you on that one."

Nate frowned. "There's no *data* because there's no way to prove it's not learned behavior. You can never isolate a person's nature from the environment they grew up in. And claiming so is dangerous."

"How could facts be dangerous?"

Nate was leaning in to hear her, close enough that it would have been uncomfortable if he hadn't been so absorbed by the conversation.

"Because think of how stuff like that could be used. It would be an excuse to stop pushing for more women in STEM or management or government. It would make it easy to write off the differences as inevitable and not a social justice problem."

"Inconvenient statistics are still statistics."

"That's too reductionist. Even if there *are* differences, which there aren't, how would that information be helpful? It would be grossly unethical to use trends to make decisions or treat individuals as if they should be representative of a group."

She took a thoughtful sip. "Isn't it better to do the research, though? Allow the scientists to at least *try* to find out?"

"But it will always be a chicken and the egg question. Are women less interested in being computer scientists because there are less women *in* computer science and therefore young women can't picture themselves in computer science? Or are they less interested because they were born that way?"

"Or, to return to the original point, do women naturally want men to take charge or have they been conditioned to *think* they want that?"

Nate drew back, surprised. "Exactly."

She looked at the ceiling, as if to consider her own question.

"I think it's probably some of both, right? I mean, I grew up watching *Pride and Prejudice* and falling in love with Disney princes and heroes who saved the day. So I suppose I've been conditioned. But I do think there's an evolutionary aspect to it, that women are drawn to traditionally strong men because they'll make healthier offspring and protect them, right?"

Nate took a big sip of his cider, trying not to think about the huge, muscled rowers around him and his own underdeveloped pecs.

"So it's probably somewhere in the middle," she concluded.

"Maybe," he admitted, glad Tiffany wasn't here to witness such a concession of ideals. "But don't you think the world would be better if we evolved past our own base instincts?"

"Sure," she said, swirling her bottle. "But that's like saying wouldn't it be better if we didn't die? That's not the world we live in."

"People can change."

"I think human nature works on a different scale than you're thinking."

"So we should just give up? Act like chimpanzees and gorillas?"

The girl laughed and the sound was bell-like, crystal clear and filled with a richness that made Nate desperate to hear it again.

"I think we shouldn't try to deny the world as it is," she said, still grinning. "It seems like a foolish venture to pretend things aren't as they are."

"Well, I like to believe in what *could be*."

"Of course," the girl said, saluting with her almost-empty bottle. "But we aren't there yet."

Nate whistled. "We sure aren't." He paused, knowing full well where this was going. But she hadn't lost her shit yet, had she? He'd been waiting for it, the lightning-strike of outrage, the openmouthed scandal, the explosion that would let him shrug her off, walk away, and go back to hunting down the reason he was at this party in the first place.

She wasn't making it easy on him.

"So if you think—"

She cut him off, holding up one finger.

"I need to use the restroom," she said, placing her bottle down with a soft *clink*, barely audible over the din of beer pong in the other room. "But I do want to continue this. Will you still be here when I get back?"

"You aren't getting rid of me that easy," he said, lifting himself onto the table with an expectant smile. She laughed again, and he felt warm, light, as if he might float right out of the damn kitchen.

As she edged into the crowd, Nate found his eyes following her quite against his will, even after she'd disappeared through a knot of ludicrously tall and well-built athletes. For once, Nate wasn't looking at them as potential bedmates but as competition for the pretty girl with the strong opinions.

Uh oh...

No, it was fine. He wasn't *interested* in her, not really. She was beautiful, sure. Distractingly so. But he was only sticking around to set her right, to stand up for his beliefs and make sure she didn't walk away from this with the false impression that she'd won ground. It was *important* that he talk to her about these things, show that he

34

cared enough to fight for the correct ideas. Maybe he could even change her mind. What did it matter that he was thinking about her eyes, her hair, the fact that her voice sounded like an aural manifestation of honey? He was just like that. It didn't mean anything that his stupid romantic brain had already zoomed into overdrive because that's not what tonight was about.

Oh man, she and Tiff would be a disaster, he thought, chuckling to himself.

His chuckle cut short when, all of a sudden, Ross appeared.

He was alone, a bit unsteady on his feet, stumbling toward the keg on the opposite side of the kitchen. There was a hazy vagueness to his smile that Nate knew all too well, the perfect blend of bad-idea drunk and still-consenting sober.

This was his chance. He could sidle up, make some clever joke about finding a place to "chat." He'd been pining over this kid all Christmas and this was *exactly* the opportunity he'd been hoping for. Nate shoved off the counter, straightening, planning his entrance...

What about hockey girl?

If he left, she'd come back to an empty spot. He imagined she wouldn't be too offended by his disappearance—after all, people came and went at parties all the time.

But their argument...

Nate stood frozen, tugged in both directions. He watched mutely as Ross finished filling his red plastic cup and ducked back into the fray, as the party absorbed that mouth-watering pair of shoulders as if he'd never been there.

Nate was still there when hockey girl returned with another two ciders.

"Wanna duck outside?" she asked. "It's too loud in here."

35

Chapter 6

What on Earth am I doing?

But there was no time for Marina to answer her own question, because the boy with the bright hair was tapping his chin, leaning against the porch railing, contemplating their game. She'd never heard of Truth or Drink, but he'd explained it like a challenge and she'd never been good at turning those down. So now she was four ciders and two shots in, holding a big cup of suspiciously delicious Jungle Juice that one of Ben's housemates had handed her. Austin still hadn't come looking for her, and Marina found that she wasn't all that upset about it.

Although she did wish there was an easy way to get out of this game.

"Alright," Nate said, gesturing a little too emphatically. "I've got one. Number of sexual partners."

Marina snorted to hide the flush of embarrassment climbing up her neck. "You don't pull your punches, do you?"

"Well? You gonna answer or what?"

Marina drank.

"Oh *ho*, interesting! You know what they say about Catholic schoolgirls."

"I really don't," Marina said, wiping sticky juice off her lips.

He looked up at the roof of the house's enclosed porch in an expression of perfect innocence. "Your turn."

"What do they say about Catholic school girls?" Marina asked to buy more time.

"That they're virtuous and pure?"

Marina planted her hands on her hips.

"Fine," he said, waving a hand. "That they're fucking wildcats in bed."

Marina coughed in surprise.

"I'm sorry," he said, ducking his head with a surprisingly adorable look of embarrassment.

"No, it's fine," she said, pounding her fist against her chest. "I never said you were wrong."

His eyes widened, and she couldn't help but laugh.

"Anyway, my question. Hmmmm." She drummed her fingers against the arm of her puffy winter jacket. They'd had to fetch them within five minutes, but it was worth it to get away from the music and shouting and one particularly exuberant game of Slap-Cup. "Ok, here's one: how many times have you fallen in love?"

"What are we, eighth graders?"

"Does that mean you plan to drink?"

He rolled his eyes, but Marina was watching the way his cheek twitched, as if he was clenching his teeth.

He drank.

"Ok, ok," he said before she could comment, "I've got one. What's the most embarrassing thing that's ever happened to you?"

Marina considered her cup. She could drink, oh how she wanted to. But that didn't seem in the spirit of the game.

Dammit.

She looked up through her eyelashes, blushing furiously, at once wishing she was somewhere else and, oddly, never wanting to leave this porch.

"I was working in the ER last year, doing an internship for an anatomy class required for my major. And the attending I was working under pulled me aside, asked if I wanted to see something cool." Marina could feel her whole body heating up, as if she was back in the moment, under the sterile hospital lights, surrounded by the chirps and beeps of lifesaving machines. "There was this guy who'd sliced his toe open. It wasn't even bleeding that badly, but part of the bone had come off and they had to figure out if it was still attached to the tendon." She shuddered. "Anyway, the doctor started prodding around the wound, which was numbed but the poor guy could still feel pressure. And watching his expression, I could imagine what it felt like." Marina was back in the moment, looking at the gruff gentleman from Dorchester as he winced and gritted his teeth. She swallowed. "I... stepped out of the room. And fainted right in the middle of the hallway."

He began to snicker. "Really?"

"Yes," Marina said, kicking him gently. "Don't laugh! They had to admit me to make sure I didn't have any brain damage."

He struggled to look serious. "And did you?"

"No." Marina tucked into her shoulders like a turtle. "But I needed two stitches."

"I'm sorry."

She glared at him. "You don't look very sorry."

"Hey, you're beating me at my own game! That makes me sorry."

"That's right, it's my turn." Marina narrowed her eyes. Her gaze scraped over him, tracing his brazen smile, looking for a weakness.

That's when she finally noticed his shirt, visible through the open buttons of his coat.

"Hah, that's great! Where did you get that?"

"Is that my question?"

"No!" Marina threw up one hand. "No, that's not it." She scoured her brain. *I need more practice doing stuff like this.* "Are you straight?" she blurted without thinking.

"Nope. Queer and proud, baby."

Marina was surprised by the disappointment that curled around her spine and tightened, cutting off her breath, dimming her smile.

She leaned back, taking a sip even though it wasn't her turn. "Have you always been?"

"One question only," he said, waggling a finger. "But yeah, was kinda born this way. You know how it is."

"Can't say I do."

"What, never daydreamed about the sexy nuns at school?"

Marina laughed, but even in her own ears it was a hollow, lackluster sound.

What is wrong *with me?*

"I can't say any of them were particularly sexy."

"Poor things were probably repressed as shit."

"What would you know about being repressed?"

He tilted his head back, grinning as if to himself, and Marina couldn't help but notice the strong line of his jaw, the curve of his clavicle, the jut of his Adam's apple.

She compelled herself to focus on his face.

"Believe it or not," he drawled. "I wasn't always so fabulous. In fact, I was pretty strait-laced until high school."

"What changed?"

"Theatre," he said simply, looking sideways at her. "Turns out I was a total ham."

"I'm shocked." Marina leaned back on her elbows, staring at the frosted windows. "Do you still perform?"

"Naw, not since I graduated. Too much to do."

"Like what?" Marina asked, knowing she should cut her losses, leave now, stop whatever-this-was and find Jordan. But she found herself wanting to hear the answer.

"Hockey, as you know." He took a sip and she watched the movement of his neck as he swallowed. "My roommate is really socially engaged, so she keeps me pretty busy."

"You mean like protests and stuff?"

He looked at her, meeting her gaze the same way he had in the kitchen, only now his eyes were slightly glassy, a little unfocused.

She couldn't look away.

"Sounds like you don't approve," he said.

"People protest a lot these days."

"There's a lot to change."

"And you skipping class is going to fix it?"

They were leaning in, and Marina couldn't deny that there was a gravitational pull here, a yearning to make him understand, to keep him talking.

"Hopefully," he went on, "it'll make powerful people pay attention. Protests have changed the world before."

"You're awfully concerned about changing the world."

He jerked back, for the first time looking truly surprised. "Isn't everyone?"

Marina considered. "I'm concerned about changing myself, my life, and my community. The world is a pretty big place. I'd rather focus on the things I have power over."

"That's showing your privilege."

"Privilege?" Marina could feel herself swelling, thinking of the tiny ranch house she'd grown up in, the raw skin on her mother's hands, the burn scars that made train tracks up her father's arms. "Who are you to say I'm privileged? You don't know the first thing

41

about me."

"Well, you're here, right? At one of the most prestigious schools in the country. You're healthy and educated and obviously smart enough to use it."

Marina opened her mouth, but nothing came out. She closed it, staring through the open door at the milling students in their elegant sweaters and trendy boots. It was a room full of the kinds of people she'd spent her whole life looking in on. But whose fault was that?

After all, she was at the party too.

"I guess you're right," she said, feeling like the words were pulled out of somewhere deep inside her.

He shrugged. "It's always hard to recognize your own privilege. Hell, I've got a whole stack of things to be aware of. White, male, straight-appearing some of the time—"

Marina's gaze snapped to him. "Straight-appearing?"

He flashed her a thumbs-up. "A perk of bisexuality." He considered. "One of many."

Marina rolled her eyes, but she felt like there were tiny fireworks popping in her chest, and from the recesses of her subconscious, a tiny voice whispered, *back in business*.

Chapter 7

Nate frowned. "It's... cold."

Hockey girl chuckled and a plume of mist fogged the air in front of her face.

"You look like a dragon," Nate informed her, squinting against the blur of the world.

"Just keep walking."

They were outside, but Nate couldn't quite remember when that had happened. There was a blank chasm between the house, the game, the lights of the enclosed porch playing off her long eyelashes... and here. Where was he? He squinted, mentally listing off the facts he could gather. One: he was somewhere in Cambridge. Two: he was unsteady, trying to keep his footing despite the snowdrifts that insisted on trying to trip him. And three: there was a woman under his arm.

He exhaled, watching his breath coalesce and dance, almost cloud-like. "Fucking gorgeous."

Nate wasn't sure if he was talking about the evening or the person.

She huffed. "Yeah, sure, just don't fall and crack your head open."

"You'd like that," he said, nodding and then immediately regretting it. "Then you'd win."

"What an awful thing to say!"

"I'll bet you were thinking it, back there. When we were arguing."

43

"We weren't arguing," she said reasonably, helping him navigate a jagged patch of sidewalk, prickling with fresh ice. "We were debating."

"Same thing."

"Only to the lazy mind," she said.

Nate frowned, trying to puzzle through that statement. But his thoughts bunched and knotted around it, pulled in all directions. So instead, he turned to her, almost tripping on a snow-covered root in the process.

"How come you're not drunk?"

She exhaled heavily, creating more fog. "We Cubans have a high tolerance. I've been drinking since I was fourteen."

"Whaaaaaat?" Nate drew the question out, swaying to a stop as she turned to look at him.

"Where my parents come from, it wasn't a big deal for kids to drink. They've been letting me have wine at the table since I was in middle school. I guess I learned my limits."

Nate made the half-conscious decision not to take offense.

"Wait, so your parents are... immigrants?" he asked.

"Not just them."

"Huh?"

Her smile was oddly strained, as if he'd touched the center of a bruise. But he was in no state to puzzle out what it meant.

"You didn't realize I was Latina?"

"Latinx." Nate corrected automatically.

She put her hands on her hips. "Shouldn't I get to decide my own ethnicity."

This made Nate's brain swim.

"I... guess you're right." He felt his eyebrows pull tighter together, the space between them slightly numb from cold and intoxication. "But wouldn't you want to use the most respectful term

44

for… yourself?"

"I don't think it's more respectful to use a term a bunch of American intellectuals made up. My culture was doing just fine before people like you decided to change its label."

Nate was swaying, the cold tapping on the edge of his thoughts like a bird at the window, but he ignored it. She was watching him, her dark eyes reflecting the lamplight and the distant, almost invisible brush of stars.

"You're… surprising."

She smiled, reaching for his arm again. "And you're wasted. C'mon, let's get you home before you freeze to death without even noticing."

"I think I left my friend back there," Nate muttered, struggling to look over his shoulder in the general direction of the house where he'd forgotten Leo, forgotten damn near everything except her.

"Um, I believe he went home with someone."

Some vestigial part of Nate's brain whirred, clicked.

Please don't let it be Ross.

But even the thought of Leo and Ross kissing, caressing, maybe even fucking, didn't bother Nate as much as it should.

"Tell me something," Nate said, blinking into focus. "Do you really believe in God?"

He was satisfied by a surprised laugh from around the vicinity of his armpit, accompanied by a gasp as they almost slipped on a patch of slick ground.

"Why do you ask?" she panted.

"Seems weird. You're an MIT student. You're smart."

"Believing in God has nothing to do with being smart."

Nate was overcome by a heady recklessness, like he was standing on the edge of something tall and steep and preparing to jump.

45

"But there's no evidence," he said. "There's no reason to believe that there's some big man in the sky looking down on us."

She pulled him around a big puddle, rimmed with salt. "There's no reason not to either."

He snorted. "There's no proof that fairies don't exist, but I assume you don't believe in those."

She was silent for a long moment, the air around them filled with only the rasping of their breaths, the little explosions of steam. Nate wondered if he'd insulted her and then wondered why the idea bothered him so much.

Finally, she spoke.

"I think there's plenty of evidence that humans are made to seek meaning. We're designed with an internal compass of right and wrong, good and bad, joy and sorrow. And more than that, we were designed to ask the important questions, questions that run deeper than just science. Look at the history of art, writing, philosophy. The things we dig for are so much bigger than just the visible, tangible world around us. And I think that there's no reason for that drive to exist if there wasn't a purpose for it."

"You do believe in evolution, right?"

"Of course."

Nate laughed. "Just checking." But then he swallowed, slowed, and tipped his head up to squint at the rolling cloud cover, lit from below by city lights. "You don't think it might just be... wish fulfillment?"

She paused with him, letting his arm grow heavy around her shoulders, not quite leaning into him but not pulling away either. "If it was just wish fulfillment, then it would be easy, right? There would be no hell, no threat of failure. And it wouldn't be so difficult to do what's right."

Nate snorted. "Like the church would know anything about

what's *right*."

She didn't rise to the bait, instead saying in a thoughtful tone, "I believe in God because God makes my life better. He gives my life significance and direction and purpose. Maybe He's real, maybe He's not, but I don't think it really matters in the end. Because I'm happy." She turned to him and Nate had the feeling of being in a spotlight he hadn't asked for, hadn't prepared for. "What do you have that gives you what you need?"

Nate straightened, drawing back his shoulders even though it meant pulling away from her. "I have justice and activism and the pursuit of a better world."

"How can you be certain you know what that is?"

Nate opened his mouth, but his thoughts were muddled and messy and, worst of all, distracted by the way her skin twinkled with frost.

"I declare an ambush," he announced. "You're unfairly advantaged in this argument."

"Debate." She reminded him.

Her lips curled and Nate wanted so badly to lean in and kiss her that it ached. But before he could, she was hauling him forward again.

"Come on, we're almost there."

"How do you know where I live?" he mumbled, hating how garbled he sounded.

"You told me, silly."

"Oh." Nate's feet were leaden and numb, clumsy as he slipped and slid over the frozen ground. He was still going through what she'd said, picking through the scattered thoughts he could grab hold of. Then he paused, swaying. "You know what I believe in? Space. Stars." He jabbed his finger upward. "The moon. I can trust in the moon."

47

"Even though it changes constantly?"

"But it changes *predictably*. Unlike everything else." Nate found himself thinking about Tiffany, whose moods shifted like a hurricane's direction.

Not that he was any better.

"Well," Marina said when he didn't go on, "you don't seem like the type who would enjoy routine anyway."

She led Nate up to the open space in front of his apartment building.

"Here so soon?" he said, head lurching up in surprise. Did he imagine the slight sadness in her smile?

"Don't forget to drink some water."

Nate offered his best roguish, sideways grin, which felt just a little too disheveled to be called sexy. "Wanna come upstairs?"

Her breath burst out in a laugh. "Now?"

"No time like the present."

She eyed him. "I feel like I would be taking advantage of you."

"Please do."

"Isn't that kind of the opposite of what they taught us freshman year?"

"First year." He corrected again without thinking. Nate leaned in, close enough to see the detail of her eyebrows, the chapped crinkle of her bottom lip. "I give my full consent."

She stepped back, shaking her head and smiling, as if to herself.

"Consent doesn't count when you're drunk, as you well know Mr. Politically Correct. Get some sleep, and we'll revisit this another time."

Nate clutched his chest in mock horror, but inside his spirit soared and danced.

Another time.

"Oh, parting is such sweet sorrow," he called, sweeping his arm wide. "How will I endure the pain?"

"Stop, stop, stop," she said, grabbing his hand and pulling it in. He could feel her breath on his face. "You are a ham."

"I warned you."

"And I'll warn *you* that you might not feel too great tomorrow if you don't rehydrate."

Nate blinked. "Fair point."

"Good night sir."

It felt like Velcro, her pulling away and leaving him so much colder than he'd been only moments ago, even though the night air was the same. He watched her walk down the driveway of his building, his fingers curling in a royal wave, her looking over one shoulder with a half-coy, half-worried expression that felt like all the things he'd ever wanted to see in another person. She cared about his safety, was thinking, even now, about him getting home in one piece. She'd turned him down not because of disinterest but for his own good. Even though he disagreed with her on pretty much everything, here she was smiling at him as she rounded the corner and disappeared into the night.

It was only after she was gone and Nate had trudged up the stairs to their three-bedroom on the top floor that he realized he'd never asked her name.

Chapter 8

Marina was wandering. She knew Jordan wouldn't be home yet—when she and whoever-he-was left the house, Ben had been holding court in the dining room. The music was still pounding, and the food bowls were still out, college life rolling on around her as it always had.

But for the first time in her life, Marina had walked out with a stranger.

Who am I turning into? she thought ruefully, staring at the sky as she drifted toward their apartment. She fought the urge to whistle. Had she actually *enjoyed* the evening, against all expectations? Was she becoming… normal? Already she found herself wondering when Ben's house might host their next party and who would be there.

If *he* would be there.

She'd heard someone call out as they'd left, one of the rowers with a half-zip sweater, face blurred by the smog of the room.

"Hey, Nate!" he'd shouted.

Nate.

She shook herself like a wet dog, letting the cold shiver through her.

He was handsome, sure, despite the awful hairstyle. And it was normal, natural even, for her to appreciate his tall, narrow build, the way his arm draped around her, the dimples when he smiled.

There was no harm in thinking about his laugh. No danger in the way the night had narrowed to the amused intelligence in his bright eyes, the inviting curve of his lower lip.

But Marina had made the deliberate choice *not* to ask for his number, not even for his name. What was the point? He lived in an entirely different Boston than she did, a place of casual sex and heavy drinking and unnatural dye jobs. She imagined that the people in his circles would be the very same ones who gave her cross a side-eye and talked over her in class. Worse than that, what would Jordan and Ben say if they knew who she'd walked home with? It felt like she and this Nate character were polarized in all the wrong ways, the tidal forces of their lives in complete opposition.

She sighed, watching her breath as it fled from her.

It wasn't faith that kept her from accepting his invitation to go upstairs. A part of her wished it was, but the Salinas family had never been puritanical about sex. Her parents had given her condoms for her *quinceañera*, and the jokes they let her younger brother tell at the dinner table could have made a pole dancer blush. No, Marina had never made any conscious effort to avoid the big It, but her rigorous ambition had filled out the edges of her life, leaving no space for things like kissing, touching, exploration. And now, at the age of twenty-one, Marina felt like a pariah at a place like MIT. A virgin in college? One who wasn't intentionally holding out for marriage?

What a joke.

She could imagine admitting this to Nate, watching his sly, excited smile freeze, perhaps droop. Maybe he'd be kind and offer for her to come upstairs anyway. Maybe he'd get nervous, rambling on about how it didn't matter, that he was *fine* with it. No big deal.

But it did matter.

Marina knew all too well how much it mattered. It was why she hated dating in Cambridge, why even the idea of Austin was overwhelming. She'd discovered quickly that life in the northeast meant that no one was a virgin who didn't choose to be.

Except her.

She kicked the nearest snowbank, filling the air with sparkling shards of white.

No, this cute boy with the infectious smile was a dead end. A waste of precious time. Nothing to lose her head over. They'd be doomed from the start, and not just because of their politics. What would someone like him, someone charming and experienced and well-versed in drinking games, want with someone like her?

And, she reminded herself sternly, *what do I want with someone so unsuitable?*

Besides, it hardly mattered now. They hadn't exchanged names and *clearly* didn't run in the same circles.

She turned onto her street with a sigh.

In all likelihood, they'd probably never see each other again.

Chapter 9

Nate had to see her again.

It was the first thing he thought when he woke up, head pounding, mouth sticky, a groan leaking out of him before he could stop it. He felt like he'd been hit by a runaway bus, like his veins had been filled with lead. For a moment he couldn't remember where he was, what he'd done, what had happened. But that directive pulsed, a single bright light in his mind.

He had to see hockey girl again.

"Argggg," he complained as he rolled over to grab his phone.

Even though all he wanted to do was stay inside and binge *The Expanse*, he couldn't, because he only knew two things about the young woman from the night before.

She played hockey and she was Catholic.

Which meant that, unless he wanted to wait for the next game against her team, if there even was one, Nate had to drag his hungover self out of bed and haul ass to the religious center on campus before mass ended.

Whenever that was.

Catholic mass MIT, Nate typed in, squinting against the aggressively bright light of his phone screen.

He scrolled through the Sunday mass schedule. The first option was 9:30 a.m.

It was 10:20.

"Fuck," Nate moaned, kicking out of the tangle of his sheets and groping around for his jeans.

"You're up early," Tiffany said in greeting when Nate staggered into the kitchen.

"Coffee?" he asked.

"In the pot." She watched him from the corner of her eye as he poured a steaming mug and drank it scalding hot. "What's the rush?"

"I... have a meeting." Nate coughed as his throat burned, but the caffeine was more important than avoiding pain right now. "Did Leo come home last night?"

"How am I supposed to know?" Tiff said with a shrug.

Nate glanced at his roommate's door. Closed, but that didn't mean much. For all they knew, Leo was still in someone's bed halfway across Cambridge.

"Did you have a good night?" Nate asked, trying to gather his wits before he went out into the howling cold.

"Sure did," she said, typing as she spoke. "Did you hear about that asshole comedian who they tried to hire to SNL? Got what was coming to him if you ask me."

"They fired him?"

"Of course they fucking did," Tiff said, glancing up. "The dude made a joke about Black Lives Matter being founded on a lie. Can't have that shit on national TV." She looked back at her screen. "I'd like to think my viral tweet pushed the scales."

Nate nodded, but found himself wondering what hockey girl would say if she was here, how she'd probably surprise him with some insightful counterargument for why the joke was funny, or maybe why the guy should be allowed to say it. She was wrong, *obviously*, but Nate, in all his infatuated absurdity, still wanted to hear

56

what she had to say.

He rubbed his face. Maybe when he finally got her name, she wouldn't haunt him so much.

And he'd be a better roommate.

Making himself pause for a moment, Nate dropped his hands and examined Tiffany. She was still typing, still focused on whatever battleground she'd moved on to. He wondered if she'd slept at all.

"Hey," he said carefully. "You ok?"

Her eyes sliced to him, painfully sharp. "Yeah. Why?"

Nate shrugged. "Just checking."

Tiffany's gaze lingered on him for a long, piercing moment. Nate did his best to hold it, trying to tell her without words that he was there for her, that she could talk to him if she wanted. If she needed.

Finally, she looked away. "Just family stuff. My sister's fiancé is being a dick, as usual."

Nate fidgeted with his mug handle. "I'm sorry."

Tiffany's face pinched in rage, eyebrows almost touching. "These alt-right fuckers are like a disease. If you don't stop them, their bad ideas just *infect* everything. Families, campuses, government. You name it, they'll ruin it."

"Amen to that," Nate said, toasting and draining the rest of his coffee.

"But they'll see," Tiff said, resuming her typing. "I'll show them they're on the wrong side of history. You watch."

Nate smiled sadly, even though she wasn't looking at him anymore. "I don't doubt it for a second." When she didn't offer anything else, he put his mug in the sink. "Well, gotta go. Places to be."

"Have fun," Tiff called, glasses reflecting the blue glare of her computer screen.

Feeling inadequate and confused and wondering if he should have said more, Nate was so distracted that he almost collided with Leo in the stairwell.

"Everyone's up early this morning," Nate said, clapping Leo on the shoulder with an overly cheerful laugh. "Walk of shame?"

"I think you mean prance of pride," Leo said, grinning. "You're not mad I ditched you, right?"

"So long as you weren't with Ross," Nate said, surprised to find that he didn't really mean it.

"Naw, bro, I'd never be that cold. Where you off to?"

Nate grinned, ear to ear. "Church."

Leo snorted. "Well if you don't wanna tell me..."

"Later!"

The bike ride to campus was brutal. Icy wind scratched long claws over his cheeks; frigid air bit at his eyes. He slipped and slid over salted roads, his thin tires barely able to maintain their grip on the iced-over bike lane. The piercing sunlight threatened to blind him. He'd forgotten everything but his coat and helmet and was hungover enough to regret it. But at least the cold was bracing, jarring him into some semblance of himself.

What the fuck am I gonna say?

Nate tried to imagine pickup lines that would work with her, but all of them fell flat in his mind. She was too clever, too composed to fall for anything as silly as *I believe we had unfinished business.* But what else was he supposed to do? He'd spent his whole life flirting into or out of pretty much any situation, but this mysterious, Catholic, opinionated, *conservative* woman seemed to have ripped all that off like a blanket he'd been cowering under and never realized it. Now he was exposed and vulnerable and *raw* and didn't understand why he liked it so much, but he sure as shit wanted more.

He skidded to a stop by the MIT chapel, all but sliding right into the handrail. *How did she get me home last night without us both breaking our necks?* From outside, he could hear piano music and voices, building to a high crescendo. Was she singing with them? Standing, or perhaps kneeling, as she worshiped what Nate had, until last night, considered quite ridiculous?

Was she thinking about their conversation with the same obsessive fervor that he was?

Finally, the music ended. People began to trickle out. Panic rose in Nate's chest. Was there a back door? Would she stay behind for some kind of Sunday school? How did these things even work? He lingered by the nearest tree, trying to look casual with his arms and legs crossed, lounging like a model but feeling like a dumbass.

Just when he was beginning to think — with an overwhelming sense of dread — that he'd be forced to go inside and risk bursting into flames, she appeared.

And *damn*.

She was even more beautiful in the daylight, wrapped in a thick coat and fluffy scarf, hair sleek and black. She was laughing, pink-cheeked and happy, accompanied by a tiny Asian student with cherub cheeks and kind eyes. What would her friend think of him? Nothing good, probably. Nate tried to think of a way to get hockey girl alone, but his abused, recovering brain didn't work fast enough because they were already making their way down the ramp, into the morning.

Toward him.

He cleared his throat.

She looked up.

For a single, glittering moment everything stopped. Her eyes met his, and Nate tried his best to decipher the thing that flashed through her expression. Excitement? Relief? Horror?

He cleared his throat again. "I, um, never caught your name."

The Asian girl looked between them, gaze ping-ponging between Nate's bright hair and her friend's shocked face. She jerked her friend's arm a little.

Hockey girl shook her head, as if to clear it. "It's Marina. Marina Salinas."

He grinned. "Nathan Campbell. Call me Nate."

"Sure," she said.

"I'm Jordan," said the friend, grinning even wider than Nate. "And I'm late for something." With a flash of teeth and a bob of her hat's pompom, she ducked past them, leaving Nate and Marina alone.

"So, er, thanks for last night." He coughed. "I probably would have turned into a popsicle or something without you."

"I'm sure you would have been fine."

He glanced up. "I'm not."

An awkwardness spread between them like spilled oil, and Nate wondered if maybe this was the reality of it, if they only worked with alcohol or hockey filling the chasm of differences between them. But he didn't want to give up that easily, not when whatever-this-was had gotten him up early on a *Sunday*.

"Do you wanna… get a drink or something?"

She lifted one eyebrow. "In the morning?"

"I mean, or something to eat," Nate said, ruffling his hair.

"I have brunch plans. With Jordan, actually."

Nate glanced over his shoulder to where the other girl had disappeared into the crowd of students on their way to breakfast or, god forbid, the library.

"Well, what about tonight?" He turned back, grinning sheepishly. "I could sure use some hair of the dog."

Marina was looking at him, lips pursed as if the *no* was already formed and ready, a bomb waiting to be dropped. Nate had been rejected tons of times. At bars, at parties, even in class. It was almost always swift, decisive, instinctual. Usually, that made it easier—at least the person in question knew what they wanted. No point wasting time, right?

But the refusal he could see forming in Marina's eyes wasn't like that. It was slow, almost reluctant.

He leaned in, pushing the advantage. "I'll buy you dinner."

Her laugh was sudden and bright. "I should hope so!"

"Oh yeah, I forgot. You're a traditionalist. Shall we say... seven?"

There was a glimmer in her eyes that he wished he could bottle up and save. "Where?"

"The Field? It's right in Central Square."

"I know it. Terrible food."

"Hey! I love their buffalo wings."

She rolled her eyes. "You would."

"So it's a date then?"

Nate hadn't meant to use the word, but somehow it had snuck through his defenses.

He blamed the hangover.

"I... I didn't mean..."

She smiled, tossing her scarf over one shoulder as she made to follow her friend.

"It's a date," she called back.

"Hey! I don't have your number!"

"Better not be late then."

He watched her go, marveling at the way she waltzed through the snow and the sunshine as if she owned it, as if it had been made for her.

Well, Nate thought, burrowing his hands deep into the pockets of his coat and letting the smile spread over his face, uninhibited and wild. *I guess she believes it was.*

Chapter 10

Marina had walked by The Field plenty of times, almost every day in fact. But having precious little experience with bars, much less going into one by herself, she eyed the front door with suspicion. Standing out front with numb feet in well-worn boots and cheeks raw from the cold, she tracked her gaze over the fire truck red facade and brown-gold lettering. It reminded her of a schoolhouse, with its old windows, or maybe an independent bookstore.

This can't be so bad, she thought, swallowing heavily and stepping inside. She offered her ID to the bouncer. *People do stuff like this all the time.*

She was early, but that was normal. Jordan and Ben liked to make fun of how much time Marina wasted, always showing up fifteen minutes before she was supposed to. She knew they only meant to tease, but what they didn't know, what Marina never said, was that her phobia of being late was about more than just politeness. Her parents had raised her to never, ever, *ever* let herself slide into Hispanic stereotypes.

You are American, they'd drummed into her and her two brothers. *You are American first, and you will not reflect badly on this family.*

And so Marina and her siblings were always early, always well-dressed. None of the Salinas children cursed or spoke Spanish except in private. Her brothers played sports like track, rugby, swimming. She'd enrolled in chorus and took yoga classes with her mom. Her parents were determined that the only thing that would ever mark them or their children as foreign would be the color of their skin, and even then, only in certain seasons.

As Marina took her seat at the bar, she wondered what Nate would think about that. What his friends would say about the choices Marina's parents had made. Would he accept their decision to assimilate and suppress their culture? Or would he be repulsed by the fact that they'd felt like they had to?

For some reason, she found herself wanting to know.

Some minutes later, the door flew open and a gust of freezing air made the whole bar shiver.

"Made it!" Nate said triumphantly, plopping down in the open seat next to Marina.

She laughed. "Were you worried?"

He grimaced, ducking his head to avoid the question. "Did you order yet?"

"I just got here," Marina lied, scooting over to let him in.

"What do you want?"

She asked for a red wine, craving something warm and savory. He ordered that and some local craft beer she'd never heard of, winking at the bartender.

Marina swallowed.

I'm already here, she said to herself as Nate settled into his chair and began the process of shucking layers. *I've already committed to this. It's just a few hours, nothing more.*

Nate grinned at her, glancing around with a conspiratorial expression.

"To be honest, I'm glad I got in. It would have been a bit awkward if I'd had to knock on the window to get your attention."

Marina frowned in question and Nate flashed the ID he was sliding back into his wallet.

"You're from Wyoming?" she asked.

"No," he hissed, eyes sparkling with mischief.

Marina's whole face flushed. She scanned the bar like a criminal, as if the bouncer's hand was about to crash down out of nowhere and drag her outside.

"You have a *fake ID*?" she whispered, leaning in close and trying not to think about the front curl of his faux-hawk tickling her forehead.

"Of course," he accepted his beer. "All the kids in my high school did."

"I doubt that."

"What do you know about where I went to school?"

Marina exhaled. "Apparently nothing. But it sure doesn't sound anything like my hometown."

Nate relaxed into his barstool, hooking one elbow over the back of his seat. "Where'd you grow up?"

She gave him an *are we doing this* look and he laughed.

"What? Gotta start somewhere, right? Unless you'd rather we go back to *debating*."

Breathing through her nose, Marina tried to hold onto her irritation, the rational feeling of wrongness.

It was harder than she'd expected.

"Roanoke," she said at last. "I grew up in Roanoke."

"And what was that like?"

"I feel like I should be in an armchair for this."

He grinned. "There are armchairs at my apartment."

Marina rolled her eyes, playing with the stem of her glass. "It was boring, to be honest. Not a lot to report."

"Except a lot of white people, I'd imagine."

Now it was her turn to squint, but not with mischief. "What's that supposed to mean?"

He put up his hands. "Nothing. I just imagine there weren't a lot of Latinx people."

"Can't you just call them Latinos?"

"No."

Marina struggled to relax her jaw, not sure if she was having fun or about to pull her hair out.

She took a sip. "No, there weren't a lot of *Latinos* there. That's actually why my parents chose it."

"How do you mean?"

"Well," Marina said. Paused. *I wanted to know, didn't I?* "My parents thought it was important for me and my brothers to... fit in. They didn't want to move somewhere like Miami, where we'd just melt into another population of Cubans. They wanted us to be as American as possible."

Nate's face had transformed into an expression of tragedy, as if Marina had described a horrible family loss.

"I'm so sorry."

Marina straightened, lifting her chin in defiance. "Why?"

"Because you shouldn't have had to do that."

She scoffed. "Of course we should. This country gave us shelter in a time of need. We have to respect its culture."

"There's nothing to respect. America's culture is an evil relic of colonialism and white supremacy."

What in the name of...?

"You can't possibly believe that," Marina said, mouth half-open.

"Of course I do. The evidence is everywhere."

"Evidence of what? *History*? I've got news for you, Nate, everywhere has history. Cuba has history too. Gross history, colonial

66

history, slave history. But I don't let those things define my heritage."

"Well, maybe your culture's done a better job of moving past it."

"Yeah, into *communism.*"

"Failed communism," he pointed out.

"Excuse me?" she said in a low, dangerous voice.

Nate was leaning in, eyes intense. "I mean, it's never really been done before, right? It's never been done *well.*"

"Russia? China? Venezuela?" Marina ticked off the names on her fingers. "How many lives need to be destroyed before we can consider the experiment failed?"

"But if it was executed correctly, to each according to their need, from each according to their capacity? It would be the best kind of system, right?"

"Except that we don't live in that world. People don't work in a perfect system because none of us are perfect, and communism fails because there aren't enough safeguards against people being horrible."

"Yeah, but capitalism is so much worse."

Marina made a *ha* noise. "Really? It's so much worse that you can say this freely, enjoy luxuries like beer and wine, own a computer*?*"

"Our lives are controlled by the rich and corrupt," Nate said in the tone of a kindergarten teacher trying to explain a simple math problem. "Our country is ruled by an oligarchy of billionaires."

"No it's not, it's ruled by *elected officials.*"

"Who are controlled by corporations and lobbyists," Nate said.

"Who are invested in the success of our economy."

"Or filling their own wallets at any human or ethical cost."

Marina put up a hand. "Fine, but where do all those corrupt

people go in communism? Do you think they just disappear? That they'll suddenly wake up and realize what terrible people they've been and give their power away? No, the assholes of the world will take what they can get, game the system, and become a *literal* oligarchy. And guess what, the beautiful country that thought it could be a utopia becomes hell on earth for everyone still trapped there. Socialism fails because of human nature, but capitalism works in spite of it."

Nate leaned back. "I apologize. It was insensitive of me to bring this up."

"I don't care about *sensitive*," Marina said, bristling at the implication. "I care about *accurate*. You're an idiot if you think communism is a good idea."

He frowned. "I think that's a bit closed-minded of you."

"Says the guy who called God a fantasy."

Marina was aware that the bar patrons around them had gone quiet, that her voice was louder than she intended. But if there was one thing, *one thing* her parents would never tolerate, it was if she brought home a *communist*.

She didn't have the bandwidth to consider the fact that her brain had already leapt to bringing Nate home.

"Well," he said with a wry smile, ruffling his ridiculous hair. "Can we at least agree that it's sad you grew up so far from home, whatever the reason."

"Cuba wasn't my home." Marina glared at her hands to calm herself down, examining the nails her mother had taught her to keep filed and round, the scars from playing in the Virginia forests. "I think children are more resilient than we give them credit for. I could have grown up anywhere, so long as I had my parents teaching me what mattered. I had a community and a church, and no one ever thought twice about the fact that my parents spoke with an accent." Now she looked right at him, her gaze level and her words strong. "If we live in some white supremacist dystopia, I've never seen any evidence of it."

Nate pursed his lips. "So you've never experienced racism?"

She shrugged. "Sure, there are jerks. But those are individuals, not the system."

"I guess I can't argue with your lived experience." His lips were twitching, inviting her in on the joke, and Marina found her ruffles smoothing, her edges softening. She smiled back.

"Isn't that exactly the problem with basing truth on lived experience?" she asked. "There's no counterargument."

"Now you're sounding like a Fox news anchor."

"Maybe I agree with them sometimes."

"God help you."

"He already does."

Nate's laugh was loud enough to make the bartender, already half-listening to their conversation, flick a look in their direction.

"I like you, Marina Salinas."

She stared into her wine, feeling strange and unsteady all of a sudden. It took a moment for her throat to clear.

"I don't think that's a smart choice."

His touch on the bare skin of her wrist, right at the edge of her sweater's cuff, was sudden enough, unexpected enough to make her jump.

"Maybe it's not a choice," he said.

She looked up, braced with sarcasm and deflection. But he was there, too close, his eyes dancing in the half-light of the bar. Had she ever noticed how blue they were? How much they looked like the Caribbean ocean or the sapphire in her mother's engagement ring? Terror and pounding adrenaline filled her as Nate leaned in, too real, too suggestive, *too close*. She knew where this was going, couldn't think past the thumping in her heart of *not yet, not yet, not yet.*

She brought the wineglass to her lips and tried to convince herself that she didn't see the disappointment cloud those perfect eyes.

"So," she said, swirling her drink and pulling on a smile. "Your turn."

Chapter 11

It wasn't the first time Nate had spent the week back to school thinking obsessively about a kiss that didn't happen, but it was undoubtably the strangest.

He kept trying to remind himself that she was *Catholic*, she was *conservative*. Tiff and Leo would never understand, and worse, might be hurt by Nate defaulting to a straight-appearing relationship and amassing even more privilege and power. He would be risking the balance of their house, their friend group, and for what? He and Marina had nothing—nothing!—in common except that they liked to argue.

Debate, he reminded himself.

Most importantly, she wasn't interested. She'd made that clear the moment she pulled away, choosing wine over him.

And yet he found himself staring at the number she'd typed into his phone, his finger hovering over the message button as class droned on around him.

"Nathan?" His eyes jerked up to find his Ethics in Contemporary Issues professor bearing down on him like Gordon Ramsay. "What are your thoughts about the ongoing border conflict?"

He tucked his phone under his leg, doing his best to look like he'd just been Googling a term.

"Well, the wall is obviously just a ploy to rally the Republican base and distract voters from the fact that they're locking kids in cages."

The professor jerked her head in approval and Nate swallowed a sigh of relief. She continued on down the row of students. "So, if we were to compare the welfare cost of the new arrivals to the moral cost on the nation of such an atrocity, clearly there is no justifiable reason to…"

Nate, almost without realizing it, found himself staring at his phone again.

"Are you even listening?" Tiffany whispered from beside him, typing notes. This was her favorite class.

"Sure, yeah," Nate said, once again watching his finger float over the message icon as if his hand belonged to someone else.

"…the emotional fortitude necessary to stand for what's right," the lecture was continuing, "for what people believe in, is undeniably harder than just sitting back and letting things happen. People throughout history have taken the easy way, saying it's out of their control, convincing themselves it has nothing to do with them. But that's how evil is perpetuated. That's how lives are destroyed."

Fuck it, Nate thought, tapping out a quick text.

<How's your first week back?>

He hit Send before he could second-guess himself.

For a moment, nothing happened.

And then those three magical dots appeared, blinking hopefully at him.

There must be a special place in heaven for whoever invented texting, Nate thought, waiting impatiently as, somewhere on campus, Marina composed her response.

"It is the obligation of a moral society to stand in favor of what's right, even when it's difficult…"

Nate was vaguely aware of Tiffany nodding beside him, her big reading glasses flashing in the morning sun.

And then his phone buzzed.

<I thought you'd lost my number.>

He grinned to himself. *Guess she doesn't pull punches either.*

<I figured you needed time to recover from the awesomeness of my presence.>

She sent back a vomiting emoji.

<What class are you in?> he wrote.

<I'm not sure the library counts as a class...>

Nate tapped the side of his phone case, watching as the professor made another lap of the classroom.

"This semester will be particularly difficult for many on campus. There are things happening in our country that affect some more than others. We must all be more vigilant than ever to shine the light of truth where it is needed."

He began to type out, <well, don't let me bother—>

Too sulky.

He deleted it.

"Therefore, your primary assignment for this course will be to document something you've done to cultivate integrity on our campus. It can be student activism; it can be volunteering. Yes?"

Beside Nate, Tiffany dropped her hand to push her spectacles up her nose.

"Can it be something we're already doing?"

"I assume you're referring to your blog?" The professor said this with the air of an amused parent, encouraging but not quite approving.

Tiffany nodded.

"I think it can be related to a platform you've already built. But try something different this semester. Engage with what you see

73

going on. And document it."

"Perfect," Tiff muttered, relaxing into her chair as the professor moved to answer someone else's question. "I already know what I'm going to do."

Nate's phone buzzed and he checked it immediately, compulsively.

Marina had written, <What class are you in?>

<Ethics> he responded without hesitation.

The three dots blinked.

"Aren't you going to ask me what I'm planning?"

"Wha—yeah," Nate said, tearing his eyes away from the screen. "What's the dastardly plot this time?"

Tiffany sniffed even as Nate felt that glorious buzz of Marina's response.

"That guy from hockey is in my social commentary class," she said. "You know, the conservative asshole?"

Nate glanced down at his phone to read Marina's message.

<Sounds like oodles of fun.> And then she followed up with, </s>

He grinned into his lap, wondering if Marina spent as much time on Reddit as he did.

"He proposed his project for the semester," Tiffany continued, "and can you fucking believe it? He's going to start a blog. A conservative fucking blog. He looked right at me when he said it too." She snorted, watching their professor write a bullet point list of requirements for their assignment on the smart board. "I'll bet he jacks off to the Dyke Digest every night and then punishes himself for it or some shit."

"Yeah, he seems like a real peach."

Nate typed out, <I mean, can't be all that different from church, right? Teaching right and wrong and morals and all that?>

"He shouldn't even be here." Tiff's voice edged into a growl. "His fanatical ideas should have gotten him kicked out already."

Marina responded, <At least there's music in church>

"Maybe they will soon."

"Huh?" Nate looked up as he finished typing out <I could start singing in class?>.

"Who are you texting?" Tiffany asked, a note of irritation in her voice.

Marina sent back a laughing face.

"No one," Nate said, making the snap decision that his conversation with Marina could wait a few minutes. It was more important that Tiffany not find out that he was chatting up the friend and teammate of the poor bastard she was setting her sights on.

He flipped his phone over on his desk.

Tiff grinned. "You got a new boy-toy?"

Nate forced himself to grin back. "Something like that."

"So long as it isn't one of Leo's workout buddies. That didn't go well last time."

"Yeah, turns out gym bros aren't really my thing."

They both paused as the professor turned back, expounding on the virtues of activism.

"So? Who is it?" Tiffany whispered at the first opportunity.

Nate fidgeted. "I told you, no one."

"Yeah, as if that's not the oldest cliché in the book. What, are they ugly or something?"

Nate eyed her. "After all your lectures about how evaluating a person on physical attractiveness is *sexist*?"

Tiffany scoffed. "The social and historical context is completely different when you do it to women. C'mon, tell me!"

"We're not... there yet," Nate said, keenly aware that he and Marina would probably *never* be there and trying not to think about what that implied.

"Fine, fine, you do you. But I want details *eventually*, alright?"

"Ok, promise."

Tiffany nodded, elbowed him softly, and then returned her undivided attention to the lecture.

But guilt still squirmed in Nate's belly.

He hadn't *lied* per se, but it felt dirty somehow, like he was devaluing his friend by holding back, silently adding to the pile of forces that threatened to erase her existence. Tiffany cared about him, about so many things. And he of all people knew how much she struggled to just be *seen*. It felt wrong to exclude her from this, to keep her at arm's length when he'd never done so before.

So why do it?

Who was he protecting?

He wasn't sure.

Nate used to think he had enough experience with unconventional love that nothing would ever faze him again. But after years of dating men, women, and everything in between, this was the first time he actually felt like he had a secret.

He flipped his phone over to find a text from Marina waiting for him.

<So did you go for cabaret? Or is that too much even for you?>

Nate found himself grinning and wondered how such a silly joke could drive all the worries right out of his head.

Chapter 12

Marina was pretending to do her homework. On the other side of the living room, she could hear Jordan's pen scratching, Ben's fingers flying over the keyboard. He was drafting the first few articles of Red Nation, pieces that he'd described in detail to both her and Jordan over their shared dinner. Marina had nodded along as he pontificated on the questionable science of climate change, the land mine debate around IQ, the issue of gun control and how the common statistics have been misused and misinterpreted.

Privately, she wondered at his purpose. It seemed to her that he wasn't really trying to change anyone's mind so much as inflame the "other side," push buttons and take revenge for what Ben seemed to feel was a campus-wide acceptance of things he fervently disagreed with. But she kept the concern to herself. After all, she had distractions of her own.

Like the innocuous little message Nate had sent twenty minutes ago, waiting for her response.

<Let's go out again>

She was almost embarrassed by the excitement climbing up her throat, beating like a heart... or a warning. Those two words, *go out*, felt electric, loaded, heavy, thrilling.

Were they going out? Was that what this was? Had she acquired a boyfriend without even realizing it?

Stop it, Marina.

Here she was, thinking like a country kid again.

In her scant experience dating in Boston, Marina had learned that her definition of "go out" was very, very different than the definition used in the northeast. In Virginia, to be dating was to be *an item*, loyal and exclusive and, theoretically, on the road to marriage. Here, it was a casual thing, a throwaway term flung out without thought or consideration.

Oh yeah, we're going out.

I'm going out with them again.

Wanna go out?

That's all this was. Nate was feeling the waters, just like anyone else who had purple in their hair.

So why did it feel so different?

She typed out her response.

<What did you have in mind?>

Ben clapped just as she clicked *send*. "Check it out! I've earned my first leftist tears."

Marina looked up to find Jordan reading over Ben's shoulder.

"Who's Cunt Commander?" Jordan said.

"Three guesses," Ben answered with a smug smile.

"That girl who writes the gay newspaper?" Marina asked, reluctantly putting her phone aside and pushing to her feet. "What did she say?"

"Read for yourself."

Marina bent over Jordan's head, scanning the page. It was Ben's blog, black script on a white background with a logo of stampeding red elephants. The article was titled "The War on Science," crowned with a stock photo of a man and a woman standing back to back, arms folded. A stream of comments was appearing almost as fast as Marina could read them.

<You don't know shit about anything, you misogynistic pig.>

<This article is transphobic and violent.>

<How dare you twist the facts for your agenda. You're going to get trans people killed.>

<Fuck. You.>

Marina looked up with her eyebrows raised. "I guess you hit a nerve."

Ben leaned back, folding his hands behind his head as if he were lounging on a beach and not in a drafty apartment at the end of January. "I guess I did."

"She just wrote that she's gonna report this," Jordan said, eyes scanning up and down the page. "Ben, do you really think this is a good idea?"

"We're at MIT, not Berkeley. They can't expel me for using statistics."

Marina shook her head, returning to her own plushy armchair. "I'm not sure calling them a bunch of witless morons is statistics."

Ben's grin was wolfish. "What are you talking about? That's the most accurate thing I said."

"Not very Catholic of you."

He shrugged. "I fight in the name of truth. I'm sure Jesus would approve."

Marina met Jordan's gaze and they exchanged a *what can you do* eye roll.

"Did you hear they're fighting to make reassignment surgery a medical right, covered by their insane proposals for universal healthcare?" Ben said, retrieving his laptop from Jordan. "They're teaching preschoolers that their gender is an option. It's ridiculous. And I won't even get into the list of *acceptable pronouns*."

"I doubt that," Marina muttered, pleased when Jordan snorted into her tea.

"Marina, this is serious stuff. What happens when we start having kids? How are we going to protect them?"

"By not living in California?"

Ben was stretching, wrapping an arm around Jordan's shoulders thoughtlessly, instinctually. Marina felt a tug in her chest at the way her friend leaned into her boyfriend of three years, as if she was already a part of him.

Ben gestured with his free hand. "It starts there, but it'll spread if we don't fight back. You'll see. They'll be coming for our children."

"I'm sure they mean well." Marina glanced at her screen, where a new message from Nate blinked.

<Ever been to the Museum of Science?>

She grinned.

<Only dozens of times.> Then, worried it would sound dismissive, she tapped out. <Let's do it.>

"You know what they say about good intentions," Ben continued from across the living room. "Besides, someone needs to stand for truth. These activist idiots are trying to shut down logical arguments with emotion and guilt, the same way they do with racism. It's all just a power play."

"Please tell me you're not going near *racism*," Jordan said in a soft voice.

"Of course I am! Red Nation has no filters. I will not be censored on my own blog."

"You mean your social commentary project?" Marina pointed out, watching the three blinking dots as Nate typed out his response.

"*Exactly*. Don't you two get it? This is what commentary is *supposed* to be. An honest reckoning of the *facts*."

Marina glanced up. "Sounds like you're doing plenty of editorializing."

"Only because they're setting the tone."

She chuckled, trying to ignore her impatience.

How long does it take to respond to a stupid text?

"Well, I think you should be careful," Jordan said, frowning. "It could be dangerous to upset this girl."

"Ideas are not dangerous," Ben said. "Words are not dangerous. And anyone who thinks they are didn't pass first grade."

"That's some respectful debate right there," Marina said, voice heavy with sarcasm.

Finally, there was a cheerful *ping*.

<Saturday morning? I know you have plans on Sunday ;P>

Marina chewed her lip. It was the first weekend of the semester. She wouldn't have that much work to do, so what was the harm in a day at the museum? Besides, it was a *science* museum. If she focused on the biology and engineering exhibits, it counted toward schoolwork, right? And neither of them had said it was a *date*, just more time together to argue and bicker and probably find more reasons they were entirely incompatible.

Excitement bubbled through her body like carbonation as she answered.

<You're on.>

Chapter 13

Nate had been to the Museum of Science more times than he could count. Growing up in the suburbs of Boston, his schools were either too lazy or too enamored to think of any other kind of field trip. It was, he had to admit, a perfect place to take a class of rambunctious kids. Eventually, the standard displays had become so familiar to Nate that he'd started to explore the hidden corners, the elevators, and even once made his way down to a lab, forcing several surprised technicians to pause in their restoration efforts and locate the group Nate had slipped away from.

But returning to this well-trodden ground with Marina felt like seeing it for the first time. For once, he wasn't irritated by the shrieking mobs of toddlers and frenzied parents. He wasn't bored by the plaques that changed only on rare occasion. He hardly noticed them.

Because he was watching *her*.

"Isn't this fascinating?" she asked, pointing to the supersized swirl of the inner ear. "It's amazing that they were able to figure all this out."

Marina, when offered the choice, had brought them straight to the Hall of Human Life.

"Did you know the middle ear has some of the smallest bones in your body?" she went on, pulling back from the model and leading

83

them toward a massive screen, gyrating with an artist's rendition of DNA.

"I didn't even know the ear had bones. Isn't it all cartilage?"

"On the outside. We actually don't know all that much about the inner ear. It's very difficult to treat. I used to work on this big investigative project reporting on the cure to tinnitus. You'd be surprised how little we can do for it in the modern world."

"What happened to the project?"

Marina ducked, suddenly very interested in a huge display of the food pyramid. "It's over. Well, my part in it is."

"What do you mean?"

"The project branch that was at MIT ended last semester. They liked my writing and invited me to continue with the summer course if I wanted." She glanced up. "But it's at Stanford."

"Woah, that's awesome! Can you go?"

"I have the application at home," she said, and Nate got the distinct impression she wasn't telling him the whole truth. He followed her into the next room.

"Sweet. You'll like California." He paused, considering for a moment. "Well, some aspects of it. I imagine you'll have lots to say about the politics."

He grinned at her, but she didn't smile back, focusing all her attention on a plastic human skeleton.

"What is it?" he asked. "Got something against the sunshine state?"

She looked at the ceiling. "I don't like beaches."

He folded his arms. "What kind of scrooge doesn't like beaches?"

"The kind who grew up hiking." She adjusted her coat in her arms. Despite Nate's offer to pay, she'd refused to check her jacket at the front desk. "Besides, I already have a job this summer."

"Is it as cool as this one?" Nate said suspiciously.

"Can we talk about something else?" Marina asked suddenly, sharply. "Look at this, you can see the whole retina."

Nate's eyes narrowed, but he wasn't about to push. Who was he to know what kind of trauma made her so nervous about California? Maybe it was anxiety about flying or dealing with so many people of a different background, or maybe the internship was associated with some bad memories. But still, something wasn't right. He could see the tension in her shoulders, the nervous flicker of her smile. Time to do what he did best.

Distraction.

"So, I have a very important question," Nate said, sauntering up behind her. "Star Wars or Star Trek?"

Marina's surprised laugh was a welcome relief. "Excuse me?"

"C'mon!" Nate said. "I know you, of all people, have an opinion."

She pursed her lips. He waited patiently, sidestepping a small boy jumping up and down in excitement in front of a display on kitchen molds.

"A few years ago, I would have said Star Wars for sure," Marina said at last, leading them out of the biology hall and into the exhibit on optical illusions. "But now, I guess... neither. I was never really a Trekkie."

"Wait, wait, wait," Nate said, holding up his hands beside a swirling print that seemed to waver and undulate even though he knew it wasn't moving at all. "You *didn't like* the new trilogy?"

Marina's look of outrage could have been weaponized. "You *did*?"

"Of course! The Last Jedi was a masterpiece."

"You're joking."

"Not a bit. I thought it was surprising and—"

85

"Subverted expectations?"

"—diverse," Nate finished.

"Oh, yes, full of diverse but *useless* characters."

"You really are a Reddit troll, aren't you?" Nate said, fighting the urge to grin.

"No, I'm a person with *eyes*. Rose Tico was totally superfluous to the plot. She brought absolutely nothing to the story and her storyline didn't change anything."

"Which was surprising, wouldn't you say?"

"Bad storytelling is not surprising. It's just bad."

Nate leaned against a pillar in the middle of the exhibit, letting a group of tourists amble past them. "I thought it was great. The visuals were spectacular."

"Sure, if you don't mind that they created a huge plot hole out of all the old movies. If they could just ram ships into other ships, then why bother with any of the big space battles?"

"You gotta admit it looked cool."

Marina rolled her eyes. "Again, looking cool does not make stories good."

"And the morals were necessary."

"Urg, *morals*? They were just pumped in there like any movie nowadays. It was so forced, and for what? To show that white men are all evil, useless, or pathetic? To *let the past die*? I don't think either of those are the messages we want to be sending kids."

"But our past is horrific," Nate said, hardly paying attention as they followed the crowd into the Theatre of Electricity. "The modern world is built on a foundation of murder and oppression and economic injustice, all of it structured to keep the white supremacy in power."

"I was wondering when white supremacy might come up," Marina muttered.

"If we don't let the past die, then how can we ever move forward?"

"By learning from it, perhaps?"

"True, but we need to stop the hero worship of racist and misogynist historical figures. We can learn from our past and still refuse to idolize assholes."

"Don't you think that's throwing the baby out with the bathwater? I mean, sure," she lifted her hands, "terrible things happened. No one is denying that. But the part that bothers me so much is that people are always ignoring the *context*. Columbus might have killed a ton of people, but he was acting in a time when that was acceptable."

"You're going to defend *Columbus*?" Nate said, voice rising in dismay.

"Shhh!" Marina glanced around them, chuckling to herself. Then, in a lower voice, she continued, "Yes, I am. Because maybe he was a bastard—"

"That's an understatement."

"—but he also discovered America—"

"No he didn't, the Vikings did."

"Are you going to let me finish?" Nate looked at the ceiling in his best impression of an innocent schoolboy. "Columbus was an incredibly brave explorer, perhaps driven by gold and fame, but still. He did something that changed the world."

"Yeah, and not for the better. He started a genocide that killed ninety percent of Native Americans."

"Maybe he's a bad example. Ok, let's look at our Founding Fathers."

"A bunch of rich old white men who didn't value women or people of color?"

"*Or*," Marina interjected, "A group of visionaries who created one of the wealthiest and most free places in the history of the *world*. Not to mention that they wrote the very same Bill of Rights that paved the way for true equality."

"We don't have true equality."

"But at least we're trying. America is amazing, Nate. You won the genetic lottery by being born here."

"I won the genetic lottery by being white."

Marina cocked one hip. "Isn't that racist?"

"No, it's recognizing my own privilege. You won the genetic lottery too, by the way."

She folded her arms under her breasts and Nate tried not to let it distract him. "How so?"

"You're smart and healthy and stunningly beautiful."

Her arms relaxed. "What was that now?"

"Looks can be a privilege too," Nate said, trying furiously not to blush. "Studies have shown that pretty people get away with a lot more."

"What about people with purple hair?" she said, eyes flicking up to his head. He noticed that her cheeks were redder than they'd been moments before.

"It's not just purple," he pointed out.

"I'm sorry, *rainbow* hair."

"What do you have against my hair? I think it makes me look edgy."

She tilted her head to one side, eyes slanting up. "That's not the word I'd choose."

Nate was grinning, giddy, as if the electrified cage in front of them was in his chest and not taking up the two stories of the giant room. He opened his mouth to continue, but just then the performer walked out and swept their arms wide in welcome. As the actor showcased the power of static and made the whole audience gasp with a thunderclap, Nate found himself watching Marina instead of the stage. He loved the way her face opened in excitement, the way her eyes flew wide. She was so present, so in tune with the world around them. Not once had she whipped out her phone to check messages or taken a selfie. Not once had she brought up Twitter or Instagram or consulted Google.

It was totally new to him.

And wonderful.

The show finished in a burst of light. As their eyes recovered from the flash, Nate, in a rush of pure instinct, asked the question that had been on his mind all morning.

"I'm having brunch with my parents next weekend," he said quietly under the babble of the shifting crowd. "Do you want to meet them?"

The look she gave him was inscrutable. "You want me to meet your parents?"

Nate shrugged. "Sure. It's not that big of a deal. My parents are chill."

Again, her eyes flashed to his hair. "I imagine they are." She was fingering the cross around her neck, flipping it over and over. "But…"

Understanding hit him like the bolt of manufactured lightning they'd just witnessed.

He'd been so tangled up in his excitement, in the humid warmth of the museum, that he'd forgotten about the world outside. He'd forgotten that his parents had spent long dinners railing against the evils of religion, lecturing Nate about the dangers of conservative ideas, and wondering aloud if they could remain friends with their neighbor who had supported a Republican candidate.

What would they think of someone like Marina?

What would they *say*?

But he'd already asked the question, and besides, his parents had accepted every other person Nate had brought home. They should be able to accept this too.

Shouldn't they?

He grinned. "Are you telling me that you, a starving undergrad, are about to say no to free food?"

She returned his smile reluctantly, unwillingly. But it still made his heart stutter.

"Heck no."

Chapter 14

Marina could feel the dread building in her chest as they neared her apartment on their way back from the museum. It was still early afternoon, barely five. She'd told Nate—truthfully—that she had plans to watch a movie with Jordan that evening. It was ladies' night, one of the few evenings a month where Ben met with his men's group in the Catholic Center and the two of them could watch *Downton Abbey* and paint their nails and giggle about hot actors and lovely Jane Austen fantasies. But the whole long, cold walk back, Marina had been debating, weighing, thinking, obsessively circling one question.

Should she invite him upstairs?

If this was what she was beginning to suspect it was, then he should meet Jordan. Marina would want to hear her best friend's opinion of him, even though she could already guess what it might be. But it was important, wasn't it, to take this step? Nate had asked her to meet his parents. The least she could do was have him meet her roommate.

Right?

"You ok?" Nate asked as a silence fell between them.

"Oh, yeah, sorry." She tucked a stray hair behind her ear. "It just gets dark out so early this time of year."

His eyebrows drew together, as if to say *you're really going to bring up the weather?* "I guess it does. More time for us night-owls though."

"Not the healthiest of lifestyles," Marina pointed out. "Studies have shown that people do better adjusting their schedules with the sun."

"People in Alaska must be screwed then."

She chuckled. "I suppose."

They were only four blocks from home. Four blocks for her to decide what this was and what she planned to do about it.

"So," she said to drown out the buzzing anxiety in her mind. "Your parents. What should I know?"

"They're both professors," Nate said, kicking at a snowbank. "English and History at Tufts."

"Wow."

Nate laughed. "I guess. They always just seemed like nerds to me."

"And you're an only child?"

"How could you tell?"

Marina looked away, grinning to herself. "Lucky guess." She burrowed her hands into her pockets, clenching them into fists. "I can't imagine life without siblings."

Nate shrugged. "I had a lot of friends."

"I'll bet your friends didn't break your toys and steal your stuff."

He grinned. "You'd be surprised. My friends were assholes."

"Yeah? Well try being the middle child between two brothers."

His smile flickered, and Marina wondered if this was a touchy subject. One of her high school friends had been an only child, and she'd often looked wistful when Marina returned from screaming at Alvaro or throwing things at Nick.

"Should I be worried about one of your brothers showing up with a gun?" Nate asked, his grin back in full force.

"I mean, Nick does have about three dozen."

"*Guns?*"

"Oh yes," Marina said, pretending not to notice Nate's horror. "He collects them."

"Fucking hell, that's terrifying."

"Why? He's certified to teach at the local shooting range. He knows everything there is to know about them. It's not dangerous."

"No one needs that many guns."

"No one needs more than one car, but you don't seem to mind people collecting *those*. They kill more people, are bad for the environment, and are, in the case of sports cars, a total waste of resources. But I'll bet none of your friends protest car fanatics."

"Yeah, because no one's driving their sports car into a school and running people over."

Marina pursed her lips. "Those are awful instances, but they're statistically very rare."

"I think we can do better than rare."

"But what about all the killings *prevented* by people with guns? What about the armed citizens who've stopped mass shootings?"

"There can't be that many of—"

"There are tons of them, but of course they don't get any media attention. Prevented tragedies don't sell newspapers."

"What about better regulations? Mental health checks?"

"But who would dictate the regulations?" Marina said, spreading out her hands. "Who gets to choose who's mentally healthy enough to get a gun? You? My brother has memory issues after six concussions. Does that make him mentally unfit?" She put up her palm to stop the response she could already see forming. "Of course,

93

if someone has expressed murderous intent they should be stopped. And many of them are, even in the current system. But surely you can sympathize with the fact that people get nervous when their government starts talking about restricting a constitutional right on something as vague as 'mental health.'"

Nate huffed and his breath fogged the air between them. "Well, I get nervous that anyone can waltz into a Walmart and buy a pistol."

"My brother doesn't. Do you know why? Because he's already wearing one." Marina rolled her shoulders. "Besides, Boston is a gun-free zone."

"People still get shot."

She looked at him. "Exactly."

Without her noticing, they'd reached her apartment building. Strange, how much he could distract her from even the most potent of anxieties. She stopped behind the row of parked cars jammed into their tiny Cambridge parking lot. Looking over her shoulder, she found Nate shaking his head in apparent disbelief.

"Well, as usual, it's been… illuminating."

Marina snorted. "Getting tired of debating with me yet?"

"Not even a little bit."

She tried to pretend the redness in her face was just the cold, the flutter in her chest just nerves. Her eyes darted up and she could see his question, his torso leaning in.

No, not again. I'm not ready for that, can't face that yet.

"Do you want to come upstairs?" she blurted.

Nate blinked.

"My roommate is home," Marina clarified. "But I'm sure she'd like to… meet you. You know, officially."

He chuckled. "Are you? Sure, I mean. I do have *rainbow* hair."

"Will you just come in?" Marina said, turning her back on him

94

and walking up the driveway before she could second-guess herself.

Oh Lord, please let Ben have left already. Please let Ben be gone.

Thankfully, Jordan was alone on the couch, working on her advanced calculus homework.

"I'm supposed to be good at math," she wailed as Marina walked in, and then fell silent when Nate stepped in behind her. "Oh."

"Jordan... this is Nate," Marina said.

They both waited for her to elaborate.

She didn't.

"Nice to meet you," Nate said at last with an awkward wave. "Sorry about the math."

Jordan smiled, ducking behind her curtain of black hair. "I guess I wish the Asian Math Gene made studying as effortless as people think."

Nate made a *pshh* sound. "That's a stereotype perpetuated by racists."

Jordan's eyes widened. They flickered from Nate's face to Nate's hair and then to Marina.

Who is this guy? her expression seemed to ask.

"What if Asians *are* really good at math?" Marina asked, taking off her coat and ignoring Jordan's unspoken question. "Broadly speaking."

Nate frowned. "We've been over this. It's racist to make any kind of generalization about people and skill sets. IQ has nothing to do with genetics or ethnicity."

"But what if it's cultural," Marina pointed out, trying to ignore Jordan's eyebrows rising, impossibly, higher. "Maybe they value certain subjects more than others."

"So? It's still dangerous to generalize."

"Statistics aren't dangerous," Marina said with an exasperated huff.

I sound like Ben.

But Nate was already responding, leaving her no time to process that thought.

"Of course statistics are dangerous. Everyone knows how easy they are to manipulate. You can make any data set say anything. Scientists need to be careful about what they say and how they say it. Look at that whole debacle with vaccines and autism."

Marina bristled. "That was based on totally falsified science."

"Whatever data you're thinking about could be falsified too."

"But how much are you going to write off that way? What about climate change? The scientists working on those studies have clear biases. Are we going to dismiss everything *they* say because of their agendas?"

Nate leaned back, ruffling his hair. "Fuck, are you a climate change denier?"

She cocked one hip and folded her arms. "I think it's more complicated than Greta Thunberg makes it out to be."

Nate slapped a hand to his forehead in an exaggerated *oh no* gesture.

"I can't believe I just went on a date with a *climate change denier.*"

"Oh, I've got worse than that."

"I don't doubt it." He shook his head, looking to Jordan for support. "Your friend here is quite something. Downright full of opinions."

"You're one to talk," Marina grumbled, unable to hold back the grin tugging up on her cheeks.

"Did you guys have a nice date?" Jordan asked, and even in her quiet voice, Marina could hear the emphasis on the word *date*.

"Museum was packed, but Marina taught me some cool stuff

about ears."

"And I educated him about Star Wars," Marina said, plopping into her favorite chair.

"*Au contraire, mademoiselle*, I believe it was I who was educating *you*." He turned to Jordan. "She was trying to diss on the new Star Wars trilogy."

Jordan frowned. "And you weren't?"

Nate threw his hands up. "I'm surrounded by people with terrible taste."

"I think you are, but not in this room," Marina said, yanking off her boots. "Do you want something to drink?"

"Beer?"

Marina suppressed a grimace, making the conscious decision *not* to look at Jordan.

"We have tea and hot chocolate," she said, padding into the kitchen. "And no, nothing to spike the hot chocolate with."

"Tea then!" Nate called.

"What are you studying?" Marina heard Jordan ask in a timid voice.

Terror pulsed through her. They were talking without her supervision, without her guidance.

What am I doing?

Marina could practically hear Jordan's thoughts as Nate described his plan to major in Urban Planning and minor in Political Science so he could go into ethical city planning and development. It was as if she was seeing Nate clearly for the first time: that ludicrous hair, that self-satisfied smirk, the way he casually said controversial, inflammatory things as if they were fact, things like *our incompetent dumbass president* and *because we live in a dystopian hellscape*. It was easy, when they were alone, to challenge him, poke him back, pretend it was just a game like debate club or chess.

97

But here?

Jordan responded politely, asking sterile, innocuous questions about classes and upbringing. But Marina knew what her friend was thinking.

Because if she had any sense, she'd be thinking it too.

I must be losing my mind.

Pushing the warning bells in her brain aside, she poured hot water over the tea strainer and carried their teapot back into the living room with three mugs.

"So you're both in biomedical engineering?" Nate asked, accepting his mug.

"She's pre-med," Marina corrected, offering another to Jordan. "It's how we met. We were roomed together because we're both interested in healthcare."

Nate blew steam off the surface of his drink. "Then you must know firsthand what a mess our medical system is."

"It is," Jordan said, her soft voice somehow carrying. "But I'll bet not for the reasons you think."

Marina sat back, clenching her teeth and trying to look relaxed.

Nate frowned over the edge of his mug. "What do you mean?"

Here we go.

"It's a mess because Obamacare was a huge mistake," Jordan said. She looked deceptively innocent with her small hands wrapped around her favorite floral teacup, but Marina knew just how well her roommate could hold her own. She was dating Ben, after all. "See, the problem is that we used to have more of a purely capitalistic system. Which worked ok. Obviously, like all capitalism economies, there were people who fell behind or got the short end of the stick."

"Short end of the stick?" Nate said, eyes wide, voice incredulous. "Is that what you call forcing poor people to decide between bankruptcy and death?"

"But mostly," Jordan rolled on, "it was functional. Costs were kept low by a competitive market and people were given top-notch care."

"Yeah, until they had a chronic condition," Nate said, tea forgotten. "Or were *broke*."

Jordan inclined her head. "Sure. Again, it sucked for a few but worked for the many. Obamacare was meant to socialize healthcare, which is a good idea—" Nate's eyebrows rose in surprise "—in concept. Medicine doesn't play well with capitalism because you can't decide when and where to get sick. You can't evaluate options and carefully pick the best one for you. So, believe it or not, I actually support universal healthcare."

"Color me surprised," Nate mumbled.

"But we can't have it both ways. Right now, the system is half-socialized, half-capitalist, and that's making everything more expensive. When the government's paying, hospitals can charge whatever they want. That makes insurance companies unable to keep up, so only the big ones survive. Which means they can also charge whatever they want. The poor are covered and the rich can pay, so who's hurt the most? The middle class, who were the people who were, for the most part, doing just fine before Obamacare."

"I don't think they were doing *just fine*," Nate began, but Jordan spoke over him in that small but powerful voice.

"There's also the problem that we can't give everyone the BMW treatment. That's the issue with our current system, that there are some procedures that are ridiculously expensive and questionably necessary. We have amazingly advanced technology, which is wonderful, but we can't afford to use every single measure on every single case. Where do we draw the line? Who is turned away? If we try to give everyone the level of care that the rich and powerful get with their top-notch insurance, then we'll bankrupt our country and our medical system will be knocked back into the fifties. Which nobody wants."

"So you're saying poor people just get to die then? Or that some committee will decide who gets chemo?"

"No," Jordan said calmly, evaluating Nate over her teacup. "I'm saying that the idea of giving every American the best care our modern system offers is a fantasy. There must be restrictions. Every socialized system draws hard lines, lines that make people uncomfortable. We need to be able to have those conversations before universal healthcare is an option. That's all."

Nate was frowning and Jordan's face was expressionless, and Marina had sunk so deep into her own thoughts that she wondered if she might go mad.

"So," Jordan said at last. "Are you staying for the movie?"

"Oh, right," Nate said, putting his mug down and rising to his feet. "Sorry. I don't wanna interrupt roommate night." He smiled at Marina in a way she couldn't quite decipher. "Thanks for joining me today. See you soon?"

She rose to see him out, walking him to the door and struggling to keep her voice as normal as possible when she said goodbye. He didn't try to kiss her, but he touched her arm in a way that made her heart flutter and her mind race. But *why*? Why did she feel so drawn to someone who disagreed with her on *everything*? What kind of relationship could they possibly have?

Marina made her way back into the living room, waiting until the last possible moment to look at Jordan.

"So?" she asked, doing her best not to sound as terrified as she felt.

Jordan cocked her head. "What's going on, Marina?"

She plopped down. "You don't like him?"

"I don't know him. But he doesn't seem like… your type."

Marina rubbed her face, trying to knit her tattered thoughts together.

"I know. It's just, we started talking at Ben's party and…" She trailed off. And what? She'd developed a crush so quickly, so powerfully, that it felt like planetary magnetism?

"You're going to keep seeing him?"

"I'm meeting his parents next weekend," Marina admitted, looking at Jordan through her fingers.

Her friend's eyes widened with concern.

"It's not that big of a deal," Marina added quickly. "He said his parents like meeting his friends. I don't think it's serious or anything."

As if I understand Nate's idea of serious.

"Just be careful," Jordan said in a wary tone. "This doesn't seem… like you."

Marina studied the toes of her socks, decorated in an elaborate pattern of snowflakes. No, this didn't seem like her at all. She was sensible, careful, the last person to do anything impulsive. She always made six different pro and con lists before choosing a direction.

What would that list look like for Nate? What would be in the "pro" column for him?

That he makes me feel alive? That I can't stop smiling when he's around? That I think I'm falling for him, whether I like it or not?

Marina bit the inside of her lip. Her brain felt worn and weathered from the endless cycle of her thoughts.

I'm not going to make this decision right now, she told herself, doing her best to shove Nate and everything about him out of her brain.

So, with an overbright smile, she asked, "What movie are we watching?"

Jordan grinned. "Anything but Star Wars."

Chapter 15

"That motherfucker needs to go," Tiff said, pacing back and forth in their narrow living room and swelling like a bullfrog. "He's transphobic and Islamophobic and misogynist and probably a neo-Nazi. I can't *believe* they're letting him poison campus like this."

Nate was lounging in his favorite saggy part of the couch, eating Smart Popcorn and half-watching *Rick and Morty* as it played behind her. But even Tiffany's outrage couldn't hold his attention. He was too excited, too distracted with the knowledge that his parents were coming in just *two days*. How was he going to introduce Marina? As a friend? Would she be insulted? Was the alternative worse?

And, in the back of his mind, the humming challenge to crown them all:

When was he going to kiss her?

"Sorry, Tiff," Leo said, tossing back a handful of walnuts. "But you can't get someone expelled just because you don't like them."

"Don't you two *get it*?" she snapped, stopping right in front of the TV. "He's normalizing terrible ideas. He's making our classroom into an unsafe environment. He's infecting MIT! Do you even *care*?"

Nate's gut twisted. She was right; he was letting his own distractions get in the way of the greater good. Of course *he* didn't have to worry about this douchebag's presence—Nate was white and wealthy and, currently, straight-appearing. But Nate's nonchalance was only possible because of his advantages. Tiffany and Leo didn't have the luxury of laughing off white supremacy like a bad joke.

He made himself focus on Tiffany's face.

"Can you ask to the professor to intervene?" Leo asked.

Tiffany tightened her fists. "I tried."

"Do you think you could, you know, tell him?" Nate said cautiously, rolling a bit of popcorn between his fingers. "Like, about what you're going through? I'm sure he'd be nicer if he knew—"

"And throw more fuel on his toxic masculinity crusade? I think not."

"He'd probably just use it as ammunition anyways," Leo said, setting aside the bag of mixed nuts with a scowl.

Nate frowned, thinking of Marina. "But if you could just *talk* to him, get him to consider—"

"No," Tiffany said, eyes glittering with a little more than rage. "No, I shouldn't be forced to reveal personal information about myself just to feel safe in my own fucking school. I'm paying money to be here!"

"So is he," Nate said in what he hoped was a kind but reasonable voice.

"Fuck him. And fuck his money. Everyone knows his dad is some sleazy real estate mogul from Texas. That's how he rents such a nice house."

"It was a nice house," Leo said, resting his elbows on his knees.

"He can take his capitalist blood money and use it to get into a different school," Tiffany continued. "Or buy himself a soul. Whatever, so long as he's *gone*."

Nate pursed his lips, thinking of Marina. This guy was her

104

friend, wasn't he? His arm had been around that short girl, Jordan, at the party. Were they a couple?

Should it matter?

He didn't want to hurt Marina, but if it was true that this kid was making an MIT classroom into an unsafe environment, then shouldn't Nate do the right thing and support Tiff? Or at least not hold her back? Marina would understand that he was working for justice, that he was being true to himself.

Wouldn't she?

"What are you gonna do?" Leo asked, folding his hands behind his head.

Tiffany tapped her chin, staring at her reflection in the dark window. She was pretty, blonde and athletic with big eyes magnified by even bigger glasses. Nate had hit on her when they'd met as first-years and she had informed him, in no uncertain terms, that she didn't do the D. Now, three years later, Nate wondered if she did much of the V either. He'd only ever seen her date one woman and even then, only for a month. He might have wondered if she was asexual, if she didn't self-identify as a proud lesbian on Twitter. It had occurred to him on more than one occasion that Tiff might see herself as some kind of crusader, a progressive Joan of Arc, too busy with her mission of making the world acknowledge her to waste time getting laid.

Too bad for her.

"Well," she said at last in a low, thoughtful voice, "if he's so determined to spew this shit, maybe I let him hang himself with it."

Leo kicked back, settling into the couch. But Nate felt that distinct, familiar prickle that warned him of a nasty feud roaring toward them.

"What do you mean?" he asked, crumpling the edge of the popcorn bag.

Tiffany began to pace again. "If he keeps doing this awful Red

105

Nation blog, eventually the professor will have to acknowledge that it's putting students in danger. I'll keep posting comments under different names, egg him on, make sure he feels like he's getting to me. Eventually, he'll go too far. He'll say something even MIT won't be able to ignore."

"What if he doesn't?" Nate asked, thinking about how well Marina had met him on every mental battlefield they'd encountered.

"Oh, he will," Tiffany said, her fingers clenching and unclenching like an angry pulse. "He's a garbage pile of a human and he can't hide how gross he is forever."

Nate nodded, but secretly he wasn't so sure. If this kid was anything like Marina, Tiffany wouldn't have an easy time trapping him.

"And besides," she said, finally settling into a wooden chair dragged over from their dining table. "Maybe I can rally Twitter to help. If he goes viral in a bad way, it'll teach that cocksucker a lesson."

"Sounds ominous," Leo said, tossing a pecan into his mouth.

Tiffany shrugged. "I'm done rolling over for agents of the patriarchy. The internet has given marginalized people a voice and we'll use it to change the world as we see fit. They can't keep ignoring the revolution we're creating."

"But what if the other side has something to offer?" Nate found himself saying, thoughtfully, almost to himself. "I mean, no one can be wrong about *everything*, right?"

Nate looked up to find both Tiffany and Leo gaping at him as if he'd just confessed that he was joining a monastery. Leo's mouth was pulled half-up, in the act of forming a laugh, but Tiffany's eyes were wide and furious.

"How can you even *say* that?" she said in a strangled voice. "How can you say Republicans have *anything* to offer? They've ruined the environment. They support mass incarceration and modern-day slavery. They *cage children*."

"Sorry, sorry, you're right," Nate said, waving a hand. "I don't know what I was thinking. I'm just tired."

"Well, careful with that." Tiffany was up again, heading to the kitchen to get her own snack. "Entertain toxic ideas and soon enough you'll be posting unhinged rants on YouTube and spreading conspiracy theories about big tech censorship."

"Hah, yeah right," Nate said.

But he couldn't shake the feeling of Leo's eyes on him, sly and calculating; the same eyes that had watched him spend the whole party with Marina and not chase after Ross; the same eyes that had probably caught him grinning at his phone at every available opportunity. Leo was the smartest person he knew in real life. Nate might not be a physics problem, but he strongly suspected he wasn't that hard to figure out.

Slumping deeper into the couch, Nate crunched down on a handful of popcorn, keeping his gaze fixed on *Rick and Morty* and trying not to wonder if Tiffany was right.

Chapter 16

Marina was dressed in her best turtleneck sweater, her most flattering pair of jeans, her nicest pair of ankle boots, and she was still terrified.

"It's not that big of a deal," she told her reflection. "You're not officially dating. Why are you so worried, they're just *parents*?"

But her eyes kept zeroing in on that gold cross her *abuela* had given her for her fifteenth birthday. She'd never had a proper *quinceañera*. Her parents had believed it would draw too much attention, to throw a party celebrating something so *Latin*, not to mention the expense. So instead of the big, lavish ball with tiered cakes and ridiculously frilly dresses, Marina got exactly what she wanted: all her favorite home cooked dishes to enjoy with her family. Her cousins had flown down from New York, and her *abuela* had spent the whole trip complaining about how cold it was. But it was one of Marina's best memories, sitting between her two brothers with a plastic tiara from the dollar store perched on her head and a huge grin on her face.

The cross was more than just a religious symbol for her. It was a reminder of family, of how the love they had for each other could make even a humble dinner feel like the pinnacle of luxury. The symbol was an anchor to her grandmother, now in heaven, and her parents and the earthly meaning that made everything she was doing worthwhile.

But hanging in the middle of the red sweater, it felt glaringly obvious, like a sunspot on a picture. Marina could imagine Nate's parents greeting her, looking down, gaze lingering on her chest. On the necklace. He'd told her enough about them that she could piece together what would go through their minds. How they'd pretend not to notice and smile and avoid the topic of religion all night.

I'm used to it, she thought, reminding herself of all the parties, all the classes, all the random encounters on campus where her religion had made people uncomfortable. *I'm strong in my faith. Whatever happens is in God's plan.*

Her phone buzzed.

It was Nate.

<Ready for some parental units?>

Marina looked at herself one last time as she grabbed her coat off the back of her desk chair. Just as she was about to leave, she reached up and tucked the little gold cross beneath the turtleneck, turning away so she didn't have to watch it disappear.

Nate had chosen the Friendly Toast for brunch, a cozy place decorated like a vintage diner, complete with block coloring, metal-rimmed tables, vinyl floors, and masses of college students. They had to wait almost thirty minutes to be seated, which was more than enough time for the task of introductions.

Lilly Campbell was a slender, elegant woman with a sharp, short haircut, streaked with gray. She had a wide smile and had taken Marina's hand in both her own, saying how *wonderful* it was to meet more of Nathan's friends. Martin Campbell was just as welcoming, if a little less graceful. He lingered back, one arm around his son's shoulders as he kept an eye out for the waitress who had just promised them a seat. Marina did her best to smile and answer the easy questions (*What are you studying? Where are you from? Have you been here before?*).

But her insides were squirming.

Everything about Nate's parents, from their obviously expensive clothing to their easy confidence in a busy restaurant, was alien to Marina. Her parents liked to go to Olive Garden and Applebee's, predictable chains with simple reservation systems and cookie-cutter layouts. Anything in the city always had them standing in the corner, waiting for a booth to open up so they could have their backs to something solid. But Nate's parents moved through the world with effortless ease, reaching out to Marina as if they could welcome her into a universe they already owned.

It would have been fascinating if she wasn't so nervous.

"Here we go," Mr. Campbell said as the waitress came back to seat them. "Time to eat at last."

"I'm ravenous," said Mrs. Campbell, winking at Marina.

Marina swallowed.

The menu was huge and overwhelming. There were burritos, waffles, pancakes, omelets, eggs cooked in every conceivable way. Marina picked something at random, unable to keep up with the conversation and analyze options at the same time.

"So are you starting to think about next steps, Marina? Life after MIT?"

"Mom," Nate complained, stirring his coffee. "We're *juniors*."

"Not everyone's as spontaneous as you, dear."

Marina cleared her throat, taking the paper hat off her straw but not yet touching her orange juice. "Actually yes. I'm starting to look at careers in biomedical engineering."

"Oh, how exciting," Mrs. Campbell said brightly.

"Lots to fix in the medical industry," Mr. Campbell inserted with a sage nod.

"And lots of people to help," Marina answered. From the corner of her eye, she saw Nate grin into his whipped cream topping.

"Any idea what kind of work you'll do?"

"Prosthetics, I think," Marina said, stirring in her pulp. "There's a debt-forgiveness program I'd like to apply for. It pays off your student loans if you agree to work on government research for a few years."

"Would that be in Boston?"

"No," Marina admitted. "Probably more rural than that."

"That's very noble of you," Mrs. Campbell said, putting her napkin on her lap. "I don't think I could ever leave the city. It sounds lovely sometimes, to have more space and greenery." She smiled. "But I'm not sure we'd find our kind of people."

Nate winced. Marina cocked her head, ignoring him.

"What do you mean?" she asked.

Mrs. Campbell glanced up, blinking in surprise.

"Why, liberals of course. You hear horror stories about all those gun-toting rednecks in middle America, the kinds of people who voted for our president." The way she said *our president* made it perfectly clear that she couldn't imagine anyone in the world disagreeing with her already solidified opinion.

Marina forced herself to smile. "My family owns guns."

Mrs. Campbell's eyes widened in horror. "Oh, I didn't mean—"

"Lots of people who own guns aren't, as she says, gun-toting rednecks," Mr. Campbell inserted.

"And maybe not all gun-toting rednecks are bad people," Nate said, half-grinning, half-grimacing.

"Well, all the ones who voted for—"

"Here's our food!" Mr. Campbell interrupted his wife as their waitress swooped in, arms heavy with overflowing plates.

Marina accepted the subject change, letting the conversation move on to Nate's hair—apparently more vibrant than the last time they'd seen him—and some new mission Nate's activist roommate had taken up against another student. She picked at her Eggs Benedict, bobbing her head as she listened to them talk about their university jobs.

But again, Marina's imagination inserted her own parents into the scene, sitting at the table with them. Her father's mustache would be covering a frown, unable to hold back his disapproval and discomfort. Maybe her *mamá* would smile and ask polite questions as Mrs. Campbell explained her department's decision to remove Chaucer and Hemmingway from the syllabus in favor of making the reading list more diverse.

Maybe not.

A small but loud part of Marina felt like walking out, deleting Nate's number, letting this whole stupid distraction fall away like a bad dream. But that was the problem, wasn't it? It wasn't a bad dream. Every time Nate's gaze lingered on her, every time his lips quirked in a secretive, knowing smile, her heart raced. Her limbs felt electric. And all she wanted was to get him alone so they could discuss what his parents were saying. Not just nod along but dig into it and find out what he was thinking.

And maybe do more than just talk…

She took a big sip of orange juice, trying to cool herself down. Was it hot in there? How was Mrs. Campbell keeping her coat on?

"Of course some of the older professors are putting up a fuss," Nate's mom was saying. "It's endlessly frustrating how tenure keeps these old white men around. But at least we're hiring for three new positions, so change is in the air."

"That's a lot," Nate said with enthusiasm even Marina could tell was fake.

"Yes, we're already interviewing applicants. There are so many women and people of color that it's going to be difficult to decide between them."

Marina bit her lip to stop the question from tumbling out of her. *Are you hiring just based on their skin tone and gender?*

But then Nate cut in.

"What about us white dudes?" he said with a smirk.

"We have two candidates who are queer," his mother said, sharing the smile. "Although they aren't as exciting."

"Hey!"

"Sorry, honey." Mrs. Campbell patted Nate's cheek. "But you know what we've taught you. It's time to share the table with everyone."

She turned to smile at Marina with the benevolence of someone absolutely certain they'd just said something virtuous and right.

Marina couldn't stop herself. "I'm sorry, but I'd rather get a position for my talent than my heritage."

There was an awkward silence.

"Well, of course they're very talented," Mr. Campbell said with a cough. "At this level, it's hardly a scientific process."

"Maybe," Marina said, flushing. "But in science, we believe in double-blind studies. Merit-based. That kind of thing."

"Well, unfortunately there's no such thing as double-blind in the arts," Mrs. Campbell said with a sympathetic spread of her hands. "It's far too subjective and prone to internalized biases. Those with the power to do so much strive to cultivate diversity and true artistic merit because it certainly won't happen on its own. Can you imagine what the world would look like if our educational choices were ruled by public tastes? It would be a disaster. *Fifty Shades of Gray* would be given a Pulitzer."

Marina shrugged. "I haven't read it. But maybe it should be considered, if so many people like it."

Nate's eyes were huge now, with either shock or worry, Marina couldn't be sure. Mrs. Campbell was leaning in, still smiling, still warm, but there was an edge to her voice that made Marina wonder if she'd stepped over some invisible line.

"The fact that people like something does not make it worthwhile. The populace is a remarkably poor judge of quality and moral value. Look at the state of movies right now."

Marina sawed off a corner of her English muffin. "What do you mean?"

"Space battles, car chases, *elves*? Where is the nuance? Where is the art? And for God's sake, where is the *representation*?"

"I mean, *Black Panther*'s coming out," Nate said reasonably.

"At long last," Mr. Campbell said, nodding and eying his wife nervously.

Finally, Marina thought as they began to discuss how excited they all were to see it, *something we can agree on*.

Chapter 17

"Three more," Leo said, looming over Nate's bench with his best *angry coach* face.

Nate groaned, dipping his arms back down once. Twice. But on the third he got stuck halfway, his whole body as taut as industrial cables. His shoulders strained, his elbows shook, his spine pressed into the padding.

Leo grabbed the bar and pulled the weights onto the rack. "You're distracted."

Nate rolled into a seated position, rubbing his face with the rough, grainy gym towel.

"Sorry, dude," he said, catching his breath. "We can't all be as built as you."

"It's that chick from the party, isn't it?"

Nate ducked, rose without answering, and led them to the free weights area where he and Leo would finish their workout together.

It was *that chick*. Marina had been circling his brain all week, ever since the brunch with his parents had come so perilously close to disaster. And then the phone call with them after, when they'd said they were *worried* about him, that they weren't sure she was *the right person for him*. The problem was, had always been, that his parents were spot-on. Marina was all wrong for him, all wrong for his family and his friends. She was a puzzle piece that didn't fit, a square block in the round hole of his whole fucking life.

So how come all he could think about was seeing her again?

"You're crushing hard, man," Leo said, selecting a bulky pair of dumbbells. "I know the signs. Staring off into the distance, grinning at your phone when you think no one's watching, ignoring just about everything else that's going on." He grunted as he began to lift. "Whether or not you want to talk about it, I see what's going on."

"It's not a big deal," Nate said, swinging a weight over one shoulder to work his triceps.

"Sure," Leo chuckled. "Not a big deal. You do know what tomorrow is, right?"

"Yeah, the day companies capitalize on everyone's seasonal affective disorder and try to sell them chocolates and cards to fill the existential void no one wants to think about."

Leo snorted, dropping his weights onto a nearby bench with a *thump*. "Happy Valentine's Day to you too."

"It's a made-up corporate holiday. It doesn't mean anything."

"Maybe not, but your reaction sure as hell does." Leo sat down, wiping his forehead. "C'mon, tell me. I promise not to laugh."

"That's not what I'm worried about," Nate said, making a face at himself in the mirror as he completed his rep.

Leo kept still, as patient and silent as a preacher waiting for confession.

Fuck, is she converting me now?

Nate plopped down across from him, glaring at his shoes.

"Ok, it is her," he admitted.

"No shit," Leo said with a grin.

"She recognized me at the party. We spent most of the evening together on the porch."

Nate looked up, waiting for him to put things together.

118

"I saw you two through the window," Leo said, still not getting it. "Black hair, good smile. Great ass."

"But I'd seen her before," Nate went on. "At our hockey game. Remember? The first one of the season? The one against... the CCCs."

It was at once horrible and totally satisfying to see Leo's face open, his mouth curve into an O of surprise. And Nate found himself thinking about how it wasn't so long ago that he'd picked apart Leo's expressions, watched him for any hint of interest. And what had Nate even wanted? A one-night stand? A roll in the sheets? The simple comfort of a sexy body beside his?

Things felt so much more complicated now.

"Wait, you're saying she's... Catholic?"

Nate nodded. "And conservative."

To his surprise, Leo broke out into wild, gut-deep peals of laughter. "Dude, that's *hilarious.*"

Nate threw the towel at him. "Fuck you."

But Leo didn't stop, clutching his gut and all but falling off the gym bench. A few other students turned to stare and one woman on an elliptical — likely a grad student — gave them both the stink eye.

"You promised not to laugh," Nate said, struggling to keep the whine out of his voice.

"Right," Leo said, wiping his eyes. "Right, sorry." He took a deep breath, as if to gather his composure. "I'm listening. So? How did it happen?"

Nate stared at the ceiling as he answered. "She walked me home from the party."

"And you banged?"

"No." Nate swallowed. "We haven't even kissed."

"That sucks," Leo said, drawing out the U.

Nate looked at him, feeling a strong need to explain, to make

Leo understand. "I think… this is different. I want to do it right this time. Leo, I think I really like this girl."

"The Catholic?"

Nate huffed. "She's not *just* Catholic. She's smart and witty and calls me out on my shit."

"I like her already."

"And I actually *enjoy* talking to her about politics. It's… kinda fun."

Leo raised his eyebrows. "Even though all her ideas are trash."

Nate found himself standing without consciously deciding to, walking to the weights, walking back, overwhelmed by an itching need to crawl out of his own skin.

"That's the thing, what if her ideas *aren't* trash? At least not all of them. And what if she thinks some of *my* ideas are trash? And what if we can make something stronger by talking about things and finding the common ground that *isn't* trash?" Nate paused to look at his friend.

Leo's expression was wryly skeptical. "This has nothing to do with the fact that she's a total hottie, now does it?"

Nate rubbed his sweat-damp hair. "I mean, not *nothing*."

Leo rose, clapping Nate on the shoulder with one hand. "Want my advice?" He didn't wait for an answer. "Let this one go. You've got a whole school to choose from, literally, so go out there and pick a person less, er, difficult."

It was strange to know that this was the very same advice Nate would be giving himself if their roles were reversed. But his instincts recoiled from the idea like it was diseased, like it was a poison that could taint his whole life. Nate could picture it, ending things with Marina the way he'd ended countless other one-night stands or Tinder meetups. He'd sit her down for *the talk* or maybe write her a long, careful message. When he saw her around campus, he'd dive out of view or scuttle into an open classroom to avoid any awkwardness.

And always, for the rest of his life, he'd wonder what he'd missed out on.

"Naw, man," Nate said to his reflection in the mirror. "I can't do that. I need to know."

Leo shrugged in a *your funeral* kind of way.

"Alright. Then yank off the Band-Aid. This thing is too wild to draw out." Leo pulled out his phone, scrolling through emails. "Here." He handed his phone to Nate.

"The undergrad ski trip?"

"Exactly. A full weekend, just the two of you. Offer to drive her. You'll share a hotel room." Leo winked. "It's perfect."

"I don't think she'd go for that..."

"Fuck, man, you can't date some kind of nun. Your balls would fall off."

Nate grimaced, thinking about their drinking game, the number she hadn't asked for in return.

Sexual partners?

He'd stopped counting at twenty.

"Yo, Earth to Nate. What's the verdict?" Leo asked.

"Yeah," he said, shaking himself. "Yeah, ok. I'll try. But I don't even know if she skis."

Leo waggled his eyebrows suggestively.

"Sounds to me like you have lots to teach her."

Nate shoved him into the cardio area, making the woman on the elliptical huff in indignation.

Chapter 18

This is not me. I'm not someone who waits around for a boy to text. I'm not someone who falls for Marxist idiots with unnatural hair colors. I don't go on secret dates I can't tell my friends about and hold my breath on Valentine's day...

And yet Marina couldn't stop looking at her phone, still and silent beside her laptop. Her biomechanics homework was open, cursor blinking over the online assignment's empty cells, but all she could think about was Nate and how long it had been since he'd written and what he must be thinking of her.

Looking back on it, the brunch with his parents felt like more and more of a mess. But what was Marina supposed to do? She'd hidden her faith, held her tongue when she could, but she wasn't *perfect*. And besides, what was the point of starting off on false pretenses? Already, shame and regret braided up her backbone at the things she *had* hidden: the fact that she prayed every night, the fact that her brothers were the very redneck hicks the Campbells were so dismissive of.

The fact that her parents would have been horrified by almost everything in the conversation.

"*Argg*," Marina groaned to herself, letting her head fall onto her folded arms. In the other room, she could hear Ben and Jordan. To distract herself, she focused on their voices, on the pendulum back-and-forth of their discussion.

"...I think this is a bad idea," Jordan said.

"Standing against murder is a bad idea now?"

"You know I agree with you, but what if your professor is pro-choice?"

"That's her problem."

"No," Jordan said reasonably. "It's yours. You're the one who has to pass the class."

"If she fails me, I'll sue for religious discrimination."

"You'll still have failed. And besides, what about the rest of them? Like that girl who keeps commenting on your blog."

"She's a nitwit."

"A nitwit with power."

"Only if we give it to her."

"Didn't you hear about the student her magazine dragged last year? The guy who made some stupid rape joke? Ben, he was *expelled*."

"Totally unfairly. See babe, this is the problem. Bullies like her are purposely conflating speech with violence to shut down anyone they disagree with, and the institutions are letting it happen. It's a dangerous cycle that threatens our freedom."

"You can't fight the whole system in a day."

"I can fight the thought-policing tyrants one article at a time. Starting with this ditz."

Marina straightened, rubbing the back of her neck.

Maybe listening to them wasn't the best way to calm herself down.

Ben's fight with the Social Justice Warrior online had escalated. Every day, her comments on Red Nation got more inflammatory, more enraged, more vitriolic. She'd recruited friends and online personalities. Even Ben's professor was beginning to express clear distaste, allowing the girl to make pointed, unfriendly statements in class about fascists and braindead Republicans. It made Marina nervous, this cloud of battle hanging over her friends, her apartment, her life.

And, by extension, her budding whatever-it-was.

Marina and Jordan had agreed that they shouldn't tell Ben about Nate. While Jordan wasn't necessarily unsupportive, they'd decided together that, until Marina was sure how she felt about the kid with rainbow hair, it was silly to complicate everything by getting Ben involved. So, for the first time in Marina's memory, there was a secret in their household. Texts she couldn't talk about, thoughts she couldn't share. That had been the *point* of their friendship in the first place, that nothing was out-of-bounds. The three of them could discuss anything, no matter how *offensive* or *unsafe*. It was the glue that bound them together, coming undone.

How is it that I can have conversations about racism and dead babies but I can't tell them about someone I'm falling in love with.

Marina caught herself.

Was she... falling in love?

Before she could parse through the terrifying ramifications of such a thought, her phone buzzed.

It was humiliating how excited she got, seeing his name on the screen.

<I have a proposition> Nate said.

Marina was grinning, stupidly, foolishly, out of control. She typed out a quick response. <You do know what day it is, right?>

She held her breath as those three hateful dots appeared, pulsing like firing neurons. His answer came in a quick series of texts.

<Yeah, a stupid capitalist holiday fabricated by greeting card companies and corporations grubbing for more money>

Then, <Not to mention an opportunity for the ruling class to

push their heteronormative, homophobic bullshit>

Then, <Happy Valentine's Day>

She laughed, leaning back in her chair to kick her feet up onto her chemistry notebook. <Well if it isn't the life of the party over here>

He sent a winking face. <Bah humbug. Anyways. Do you ski?>

Marina's heart sank.

It wasn't the first time someone had asked her if she skied. She'd only ever heard about the sport down in Roanoke, where the more affluent kids took trips with their parents to places with fantastical names. Vale. Aspen. Breckenridge. Tignes. Marina had once googled how much a *day ticket* to one of these places cost and her mouth had fallen open. And these people went for a whole week, sometimes two! Ridiculous. Here in Boston, it seemed like students were always popping up north for a *day on the slopes*. How anyone could even think of wasting money like that was beyond her. Did they not realize how expensive college was?

Or, more likely, was debt not an issue for them?

She sighed, fingers moving sluggishly over the small keyboard. <Not really.>

He answered quickly. <Wanna learn?>

She could feel his infectious enthusiasm through the phone, and her whole body leaned in, as if in physical craving. An image bloomed in her mind: her and Nate in fluffy hats, sprinting through a pristine winter landscape, shoving fistfuls of snow into each other's faces. She pictured them tumbling down in a puff of white powder with an echoing, glorious laugh, and much later, warming their hands by a roaring fire with mugs of cocoa or mulled wine.

It was hopelessly unrealistic, almost saccharine, like something out of a bad romcom.

And she'd never wanted anything more.

<When?> she asked to delay her answer.

<Next weekend. It's a student trip up to Mount Snow. I know some people who rented a few rooms together.>

Marina paused. *Some people*? Would they be *his* kind of people, who would look at her like an alien, stare at her cross like it might burn them?

She swallowed, but he was still typing.

<I volunteer as driver> he said, and Marina imagined his boyish, pleading voice saying the words.

<Good> Marina answered. <Because my car is 600 miles away.>

<Lol. So we on then?>

It felt like a hand was squeezing her heart, reminding her that it was time to be a responsible adult. Ski trips were for rich American-born kids with parents who hadn't given up everything for a better future. Ski trips were for people like Nate, who didn't think of their time at MIT as a stack of burning money but rather as an *experience*, something to be casually and aimlessly wandered through, as if a successful future was going to drop out of the sky.

And he calls me *privileged*, Marina thought.

<Sorry> she said, hating the words even as she typed them. <I can't get away that weekend>

<Why?>

<Big exam.>

<This early in the semester?!?!>

<Alas, my prof is a jerk.>

A lie.

Her professors were all wonderful people she'd studied under before. And she didn't have an exam. So why was she committing a sin, however slight? For him? Or because she was too proud to admit

127

that she didn't have the cash?

<That sucks bro>

She chuckled, but it was a dry, wispy sound. <Thanks dude?>

<I'll just have to find another way to get you out of Boston. Seems like you'll need a break this semester, eh?>

Marina sent a laughing emoji, because she had no idea what else to say.

Chapter 19

"You know," Nate said, shrugging off his coat and hanging it on the barstool, "We *could* just hang out at my apartment."

Marina's laugh was warm and infectious and chased away the cold better than any shot. "Aren't your roommates there?"

"You met my parents!"

"And something tells me that your friends will be a whole 'nother story," she said, toying pointedly with her cross.

"Touché," he said, flagging down the bartender and ordering the seasonal Harpoon IPA.

Really, a part of Nate was relieved that Marina didn't want to come home with him, at least not yet. Of course he wanted things to move in that direction. He wanted her to see his room, read the spines of the books on his shelf, sprawl laughing on his bed. But every time he imagined leading her inside, Tiffany and Leo were there, waiting on the couch. And what would they think? How would they react to him bringing home a conservative, a *woman*? He knew they'd be accepting; of course they would! But what if it created a schism where there hadn't been one before, a feeling of otherness as Nate embraced the less oppressed side of his sexuality? Would they think Nate was "going straight," abandoning them for societal acceptance?

How could he explain to them what he couldn't even explain to himself?

When he finished paying for his beer, Nate turned to find Marina watching him with a pained expression.

"What?" he asked, settling back in his chair.

"I guess it would make me feel better if we didn't meet in a bar."

"Because of this?" he said, flashing the Wyoming ID as he slid it back into his wallet.

"Well, yeah."

Nate grinned, sitting up on one hip bone to return it to his back pocket.

"Where do people even hang out if not bars?" He lifted the pint to his lips, flashing Marina a wink. "Other than apartments, of course."

She swirled her cocktail suggestively. "Trying to get me to Netflix and chill?"

Nate waggled his eyebrows. "Or blow off your exam and come skiing with me?"

"I knew I hadn't heard the end of that."

"Come on, live a little! You're like a studying machine."

"I'm like a student," she said, emphasizing the *like*. "Studying is kind of the point."

Nate smirked. "Sounds boring."

Marina shifted to hook one leg over the other, toward him. Hadn't Nate heard somewhere that the direction a woman crossed her legs was an expression of sexual interest? Was she signaling something to him, in her own subdued way?

He'd certainly like to think so.

"Let me guess," Marina said, propping her chin on one hand. "Your parents are paying for your tuition."

Nate sniffed. "They are not."

What he didn't mention was that his tuition was paid for by a trust fund his grandfather had created when Nate was five years old, a generous pile of money in the stock market that had more than doubled in the intervening years.

But Marina didn't need to know that.

"Besides," he went on, eager to change the subject, "none of this would matter if tuition was free. Education should be for everyone, not the privileged few."

"Going to MIT is not a right," Marina said, her elegant eyebrows pinching together. "Going to an Ivy League college to study English is not a right. College shouldn't be an expectation."

"Why not? Wouldn't it be better for the economy if everyone was more educated?"

"What about tradesmen? Plumbers? Electricians? Are they not valuable?" There was a prickliness to Marina's voice that made Nate pause.

"Sorry, didn't mean anything against your folks," he said, mentally kicking himself and trying to remember if she'd told him what they did.

"I'm not upset," Marina said, holding up a hand. "I just think it's unfair to expect my family's working-class taxes to pay for people to study history at Dartmouth."

"If they can get into Dartmouth," Nate pointed out.

"But why does someone *need* to go to Dartmouth? Or Harvard or Cornell? What's wrong with state schools and community colleges?"

"*You're* not at a state school," Nate pointed out. "Because MIT offers better opportunities, opportunities that shouldn't just be limited to the super wealthy."

"I'm also not super wealthy. I'm just able to rationalize that the debt will be worth it on the other end."

"That's a bit elitist of you, to imagine that someone else

couldn't go through the same logical reasoning."

Marina shook her head, staring off into the middle distance. "That came out wrong. What I mean is that the cost forced me to think critically about whether or not to pay for the service of college. The expense means I had to carefully decide what I was going to study and why MIT would be the better option. If it was free, what would stop me from studying something less useful to society, or wasting my time by just taking the classes I want to take?"

"What's wrong with that?" Nate asked, trying and failing to keep the defensiveness out of his tone.

Marina, of course, didn't flinch. "There's nothing wrong with taking fun classes in the system we have. But the problem is that if we're going to subsidize education by the government, if we're going to socialize it, then we need to be getting value back out of that cost, right? If taxpayers are going to help cover college education, there needs to be a benefit directly to them. More doctors, more lawyers, more engineers."

"It seems like you're discounting the value of artists and historians."

"I'm not," she said. "But we already have a lot of them, and no offense, but how much do you really think your political science degree will add to the world?"

Nate straightened. "Excuse me."

Marina grinned. "I said no offense."

"That's just something people say before they offend you."

Her expression became distant again, as if another argument had just occurred to her and she needed to gather it before it flew away. And Nate knew he should fight back in her moment of distraction, press the advantage of her pause. But how could he when she looked so focused, so intelligent, when her leg was oh-so-close to his?

132

"What are you thinking?" Nate asked in a probing, amused tone.

"Well," she began slowly, glancing at him in that cautious way that was becoming familiar between them. "One also has to consider that the liberal arts have become a little bit... biased."

She paused, watching him for a reaction. But he kept his features neutral, waiting for her to continue if only to hear her voice.

"I mean, I don't know the numbers off the top of my head. But Ben says that there are practically no conservative professors left in most liberal arts colleges. Look at what happened at Middlebury or Evergreen. It seems like there's a clear political slant to most non-STEM programs nowadays, so I can't help but feel suspicious about the free-college argument coming out of the left, since it would increase their own influence on young people."

"Well," Nate said when she stopped. "If you flip that coin, don't you think it's *interesting* that so many of the educated, well-read individuals in the nation are liberal?"

Marina's lips tightened and Nate thrilled at the gleam of challenge in her eyes. He lifted his hands in a gesture of surrender.

"Not that I'm saying conservatives are *dumb* or anything—"

"Uh huh."

"—but there is something to be said for the fact that the centers of higher education slant a certain way."

Marina steepled her fingers. "I think it's confirmation bias. They've become more liberal, so they've hired more liberal professors, who then educate more liberal PhD students, etcetera. It's the same thing that's happened in Hollywood and the news. As the ideas get stronger and more popular in certain circles, people who do disagree are less inclined to speak out."

"You think there are Republican professors who are staying silent?"

"There are certainly Republican students who are."

Nate smirked. "Like you?"

She frowned. "Just because I say these things *here* doesn't mean I'd say them in class. I'm not Ben."

"Who?"

She shook her head. "It doesn't matter. What's important is that you can't deny that, as much as modern-day colleges push ethnic diversity—which is racist, by the way—there is precious little effort to push diversity of thought. Which is far more important."

Nate shuddered like a dog shaking off water, unable to stop his grin from widening. "There's a lot to unpack there."

Now it was her turn to smirk. "Do I need to explain it to you?"

"Oh no, I followed along. It's not *my* fault that none of it made any sense."

"Surprise surprise."

"First of all, affirmative action is not *racist*."

"Why not?" Marina said, cocking her head in that way he was beginning to love. "It's literally making decisions based on the color of a person's skin, or where they were born, or where their *parents* were born. It has nothing to do with who a person is."

"This country has a long history of discrimination. It's necessary to have programs that correct that."

"I agree it *was* necessary."

Nate narrowed his eyes. "Are you saying racism is no longer a problem?"

"No, but I don't think it's a problem in university administrations. As we just discussed, I think those are pretty liberal environments."

"Can you imagine if we got rid of affirmative action? Only the rich and privileged would end up in high-level colleges."

"Not if you restructured affirmative action to be based on

134

economic status," Marina said with a smug nod, as if she'd just dropped an ace on the bar. "Rich kids shouldn't be given advantages just because they're black or Latino—"

"Latinx."

She ignored him.

"We should be helping the people who had to work two jobs as they struggled through high school. The ones who can't even *think* about Harvard because of the cost. I don't want my application to be given extra weight because of my family's history. I want to be given help because I need it."

It occurred to Nate suddenly, painfully, that maybe this conversation wasn't entirely theoretical. Did Marina actually need help? Was money a weight on her mind? To Nate, it had always been a given that he'd go somewhere like MIT. *Don't even look at the price tag*, his parents had said. *Pick the best place you can get into.*

What if Marina's parents had said something very different?

Nate swallowed, trying to find a polite way to ask, a sensitive entrance into such a loaded topic.

"I think," Marina was continuing over the hum of concern in Nate's brain, "that we as a country should be altogether less focused on things people can't change. Identity politics is poisonous because you can change your political beliefs or your work ethic or your income, but if you base your identity and self-worth on something you can't change, like your race, then everything calcifies and stagnates and you get a government so divided that they can't even stop themselves from shutting down every year. How can you debate with someone who isn't able to change their mind, because that would mean changing *themselves*? What's the point of trying?"

A silence fell. Marina looked at him, frowning in question.

"Is that why you don't want to go on the ski trip?" Nate blurted before he could stop himself.

Marina balked at the sudden shift in topic. "What?"

Nate fought the urge to squeeze his eyes shut and drop his head onto the bar. *Whoops*. But it was too late to go back now.

"Was the ski trip too... expensive?" he asked, more carefully this time.

A series of expressions flashed over Marina's features— surprise, hurt, shame, anger—so quick that if he'd blinked, he would have missed them. But he didn't, and it cut him to the core.

"I told you," she said, her easy smile just a little bit cold around the edges. "I have an exam."

Nice going, moron, Nate thought, but he forced himself to return the smile, leaned back in his chair.

"Of course, Hermione."

She folded her arms. "I take that as a compliment."

"I must have said it wrong."

To his enormous relief, Marina's laugh returned in full force. "You say a lot of things wrong."

"Or you misunderstand me," he said, grinning.

"Why do I feel like you keep insulting my intelligence?"

Nate shrugged in a facsimile of innocence. "I question the intelligence of anyone who supports our fascist-in-chief."

"Oh please, he's hardly a *fascist*," Marina said with an exasperated huff.

Glad that he'd managed to distract her, Nate made a show of raising his eyebrows. "That is *demonstrably* not true."

"How so?"

"The strongman rhetoric? The chumminess with authoritarian leaders? Encouraging violence at his rallies? Demonizing of the press?"

"Who demonize him right back," Marina said.

"For good reason! He flouts the rule of law for his own

136

personal gain and puts his family members in key political positions they didn't earn. His policies hide blatant xenophobia under a banner of patriotism. These are literally the *defining* features of fascism."

Nate stared at her, hands spread, meeting her thoughtful expression with his own incredulity. After a moment, Marina waggled her head.

"Ok, you might have a point."

"At last, some sense!" Nate cried.

"*But*," she went on as if he hadn't interrupted. "I do understand why he won."

Nate gripped his beer. "Yeah, because this country is full of bigots and assholes just like him."

She rolled her eyes. "*No*. It's because there are a lot of people, especially in the middle of the country, who feel like they've been ignored for a long time. In their view, the coastal city intellectuals," Marina shot him a pointed look, "look down on their lifestyles, their religion, their old-fashioned nostalgia. Increasingly, the media doesn't represent their values. Celebrities call them names. Hollywood pokes fun. I know the President can be a bit of a jerk sometimes—"

"All the time."

"—but I think he's trying, in his own *very* flawed way, to make those people feel heard. To validate that there are reasons for them to be proud of who they are."

"By encouraging a white ethnostate and the oppression of minorities?"

She huffed again. "That's a bit extreme. And besides, do you really think that kind of language is going to change anyone's mind? Wouldn't it be better to focus on what you have in common?"

"We have nothing in common!" Nate said, outraged by the very idea.

"You and I do," Marina said with unsettling sincerity. "We both believe it's wrong to kill people, for example. I think we both believe in fairness, although in very different ways."

"That's an understatement…"

Marina smiled into her cocktail. "And we, at least, believe in open dialogue."

She paused tentatively, questioningly.

After a beat, Nate's face broke open into a wide grin.

"To dialogue," he said, lifting his beer.

The clink of her glass against his filled Nate with a strange, giddy kind of hope.

Chapter 20

Marina had lost the ability to focus.

She had her homework open in front of her—organic chemistry this time. The study sheet was color-coded and zoomed in. But the information slid out of her mind like water off feathers. She kept thinking about Nate, about the way he'd touched her arm and smiled as they'd left the bar. The heat of his body, tantalizingly close to hers.

How he'd asked about her finances.

Much as she hated to admit it, his question hadn't been judgmental or condescending but... sad. Like he wished he could fix it, swoop in and solve everything. Take care of her.

And a small, childish part of Marina wanted to let him.

She dug her fingers into her hair, leaning forward. *No.* This was wrong. She wasn't a damsel and he wasn't her champion. He'd probably be horrified if he knew she'd thought of him as one, even for a second. Despite Nate's determination to solve all the world's problems, Marina could also see how much he struggled to not step on toes or cause any offense, to play the savior without actually *being* one. He spooked at any sign of his own *toxic masculinity* and was constantly ragging on the *patriarchy*. But she'd seen that flicker in his eyes. He'd have paid for her, if she'd asked, because Lord forbid someone else's problems get in the way of his fun.

Their fun?

Marina growled to herself, rubbing her temples.

She was *independent*, dammit, stood on her own, didn't pine for some rich suburbanite and his luxurious, ridiculous life. That was envy, the worst of sins. She'd been perfectly happy all these years without skiing, so really it was just silly to pray for a miracle that would let her join him this Friday. To ask for God's intervention in something as vapid as a weekend away.

Stop it.

Trying to *force* Nate out of her head, she bent over her computer and glared at the hexagonal benzene rings and jagged functional groups she had to memorize for the upcoming exam that wasn't quite as close as she'd pretended.

But something buzzed against her thigh, once. Twice.

A phone call.

What *now*?

Marina pulled out her cell to find it glowing with her mother's name.

Oh, she thought. *Right.*

Taking a quick moment to gather her thoughts, she slid her thumb to answer the call and put it on speaker.

"Hi everyone," she said with forced cheerfulness.

The response was immediate and deafening.

"HAPPY BIRTHDAY!!!"

Marina tried to make her laugh sound sincere as she plopped down on her bed and held her phone out in front of her, still reverberating with cheers.

"How are you all?" she said when they finally quieted down. "What did I miss this week?"

"I'm helping Papi understand his new Android," Alvaro said. "It's like teaching calculus to a retard."

"*Alvaro*," her mother snapped.

"I'm sorry, *mentally challenged*."

"I'm learning fast," her father chimed in.

"He's not," Nick hissed as a baby wailed in the background.

"How's the Nicklet?" Marina asked in a light voice.

"*Cole* is doing just fine, thanks. Vanessa's almost fully recovered."

Marina grinned. "Give the Nicklet a kiss from me."

She could hear Alvaro snickering in the background.

There was a scuffle as the phone changed hands and then her mother's voice was filling her bedroom.

"You sound tired! Are you not sleeping enough again?!"

Marina rolled her eyes. "I'm fine, Ma, no need to shout."

"I hope you're spending some time outside the library, *mi niña*!"

"Yeah," Alvaro piped in, "it's boring to keep hearing about how much you study."

"Well, the library's free," Marina said before she could stop herself.

Her mother made a noise of disapproval. "We did not bring you to this country to only do things that are *free*!"

"Just things that are cheap," Alvaro said under his breath.

There was a *smack* and an "*Ow*."

"You, be quiet!" Then, back into the phone, "Tell me! What are you doing for fun on your special day?!"

"I'm afraid to answer now," Marina laughed, falling back onto her mattress with a soft *thump*.

"Is someone throwing you a party?! That friend of yours, the Oriental one!"

"Mami, you're not supposed to call her that," Marina said.

"Yeah, she's *Asian*. Get your PC bullshit right, Ma," Alvaro

141

said before his chuckle was punctuated by another outraged, *"Ow!"*

"Besides, Jordan understands that parties aren't really my thing," Marina went on over her mother's reprimand about *not swearing in front of the baby.*

It was only half true. Really, Jordan hadn't planned anything because she, along with everyone else on Facebook, thought Marina's birthday was in the summer. In an attempt to avoid the freshman-floor tradition to get the birthday person *as drunk as humanly possible*, Marina had changed the date online to something random in July. She'd never bothered to change it back, so her college friends hadn't ever had the opportunity to celebrate with her.

Which suited her just fine.

"Well, you have to be doing *something*, Marina," Nick said over the howls of an upset infant.

"What about getting your nails done?" Vanessa called from the grainy background.

"Or trying drugs?" Alvaro called from a distance Marina suspected was out of Mami's reach.

"Maybe," she said, hoping they'd drop it soon.

Her phone vibrated. A little notification appeared over the phone call, from Venmo.

Ricardo Salinas paid you $300.

"Did she get it? I think I sent it to the right person…"

"Did Papi just send me a Venmo?" Marina said in disbelief, opening the app.

"Happy birthday, honey!" her parents chorused.

"Oh shit, he's gone rogue," Alvaro muttered in the background.

"You didn't have to do that," Marina said, glad they couldn't see her blush in the dim light of her bedroom. "I don't need—"

"Do something silly with it!" her mom shouted. "Don't you

dare spend it on textbooks! You're too rational for your own good sometimes, I tell you."

There's someone else who'd agree…

But she couldn't explain Nate, not here with all of them listening.

Maybe not ever.

Shoving that thought aside, she grinned at the phone.

"Well, *gracias*. To Papi and to all of you for teaching him how to use a cellphone."

"We're going to get him on Instagram next," Alvaro said.

"What's an Instagram?" her father asked.

"Oh dear," Marina laughed. "That's just what this world needs, pictures of an old Hispanic man on the beach."

"You all know I've still got it," Papi cut in, but her mother had reclaimed the phone.

"How are you? Good? Are you eating well? Still going to church?"

"Yes, Ma," Marina said, only half-listening as her mother began to "advise" her about proper study habits and how important breakfast was. Nick's son howled in the background and she could hear Alvaro and her father laughing over the din and Marina was, as usual, flooded by the homesickness that accompanied their Sunday afternoon phone calls. But for some reason, it was more muted than normal. This time, only a part of her wanted to be in their little living room, surrounded by the people who loved her exactly as she was.

Was it because she finally had something to be excited about *here*?

"Love you all!" Marina said as the call wrapped up.

"Be good," said her father.

"Or not," Alvaro added.

"Don't listen to him!" her mother yelled.

143

"Thanks again," Marina answered, but the call was already dissolving into pre-dinner chaos. Someone had put down the phone and forgotten to hang up so she could still hear Ma shouting for someone to set the table, Vanessa calling for her breastfeeding cover, Alvaro cracking loud, off-color jokes as everyone tried to shut him up.

Marina chuckled to herself and hung up for them.

Ah, family, she mused, staring at the Venmo notification.

Three hundred dollars.

Not quite enough to cover the full cost of the ski trip, but close...

This is ridiculous, she thought, turning her phone over, returning to her homework. *What a complete waste. I could use this for...*

For what? Textbooks? That would be disrespectful. Her mother had explicitly told her not to, had instructed her to do something silly.

Perhaps something reckless too?

Before doubt had a chance to creep in, Marina tapped out a message to Nate on her laptop. <Is it too late to join the ski trip?>

He responded almost immediately, quick enough to make Marina's heart pound.

<Is Hermione taking a break from the books???>

<No one's perfect>

<Except me> he texted back with a winking emoji. And then, <You want to come?>

<No, I just asked for the hell of it /s>

Nate sent back an eye roll.

Marina grinned uncontrollably as she typed out, <So? Is it too late?>

<Nope, space still open online. Will email you the link! I'll

pick you up at your house on Friday then?>

   <Oh dear, you're going to be stuck in a car with me for three whole hours?> she texted as she transferred the Venmo money to her bank account, hoping the switch would go through in time. <Whatever will we talk about?>

   He sent another winking face. <I'm sure we'll think of something>

Chapter 21

Marina looked worse than nervous when Nate pulled up by the curb. She waved, but the gesture was timid, almost subdued. She didn't say anything as she tossed her bulky duffel into the back seat and slid into the passenger side of Nate's little Subaru Sport.

"You ok?" he asked at last, unable to bear the silence as they zoomed out onto Memorial Drive.

"I'm gonna break every bone in my body," she muttered.

His held breath burst out in a laugh. "Is that what's wrong?"

"You're belittling my impending doom."

"Oh, relax. Tons of people ski without dying."

"That's not comforting."

Nate chuckled, swerving them onto the highway and neatly avoiding a huge eighteen-wheeler.

Marina inhaled sharply. "With the way you drive, I might die a lot sooner."

"You're not a backseat driver, are you?" Nate said, looking at her as he changed lanes.

Marina clutched the grip over her window. "I'm in the front seat, now *watch where you're going!*"

"*Pshh*, I could do this in my sleep," Nate said as he weaved his way through early afternoon traffic.

"Please don't."

"So?" Nate said to distract her. "Why the change of heart? One minute you're study-Mc-study, now you're playing hooky?"

"Someone told me I should have a bit more fun."

Nate nodded sagely. "Sounds like a wise person."

"It *sounds* like someone who's going to fail their classes."

"Which is good life experience." Nate dug into the cup holder between them, groping for a moment before withdrawing a knotted cable with a pointed AUX jack on the end. "Wanna pick the music?"

"I'm not sure you'll like my taste," Marina said, but she accepted the cable.

"Don't worry, as long as it's not Gregorian chants or something, I'm cool."

"Christian Rock it is then."

"Hey, some of that stuff isn't bad." Nate glanced over to find Marina's eyebrows almost touching her hairline. "I had a car in high school that got stuck on the Christian Rock radio station." He shrugged. "If you ignore all that stuff about Jesus and fountains of redemption, some of it's pretty catchy."

"I think you might be ignoring the point."

The car's stereo system hiccupped and then something soft and crooning began to play.

"No way," Nate said, slapping the wheel. "You're a Billie Eilish fan?"

"You said anything!"

He laughed. "But we're not thirteen-year-old girls."

Marina blew out a breath. "That's pretty dismissive of thirteen-year-old girls. For your information, I find her music fascinating."

Nate leveled his best *you've got to be kidding me* look in her direction.

"Really," Marina said, leaning back in her seat. Nate was glad that she was finally relaxing, her tension leeching out of the air like a bad smell. "I feel like she speaks to what young people are feeling these days."

"And what are young people feeling these days?" Nate said, trying not to sound snide and failing miserably.

Marina ignored his tone, pulling off her boots as she answered.

"Empty, I think. Or at least confused. There's a lot of nihilism in the world right now that leeches the inherent meaning out of life. Most of our entertainment doesn't offer anything more than shallow, surface-level distraction. Directionless escapism. And it almost feels like Billie is calling all that out. Saying to the world that if you feed a generation on junk food for the soul, you get hopeless, depressed youths who revolt against the very system you're trying to shackle them with. Don't you think it's interesting that she doesn't sing about romance or fame, except to twist it into something darker? She's uncensored and cynical and *real*, unlike most public figures. Maybe that's what makes her so successful."

"So are you secretly a nihilist?" Nate said, changing lanes to get around an enormous, jacked-up monster truck.

Marina paused and the momentary hush was thoughtful and comfortable. Almost peaceful. At last, she said, "I think we all struggle with meaning, don't we? It's the human condition to have an emptiness in the center of our souls that we long to fill. Some people use activism." Nate pursed his lips. "Some use art. Some use religion. But in the end, we're all looking for something." Marina smiled. "And besides, Bad Guy is a damn good song."

"Bit raunchy for Sunday School though."

She threw back her head and laughed, and Nate felt like he could float right out of the fucking car.

"Yes," she said, still chuckling. "It is. Although you'd be surprised. I had my first Sex-Ed lesson in Sunday School."

149

"No!"

"The priest had to use diagrams."

"You're kidding!"

"It was the most uncomfortable I've ever been in my life."

"Clearly, you've never had a threesome."

Even from the corner of his eye, Nate could see Marina's smile flicker.

"And you... have?"

"No," he said quickly.

"Nate?" The tone of her voice was a warning, a half-maternal, half-professorial question that made him flush, which was answer enough. "Goodness," she muttered. "What was it like?"

Nate shifted, suddenly uncomfortable despite the plush padding of his seat.

"Kinda dull, to be honest. I was with another guy and I only really liked him. But he liked the girl and I guess she liked him back..." He glanced at her. "It was no big deal."

Marina was looking at him oddly, as if she was trying to solve a puzzle in her head.

"What?" he asked, fighting the urge to fidget.

"Do you really... like guys?"

Nate tried to smile. "That is what bisexual means."

"No, honestly," Marina said, her voice probing, cautious. "You like... both?"

"I mean, *I'm* into anything with a pulse. Not every bisexual is like that though."

She frowned. "That's a big umbrella."

"It's a big world." Nate considered for a moment. "No animals though. That's a bit far, even for me."

She didn't laugh.

"I guess," Marina said instead, each word measured and slow.

150

"I never believed bisexual was…"

"Real?" Nate raised his eyebrows. "We get that a lot. But yes, it is real. Yes, I was born this way. Yes, I can't help it." He grinned. "And yes, I wouldn't give it up even if I could."

Marina fell silent. Nate's grin faded slowly, piece by piece.

"Is that a problem?" he asked, a little more aggressively than he'd intended.

Marina stared out the front window, eyes unfocused. "No," she said at last in a careful voice. Nate waited for her to go on, heart tightening with every second of silence. It was far from peaceful now. "It's just…" she paused again, and Nate decided that long silences in tense conversations should be made illegal. "My parents think being gay is a sin. They don't hate gay people or anything, but they believe that the act of sleeping with the same gender is something God frowns upon." Her words picked up steam, like water from a burst dam. "I think they see it as a sin no greater or less than the ones they commit all the time, and they certainly don't think people should be legally punished for acting on it or anything. Separation of church and state and all that. But to them, it's a lifestyle they just can't condone."

Nate tried to wrestle down the hurt twisting in his chest. He pulled his lips up, hoping it looked natural. "Let's be honest, I was never expecting your parents to like me."

"I mean, yours didn't like me," she said in a small voice.

"That's not true," he lied and then, before she could fight him, "So what do *you* think?" He glanced over at her. "Do you agree with them?"

"I used to," she admitted, pulling up her knees and wrapping her arms around them. "But that was before I came to MIT, the land of unnatural hair colors." Her eyes flicked pointedly to his head. "Suddenly everyone here is LGBT-whatever-the-other-letters-are. And they talk about it all the time. I still think that's weird, don't get me wrong. I mean, people don't talk about liking *handcuffs* in public or anything."

"You should meet my friends," Nate muttered, but Marina was plunging on.

"I guess I've seen enough gay couples now that I just can't see any reason God would be against them. If they're happy and bringing joy into the world..." She took a breath, squeezed herself tighter, "what's the harm?"

"Doesn't the Bible say some pretty specific things about *sodomites*?"

"The Bible also says you can't wear mixed cloth or remarry after divorce," Marina said sardonically. "It might need some updating."

Nate exhaled a laugh. "Look at you, being all open-minded."

"Don't sound so surprised." Marina stretched her fingers out, holding them over the heating vents.

He took a moment to gather his courage. And then said, "You never answered my question."

She cocked her head in silent inquiry.

"Is the fact that I'm bisexual going to be a problem?"

He didn't say *between us*. Didn't say *for our relationship*. He didn't quite know what to insert into that conversational hole.

So he left it empty.

"No." She nodded once, as if to confirm it to herself. "No, I don't think so." Her lips quirked up. "Is it going to be a problem that I'm Catholic?"

Nate chuckled. "Only if you try to convert my heathen ass. That's a battle lost long ago."

"Oh, I wouldn't be so sure," Marina said, tilting her head back. "God works in mysterious ways. Maybe He'll surprise you."

Chapter 22

The hotel room had only one bed.

Marina gaped at it, bag heavy on her shoulder, furious at herself. What had she expected? If the conversation in the car had revealed anything, it was how casual Nate was about his body, about *sex*. She imagined he didn't think twice about the fact that they'd have to share a bed. Probably did it all the time.

"Place looks nice," he said, edging past her, and Marina had to fight the urge to step away, to put space between them. "Eric is hosting everyone down the hall, so we can hang out with them tonight. That ok?"

"Sure, yeah," she forced out, her words half-strangled.

But nothing was ok.

Marina felt like someone had tossed her brain in the dryer. What was she supposed to do? She couldn't tell Nate she was a virgin. He'd probably run for the hills. Maybe that was a good thing, but oh, how she wanted to kiss him. It was stupid beyond belief, but the whole drive north, whenever he went to shift gears and his hand brushed her hip, her thigh, she wondered how it would feel to touch him without the barrier of clothing. To explore one another like new lands.

Marina dropped her bag on the armchair, her whole body five degrees warmer than usual.

Maybe I should just do it?

It wasn't as though she'd been holding out. She wasn't like Jordan and Ben. Marina was the sheltered, spoiled daughter in her family, sure, but there had never been an expectation for her to be *pure*.

So why not?

Her heart thudded in her ears.

No.

She couldn't.

The idea of being just another one of Nate's stories, another exploit he'd laugh about later, turned her stomach. *Remember that one time I fucked a Catholic?* Oh God, how could she possibly go through with it? How could she pretend to know what she was doing enough to satisfy him? How could she fake it, act like it didn't hurt or that she wasn't scared?

How could she live with the lie?

Marina found herself wishing that the hotel had, in addition to another bed, a bigger bathroom so that she could throw up without Nate noticing.

"Hey." He was watching her, eyebrows creased with worry. "Something wrong?"

"No, no, I'm fine," she said airily, digging into her bag for nothing in particular.

"Are you nervous about meeting my friends? I mean, I don't know this crowd super well, mostly through my roommates, who aren't here. But I'm sure they're nice."

"No, yeah. We should go hang out. I'll be right over, give me a sec."

Nate didn't leave. He was standing awkwardly in the middle of the room, frowning as if he had no idea what was wrong.

How can he not see it? The single *elephant in the room?*

154

Marina looked up, raising her eyebrows as if it was just a joke, as if he was the one overreacting and not her.

"What?" she asked, planting her fists on her hips.

"They'll probably be smoking. You know, weed."

"I've heard of it," she said dryly.

"Is that ok? I don't have to join if it makes you uncomfortable—"

"Stop worrying," she said, waving one hand. "I'm good. It's legal in Vermont, right? And you're not driving."

Nate's lips twitched. "I think we're in for the night."

Marina almost burst into tears right then and there.

She swallowed, hard. And then said, "Great. I'll be right over."

She busied herself with her bag, not looking up, not acknowledging him watching her. Finally, after a long silence, she saw his feet disappear and the door shut behind him.

Marina collapsed on the bed, clutching her cross for support.

What am I doing? she thought for the millionth time, staring at the pattern in the carpet as if a message from God might be written there, telling her where to go, what to do, how to muddle her way through this. Everything was so *complicated* with Nate. Or no, that wasn't right. When she was with him, talking, things were simple. The world felt like an open sky, free and limitless. It was everything *around* them that was complicated. His parents and their hyper-liberalism. Her family's unfashionable ruralness and obsession with guns.

Their sexual histories.

Marina rubbed her face.

She needed to get up. Nate would come looking for her and she wouldn't—couldn't—allow him to find her like this, spiraling into the depths of her own thoughts. And for what? Nate was

155

respectful and kind. He wouldn't force it. She could say no, if she wanted.

Did she want to?

"*Arggg*," she groaned, shoving to her feet and dragging herself, step by step, into the hallway.

Don't think about it. Just don't think about it.

It was easy to tell which room was the one with Nate's friends. A deep bass pulsing made the sconces around it quiver like a chandelier in an earthquake. She eased open the door, slipped in sideways as if they might not notice a smaller target.

"It's Marina!" called a cacophony of voices.

Everyone was staring at her, smiling at her. And the faces were kind, welcoming, half-drunk.

Suggestive.

"I told them about you," Nate admitted, his eyes already a little bloodshot.

"Ma-rin-a," said a tall young person with attractively androgynous features. "That's a nice name."

"You picked a good one," added a muscled boy, clapping an arm around Nate's shoulders. "But can she tame the tomcat?" he asked, swaying, *winking*.

"Who's down for a game of King's Cup?" someone called from the back of the crowded room.

And Marina couldn't take it anymore. Her face was burning, her mind filled with that one bed, that queen mattress and single duvet cover. They all *knew*. How could they not? Everyone *else* was probably sharing beds and sleeping together with no rules and no boundaries, living in a way she would never understand or feel comfortable with. It hurt to admit, but Marina couldn't do it. She couldn't pretend to be like them, even if she desperately wanted to, because she didn't even know how to try.

Her eyes prickled dangerously, threatening to overflow.

Before her own tears could betray her, Marina spun away from the young people gathering around the table for a card game she had no idea how to play and ran.

Chapter 23

"Yo, your friend ok?"

Nate blinked. "Yeah, she's right—"

But Marina wasn't *right there*. In fact, she was nowhere to be seen.

"Oh shit," Nate said, pushing Evelyn aside and sprinting into the hallway.

The door at the end of the corridor was just swinging shut, cutting off a cold burst of air.

And Nate was already stoned.

Unfortunately, he'd always been a complete lightweight with both drugs and alcohol. Stevie had handed him the bong when he'd walked in, blabbering excitedly about some *new strain* that would *knock his fucking socks off*, and Nate had accepted the hit gratefully, needing to take the edge off what was already gearing up to be an uncomfortable night. He'd known there was something wrong with Marina the moment they'd walked into the hotel room, but what? Was she uncomfortable sharing a bed with him? Grossed out after their conversation in the car? Turned off, as girls had been before, by Nate's familiarity with dicks?

He really, really hoped not.

Nate had brushed off the pain of that particular rejection before, but he knew it would be a whole lot worse coming from her.

Stumbling for the door, Nate ripped it open without pausing to think. The cold stopped him like a brick wall. It was breathtaking, sudden and sharp in his lungs. For a moment he could only blink. A soft, thick snow was coming down, filling the air with big blotches of white, illuminated by the heavy lamps outside.

It was beautiful...

Focus.

Nate squinted into the darkness, searching. She was easy to find. Hunched shoulders, heavy boots, leaving a trail of deep prints in the fresh snow. Nate looked down at his flimsy sneakers, stylish but totally wrong for this weather. He shivered in his T-shirt, thinking of the coat he'd left draped over a chair back in their room.

"Fuck it," he said, plunging into the snow.

His feet went numb almost instantly. He tucked his hands under his armpits and lifted his knees to half-wade, half-trench through the fluff.

"Marina!"

She stopped but didn't turn.

He caught up to her. "Marina, what are you doing?"

Without thinking, he reached out and grabbed her shoulder with one frozen hand. Fighting to control the shivering muscles of his arm, he pulled her around to face him.

She was crying.

Nate's eyes widened. "Marina? What's wrong?"

"Nothing," she said furiously, scrubbing her face. "Everything's fine. I just needed some air."

"If it's the weed, I'm sorry. I—"

"It's not the weed."

The cold was seeping into Nate's chest, into his very soul. "Is it the fact that I've slept with men?"

Something flickered across her expression.

160

Nate's intestines seemed to curdle.

"It is, isn't it?" he said, releasing her arm. He hadn't realized how much he'd been afraid of this until he saw the pained sadness in her eyes, the rejection of everything he was. Why did it feel so much like being stabbed? "Look, if that makes you uncomfortable, I'm sorry but it's not like I can go back in a fucking time machine and take it—"

"Nate, it's not what you think," Marina interrupted.

He shook his head. Dammit, he should be *used* to the slut-shaming by now. He'd certainly endured enough of it, had hardened himself against it.

But for some reason it felt different coming from her.

He took a step back. "I thought we could be honest with each other. Wasn't that the whole point of all this?" He threw out his arms, gesturing at the snow. "Open dialogue, even if we disagree?" *Even if it hurts*. He blinked, surprised by the prickle in his eyes. "I guess everyone has their limits, but I gotta say, I thought you had a bit more—"

"I'm a virgin."

The words hung like the snow in the air, thick and slow to settle.

"What?" Nate said, brain scrambling to catch up.

She swallowed. "I'm a virgin. I've never had sex before."

"I know what virgin means." He shook his head to clear it, but it only made things worse. "So it wasn't that I've slept with dudes?"

"It's that you've slept with *people*," Marina said miserably. "It's that there's only one bed in our room. It's that everyone in there seemed to… smiled like…"

He could see the sobs building up in her, making her shake. In that moment, she seemed like a wineglass threatening to shatter, something beautiful and vulnerable on the verge of breaking.

Guided by a rush of instinct, he pulled Marina to his chest and wrapped his arms around her, holding her together even as her warmth grounded him.

Well, he thought, stroking her spine, *that explains a lot.*

"I'm sorry," she said in an unsteady voice.

"Don't be. It's better than what I was thinking."

"Is it?"

She pulled away from him and looked up, snowflakes clinging to her eyelashes and giving her face the impression of being coated in diamond dust.

"What?" Nate asked, suddenly nervous again.

"Don't you get it?" Her voice was strained. "It's just another problem on the pile. Our lifestyles don't fit. Our friends would hate each other. My parents couldn't even be in the same *room* as your parents, not to mention my brothers! This is just another reason that this," she waved a hand between the two of them, "makes no sense."

Nate scoffed. "Bullshit. *This* doesn't mean anything. I accept all lifestyles, remember?"

Marina frowned, folded her arms. "What if I was saving myself for marriage?"

He narrowed his eyes. "Are you?"

"Just answer the question."

It was surprising, how quickly the answer popped into his brain. Sure, the idea of being celibate for however long it took him and Marina to figure things out sounded pretty miserable. And he wasn't entirely sure how he'd survive after so long in the Tinder trenches of instant gratification. But couples did long-distance, right? People had their girlfriends or husbands *deployed* and didn't die of pent-up horniness. For the first time in his life, Nate felt that this person before him was more than just sexy, more than just funny or cool or all the discrete parts that made human beings interested in other human beings. There was something here that he hadn't felt before, ever.

And, no matter how much he loved sex, this was more important.

"It wouldn't matter," he answered and meant it.

Marina blinked and the effect under the streetlamps was dazzling. "Really?"

"Yeah," he said, stepping in closer. "I've been laid way more than my fair share of times anyway. Think of it as the universe evening out."

Her laugh was small and tentative, but there. "Well, you'll be glad to know that I am not, in fact, saving myself for Jesus."

Nate straightened. "Oh?"

"Don't sound so excited."

He wrestled his features into some semblance of seriousness. "Oh," he repeated in a deeper voice.

She laughed for real this time, shoving him gently.

"I just haven't had... the opportunity." Her bronze cheeks were the color of a sunset, all red and orange and gold.

"So you're open to the idea?"

"Not *tonight*."

"Of course not."

"But in general... yes." She was watching him, as if looking for the *gotcha*, the lie in the game. He knew that look because he'd worn it before, waiting for the person in front of him to transform, or laugh, or turn and run.

But Nate wasn't going fucking *anywhere*.

"See?" he said, brushing her hair away from the tears freezing on her lashes. "Problem solved."

"And what about... the rest?" Her voice was raspy and breathless.

"Marina," he said, leaning over her, "we don't have to have everything figured out right now."

"*You* don't," she muttered, not meeting his eyes.

"And *you* can't. Who knows what the future brings, right?"

She looked like a lost puppy, peering up at him in the dark.

When she spoke again, it came out in a whisper. "But what if everything goes wrong? What if we can't do this? What if it's a disaster?"

He closed the distance until their faces were so close that he could feel the heat of her exhale. "Marina, what if it's not?"

He held still for a moment, giving her the chance to back away. Breath fogged between them, as thick as the snowflakes dusting her hair, her shoulders, her lips. Just when he was beginning to think that she'd jerk her head to the side or slap him or offer some new and unbearable rejection, she rocked up onto the toes of her boots and pressed her mouth to his.

His arms snaked around her waist and hers were around his neck and without thinking he lifted her, straightened with her, and she wrapped him like a vine, clutching his jaw, exploring his mouth. Their tongues touched like live wires. Her fingers knotted in his hair and pulled his face to hers, holding him there. And maybe she needed to because if she didn't, Nate was sure he would fly right off into the night. The explosive joy in his chest could have cured diseases, ended wars, brought about world peace. She made a soft noise in the back of her throat that he decided on the spot was the best sound he'd ever heard. Nate didn't notice that his shoes were soaked through and his arms were bare to the falling snow. Because, with Marina in his arms, everything was what it had never been before.

Perfect.

Chapter 24

"What are you talking about?" Marina laughed, adjusting her feet on the dashboard as they drove back down to Boston. "I was awful."

"You were a natural."

"At falling."

Nate grinned. "Maybe that's all skiing is. Falling with style."

"That's flying, sir," she corrected him, pointing with a piece of beef jerky they'd claimed from the pile of leftovers. "Get your Pixar movies straight."

Marina knew she was being too giddy, laughing too easily, but she couldn't help it. Her whole body bubbled with relief and happiness, an overflowing reservoir of smiles. Sharing the bed, it turned out, had been as easy as putting a barricade of pillows between them—Nate's idea. And the day of skiing had been glorious: perfect blue-sky weather, fluffy snow, friendly crowds. Marina's ribs ached from how hard they'd laughed at her wipeouts and clumsy attempts to get back up, Nate trying unsuccessfully to help, both of them tumbling down in a heap of skis and poles and limbs. Even though they'd barely ventured beyond what Nate called the "bunny slopes," it had been an adventurous day. A magnificent day.

Marina couldn't have stopped grinning if she'd wanted to.

"Besides," Nate continued, "apparently your skin tone is

better for skiing than mine."

"Who would have thought," she said, patting her not-sunburned cheeks, "that Cubans were made for snow?"

Nate grimaced, fingers tracing the perfect goggle-shaped line between milky white and autumn red.

"Does it hurt?"

He shrugged. "Worth it."

And Marina couldn't disagree. Thinking of her pile of homework and all the responsibilities that awaited her back at home, she couldn't help but think that yes, it *had* been worth it.

She'd have to think more deeply about that.

"Well?" she said, swallowing a bite of jerky. "What's next?"

Nate threw her a quizzical look.

"If you're upending my life, you need to do a proper job of it."

Nate's grin widened into something mischievous and infectious. "Are you giving me permission?"

Marina winced. "Shouldn't I?"

"Oh, absolutely not. It's is a terrible idea." His smile turned somewhat wolfish. "I love it."

Marina chewed, not sure if the squirming in her chest was nerves or excitement. "As long as it's not clubbing."

"Clubbing it is!" Nate crowed.

"What? No!"

"Have you ever tried it?"

Marina made a face. "Loud music in a cramped room stinking of other peoples' sweat? No thanks."

"Who's closed-minded *now*?"

"Come on, can't you just take me bowling or something?" Marina half-laughed, half-whined.

"No, because we're not in middle school. Come on, clubbing is a rite of passage."

"To what? The underworld?"

Nate winked. "Take it from someone who's spent time there; the underworld is massively underrated."

Marina snorted, shaking her head. But a small, sad thought bubbled up from the depths of her mind as she wondered—for the umpteenth time—what her parents would think of him. What they would say, to a comment like that? Maybe their imaginary voices in her mind were right, maybe Nate wasn't just an infatuation but a *temptation*, leading her down all the roads she'd kept safely away from until now. Maybe Nate was her devil in the desert, luring her away from the light.

She stared into the bag of jerky.

How could something that made her so happy be wrong?

"So?" Nate asked, pulling off the highway and into Boston.

"So what?" she said cautiously.

Nate looked over at her, smug, pleased with himself. "You had fun, didn't you?"

Marina laughed. "And you're going to rub it in as long as you can."

"I think I deserve to gloat a little. It's a big accomplishment, getting you to admit you were wrong."

She blew out a breath, wishing there was more drive left, wanting the weekend to go on forever. "I wasn't *wrong*. I was just *busy*."

"Yeah, being wrong. I will accept your apology in the form of a romantic gift."

"*What?*"

They were turning onto her street.

"Flowers. Chocolates." Nate pulled his Subaru to a stop. "Top-shelf stuff too, none of that Hershey's crap."

"Hey, I love Hershey's," Marina said, laughing and shaking

her head.

"Hershey's is for plebeians."

"Now that's elitist." She stretched, sighed. "But I think we'd be here all night if we got into that right now."

"Is that a problem?"

"I need to shower," Marina complained, touching her unwashed hair, frizzy from the helmet she'd rented. "And besides, I do still have homework to do. Back to real life, right?"

Nate waved his hand dismissively. "Who wants real life?"

She pulled on her boots. "People who want to succeed."

"Party pooper."

She was gathering her things, trying to remember if she had everything, when she looked up to find Nate's face there. Only two days ago she would have frozen in horror, heart at once skipping and contracting from the closeness. But everything was different now, more exciting than terrifying.

Which was, perhaps, terrifying in itself.

"When will I see you again?" he said, and Marina wondered how many women had been asked that question by how many men and how it could still feel new and fresh and thrilling.

"I'll have to check my schedule," she answered only half-ironically, tipping closer.

"Well, you let me know when there's an opening and I'll—"

She reached around and pulled his face to hers, relishing his surprised exhale, his eyes widening and then closing, the throbbing warmth of his cheeks and lips. And oh, she could have stayed there all day, could have gladly pushed the limits of her comfort right there in the car until they were both panting and figuring out whose apartment was empty.

But she forced herself to pull back, grinning and blushing as she reached for her duffel bag.

"Thanks," she said. "For… everything."

"To many more," he said in a slightly dazed voice, tipping an imaginary hat.

Marina laughed and got out of the car, waving to him as she went inside. She felt light, floating, like her boots were skimming the ground and not crunching through layers of fresh ice. Nate didn't drive away as she tapped through the vestibule and was still sitting by the curb when she called the building's elevator, grinning at her through the tinted windows.

She blew him a kiss as the elevator dinged open, stepped inside, watched him disappear.

And then slumped against the chrome wall.

How she'd changed in just a few short days, a few short *weeks*. Marina was beginning to think of Nate as her own personal wrecking ball, knocking down all the careful barriers she'd built up around her schedule, her anxieties, her life. He was chaotic and fascinating. He challenged her, made her better.

Or at least made her different.

And she was falling in love with him.

There was no denying it anymore. Marina could feel a thread connecting her heart to his, thickening and twisting. The world outside could bombard them all it wanted, but they were stronger.

They'd survive it.

She *wanted* them to survive it.

But, as Marina stepped into her apartment, she couldn't help but wonder if maybe she was fighting for the wrong thing.

Chapter 25

Nate was supposed to be helping.

Lounging in an armchair in the student center room Tiffany had chosen, listening to the conversation swirl around him, he tried to remind himself that he'd volunteered to take notes. Tiff and her posse were planning a march for women's rights, specifically to raise awareness for trans women of color. It was vitally important to fight the mounting misogyny in the country, normalized, of course, by the asshole in the White House. Lives were at stake here. Critical freedoms were in jeopardy.

But despite all that, Nate found his attention wandering.

Without quite making the decision to open the website, he was browsing Facebook, scrolling through Marina's profile pictures. The first was of her in a lab coat, proudly holding up a prosthetic. Did she help design it? Then her between Jordan and the tall guy Tiffany hated, arms around each other, grinning from a mountaintop. Then with a dark-skinned teenager—her brother?—dressed in camo, holding guns. In a modest bathing suit, jumping into a lake. Surrounded by children in a field, pointing at something in the distance. Dressed in black with vampire teeth. Smiling over one shoulder with the hazy shapes of a party in the background.

Writing in a notebook.

Nate paused on that one, frowning as Tiff began to list ways the current administration was trying to turn their world into a Margret Atwood novel.

Hadn't Marina said something about a science writing program?

On impulse, Nate opened another tab and googled *Marina Salinas*.

The first few hits were profiles. Her Facebook, her Instagram, another woman in Kentucky with the same name. He found a LinkedIn page with Marina's picture, professionally subdued in a jacket and white button-down.

He clicked on it.

I'm just curious, he told himself as he scrolled through her research experience. *This isn't weird or anything. I just want to know.*

Although he supposed he could ask her in person…

He shook off the thought, squinting at the list of previous projects.

Primary author of a National Geographic article evaluating the current state of tinnitus research.

There was a link.

He clicked on it.

"Nate!" Tiff called, making him jump. "Did you get that down?"

"Uh," he said dumbly.

Tiffany rolled her eyes and stalked around the scattered chairs, toward him. Nate quickly changed tabs so that his "notes" were the only thing visible on his screen, just in time for her to lean over his shoulder.

"You didn't get any of it," she accused, pointing at the precious few bullet points he'd managed to jot down before getting distracted.

"Sorry, I might have dozed off for a sec," Nate grimaced. "I'm exhausted."

Eric, the only one in the room other than Nate who'd been on the trip to Mount Snow, snickered. "From your *ski buddy*?"

Their friend group had surmised at this point that Nate was "seeing someone," but the specifics about Marina had yet to be unearthed. Eric, thank goodness, had been either too high or too drunk all weekend to notice Marina's cross or her silent frown whenever issues of social justice came up in conversation. Eric hadn't even assumed Marina's gender. But Nate had the feeling of a dam breaking, his secret leaking out at an accelerating rate. If anyone found out how serious it really was...

He hitched on a smile and said in his most neutral voice, "I don't kiss and tell."

Tiff released a long-suffering sigh. A few of their friends tittered. But it was Leo's gaze, hard and knowing, that made Nate itchy.

"Well," Tiff said at last. "We're compiling our demands. After we block traffic on Vassar street and get the attention of the dean, we're going to give them this list. You ready?"

"Yes," Nate said with an apologetic nod, trying to ignore the mental tug of Marina's article.

"Good. First, we want fifty percent of new hires to be women."

"Or non-binary," someone piped up from the back.

"Or non-binary," Tiffany agreed, pacing behind Nate's chair and making it impossible for him to return to Marina's piece. "Second, we want to create women's-only spaces around campus, preferably one in every building, where we can escape from the toxic masculinity built into the structure of the school."

"Open to trans women too," one of Leo's friends added to general nods.

"Obviously," Tiff said, pausing and tapping her nose. "We

also want there to be a clear policy dealing with unsafe students, like this jerk-wad in my class. Maybe some kind of student-run board?"

"What about a Social Justice Committee?" Mimi asked, her bright pink hair in a messy braid. "They formed one at the University of Denver last year to support underrepresented people, and they're already managed to revamp the curriculum to focus on power distribution and privilege."

Tiffany nodded. "Yeah, yeah that's a good idea. And we'll assist in its creation to make sure the right people end up at the table."

Nate worked obligingly, typing up the list. Privately, he wondered if the school would—or even should—listen to the demands a bunch of twenty-somethings, half of them white, most of them from wealthy backgrounds. He could almost see Marina's scowl, hear her pointing out that, while they might be well-intentioned, it was, in fact, a bit arrogant of them to dictate instructions on how to run an institution that had stood more than a hundred and fifty years.

But he couldn't possibly say that to Tiff, who grew angrier and more strident with every message she got from home. There were enough forces in the world trying to silence her; he didn't need to be one of them.

So instead he watched from the corner of his eye as she strolled to the other side of the room, one hand in the air like a battle commander.

"We'll have to recruit help from the community," she was saying, head bobbing as if in agreement with herself. "Aesha, can you design a poster we can put up around town? We want it to be a call to arms, reminding everyone what's at stake."

"I have a few ideas," Aesha said, arms folded, grin savage.

"Guys," Leo's deep voice cut in. "I think—"

"Don't use gendered language," Mimi said.

Leo held up a hand. "Sorry. *People*, should we make it a fundraiser too? For Planned Parenthood maybe?"

Tiffany pointed at him. "Yes, totally. We can circulate with donations boxes. Maybe sell T-shirts or hats."

"I can design something and bulk order it online," Aesha offered.

Now that Tiff was on the other side of the room, Nate's attention was drifting again. He couldn't help it: no matter how hard he tried to listen, Marina was like a magnet in his brain, pulling his thoughts the wrong way, scrambling them. He slid three fingers to the side to change screens, opening Marina's article.

It began: *Imagine having a mosquito buzzing by your ear. Think about its high hum, the irritating insistence of it, the single, shrill note. You swipe at it but can't catch the little devil that woke you up in the middle of the night. You put a pillow over your head but somehow it still finds you, follows your ear canal like it wants to burrow inside. No matter how much you flail and curse, that tiny insect lingers by one side of your head in endless torture.*

Now imagine that for the rest of your life.

In bits and pieces, attention shifting constantly between Tiffany's planning and his screen, Nate read the article.

And found himself engrossed.

Marina's voice—for he could hear her speaking to him through the pixelated words—was compelling and evocative, painting a picture of tinnitus that made Nate *feel it*, almost viscerally. He'd never even heard of the affliction before, but by the end of the article he was filled with sympathetic frustration at the sad state of research and the lack of options for those with ringing in their ears.

"She's... good," Nate whispered, frowning.

"What was that?" Leo asked in a low voice as Tiff and Aesha began to brainstorm ideas for their flyer.

"Nothing," Nate said, opening his notes again. "Just dozing off again."

Leo's sly smile was laced with something unfamiliar. Concern? Frustration? "Sounds like she was wilder than you thought."

Nate's sunburn became, if possible, even hotter. "It's not like that."

"Oh? Then how come Eric says he saw pillows on the floor?"

Nate's eyes narrowed. "He didn't tell Tiff, right?"

"When did he have the chance? She's in full-on planning mode. Of course, that's not to say he won't." Leo leaned back. "Or that she won't hear about it some other way."

"You wouldn't."

"Only because I like our apartment and don't want to burn it down. But dude, you can't keep this secret forever. The truth will out, as they say."

Nate grimaced. Leo was right, he was walking a dangerous line. If Tiffany somehow put the pieces together....

He scowled, wincing as his sunburnt skin protested the uncharacteristic expression.

So what if she did? Why did it matter if he was falling for Marina? If the people in this room agreed on anything, it was that love was right in *all* its forms. If Nate was falling in love with a woman, it didn't need to invalidate Tiffany. He was just living his life, not abandoning the queer community. And who cared if Marina's ideas were bad, maybe even dangerous? He could change them. He could help her understand what they fought for, why they marched and protested and corrected in class. It was necessary. They were right.

Weren't they?

Nate ruffled his hair, keenly aware of Leo still watching him.

"I've got it under control," he said as Tiffany paced back to them.

"I sure hope so," Leo muttered. "For all our sakes."

Chapter 26

"Don't you think it's a bit... inflammatory?" Marina asked, handing Ben his laptop back over the dregs of pasta on her plate.

Ben smirked.

"That's the point."

All around them, other Catholic students were chattering away, bodies and spirits filled by the comforting tradition of Friday Night Spaghetti Dinner. Marina hadn't been in a few weeks—her free time had been taken up by something a lot less comforting and a lot more exciting lately—but she found herself lulled by the familiar faces and conversations as they swirled around her, Father Lawrence drifting down the table to make small talk and shake hands.

Leaning back, she folded her hands over her full stomach and shared a look with Jordan, who sighed.

"He's on the warpath," Jordan muttered, tilting her head back. "There's no stopping him now."

"I'm like The Juggernaut," Ben said, flexing his arms.

"Or Aquaman," Jordan said.

"Aquaman is cool now, thanks to Jason Momoa."

Jordan laughed. "I love you, but you are *not* Jason Momoa."

"Hey!"

Marina and Jordan made an exaggerated show of ducking as Ben cocked back an uneaten piece of garlic bread, a boyish smile tugging at his cheek.

"What are you three up to this time?" came Father Lawrence's voice, warm and inviting as always. Their priest was serene in a way Marina could never understand, much less emulate.

She and Jordan straightened, chorusing, "Nothing."

Father L gave them a skeptical look. "Ben?"

Ben puffed out his chest. "I'm fighting for truth, Father."

"Oh are you now?" the priest said, settling down in the empty chair on Ben's other side and taking the bread out of his hand. "How so?"

"He started a blog," Marina cut in as Ben dove proudly for his laptop.

"Red Nation," Jordan added, as if the name alone could explain everything.

"Here," Ben said, spinning his PC around.

Father L's eyebrows shot up as he read the page Marina had just skimmed, titled *The Only Thing Reparations Will Fix Is White Guilt*.

"Taking a dive into the deep end there, aren't you Ben?"

"I'm taking a *stand*," Ben corrected, folding his arms in a posture that was half-belligerent, half-eager for Father L's approval.

The pastor slid the computer back to its owner. "There are many ways to take a stand, Ben, not all of them built on anger."

"My blog isn't built on anger. It's built on *logic*."

"And I'm a cactus," Marina mumbled.

Ben shot her a dark look before turning back to Father L with a hungry expression. "Isn't it righteous to stand up for what you believe in, Father? To call out lies and falsehoods when you see them?"

Father L's smile was wry and unreadable. He took a bite of Ben's garlic bread, chewing thoughtfully. Finally, he said, "In my

180

limited experience on this Earth, I've found almost nothing that can be easily divided into truth and not-truth. Especially in politics. Real black-and-white certainty is rare, no pun intended."

"I disagree," Ben said, folding his arms.

Father L took another bite, waiting for Ben to elaborate.

"Abortion, for example."

The priest nodded, swallowing. "Yes, simple to you and me. But again, there is the matter of perspective. The truth that you and I and, I'd imagine, everyone at this table take for granted is not the one so many others accept. Their values and beliefs are just as powerful as ours, no matter how unsavory to us."

"But they're *wrong*," Ben insisted. "It's not just faith, it's *fact* that life begins at conception. There's no other way to draw the line."

Father L smiled sadly. "You can go blue in the face making rational arguments about this issue, but in some matters, logic just isn't going to help you. One must inspire change at the source."

"How?"

"By opening their hearts."

"Hedonistic baby-killers don't have hearts," Ben muttered, shredding his napkin.

Father L's face seemed to soften. He put a hand on Ben's arm.

"Of course, your bravery is appreciated. But keep your purpose in mind. After all, no amount of sanctimonious sermonizing ever converted a disbeliever."

"Even though it's fun," Jordan said, smiling at her boyfriend.

"Harrumph," Ben said, slumping in his chair. Marina was reminded of her brothers when they were young and stubborn, being told something was a bad idea and already planning to do it anyway.

"What about you two?" Father L said, turning to Marina and Jordan. "Staying out of trouble?"

"Hopefully," Jordan groaned. "I've got a tough class load this semester."

"Same," Marina said, cringing internally. "Not much else to report."

Goodness, what was Nate doing to her? She was lying *to her priest*. But it was a small lie, a white lie, just an omission really. He hadn't asked her specifically about *boys* or *dating*. It was no big deal.

Marina bit her lip, unable to shove away the slimy thoughts.

Before she could change her mind, Father L was rising, leaving the crust of Ben's bread on his plate. "Well, I wish you luck with the blog. And you both," he pointed first at Jordan, then at Marina, "be sure he makes it to the next Spaghetti Dinner in one piece, ok?"

"Yes Father," they chorused as he nodded and drifted away.

"He's wrong," Ben said the moment Father L was out of earshot. "This is important work."

"For you," Marina pointed out. "But maybe not for him. He does say the church tries to stay out of politics as much as possible."

"It's not politics. It's *facts*."

"Ben, your blog is one thousand percent politics."

He considered for a moment. "There might be an overlap."

"I'm tired of talking about this," Jordan cut in, voice sharper than usual. "What movie are we going to watch tonight?"

They began to discuss the various options on their respective lists—Jordan desperate to see Black Panther, Ben groaning that the progressive propaganda would probably ruin the story. But Marina was silent, watching her friend from the corner of one eye. Jordan's expression was overly bright, almost forced, and Marina wondered if, in her own selfish infatuation, she'd missed something. If there was trouble in the enviable paradise of Ben and Jordan's little world.

She promised herself she'd be better, more present. As soon as she figured out what the *heck* she was going to do about Nate.

182

Chapter 27

Nate was stumbling home from the bar, Leo's arm draped heavily over one shoulder, lungs aching from the cold. But he hardly noticed. The weather had become immaterial, overwhelmed by an inferno of pulsing rage.

"How dare that motherfucker. How *dare* he."

"Isfine," Leo slurred, head lolling to one side as he tried to grin at Nate.

"It is *not* fine," Tiffany cut in, struggling to support Leo's other side when she was only two-thirds his weight, if that. "You're allowed to not be fine about it."

"I'm usetoit."

Nate shook his head, seething.

They'd been having a great Saturday night, getting steadily drunker on shots and house music until some Irish *jerk* had tried to use the N-word to flirt with Leo. Nate—who hadn't realized what was happening at first—had seen Leo's face pale, his lips tighten, his head jerk in a quick *no thank you*. The man had grabbed Leo's arm, *come on, you know you want to*, and Leo had pulled away, putting his hands up and shaking his head again. *Not my type*, he'd mouthed.

Then things had really turned sour.

The dude had gone off on them, shouting all kinds of obscenities loud enough to be heard over any kind of music.

Cocksucker, welfare parasite, brainless ape. Nate had surged forward, ready to tackle the dickless prick to the ground. But Leo grabbed him around the chest and said in that low, wonderful voice, "Not worth it."

Tiffany had been almost apoplectic, getting right up in the guy's face, fists clenched, dropping every single F-bomb she could think of, until the bouncer showed up and kicked all four of them out. The drunk asshole vanished into the night and Leo had insisted on buying them another round of shots to *take the chill off.*

Now it was Leo who was blackout wasted, and Tiff and Nate both pounding with the anger of what happened. Nate was glad to shoulder it so Leo wouldn't have to, at least not until later. He was so *frustrated* by the unfairness of it, infuriated by the harsh reality of that guy somewhere in Boston spreading his vile racism and hateful existence and no one there to stop him.

"I should have hit the fucker," Nate growled.

"That would have been worse," Tiffany said, struggling to get their key in the lock as Leo leaned back to look at the stars and almost dragged all three of them backward over the railing.

"How could it have been *worse?*" Nate snapped, more aggressively than he'd meant to.

Tiffany kicked open the door, shooting him a glare from the vicinity of Leo's armpit.

"Then you'd have been Leo's white savior."

"Guys, donfight," Leo said as they all but dragged his lanky, muscled frame up the stairs.

"I would have been his *friend*," Nate said indignantly. "And besides, how come it's ok for *you* get up in the guy's face and not me?"

"Because I'm also from a marginalized identity group."

"Oh, and I'm not?"

"No, Nate, you are most certainly not." Tiffany used her hip to pop open their apartment door, and the three of them tumbled in, barely managing to keep Leo upright. "You are white and wealthy and male and shouldn't act like we need you to swoop in and save us."

Nate dropped Leo on the couch before rounding on Tiff. "So I should have just let that asshole shout at him?"

"Every time someone like you steps in, it invalidates Leo's existence a little more."

Nate threw his hands up, losing his temper. "Fine, next time I'll just let the guy keep going. And when someone grabs *your* ass in a club, I'll let them."

Tiff folded her arms, eyes glittering. "Some ally you are."

"You're telling me not to be one!"

"No, I'm telling you to check your privilege." Tiffany stalked into the kitchen, grabbing an empty glass and jamming it under the tap.

"Well it sure feels like you're the one erasing *me*."

Tiff snorted, back turned to him. "How so?"

"I'm *bisexual*! I'm a part of the queer community!"

"Something no one would know by looking at you."

Nate scoffed. "It's not like you look any gayer than—"

Tiffany spun to face him so suddenly he stumbled back a step. "What the *hell* do you know about being rejected by the world?" she shouted, voice wobbling precariously, tears beading in her eyes. "What do you know about having to fight for the right to *exist*? Your parents fucking *love* you, Nate!" She paused, gulping air, as if she could stuff the emotions back into the prison of her ribcage and lock it shut.

Nate watched her silently, heart thudding, head spinning.

"Look," Tiffany continued after a moment, "the best thing you

185

can do in the world right now is sit back and let people use their own voices."

"But I want to help," Nate said, so low it was almost a whisper.

"You can't."

The words slid into him like a knife between the ribs, a confirmation of his worst fears. Tiffany didn't see him as one of her own, not really. He was apart, separate, other. The wrong gender, the wrong ethnicity. A diluted version of what she wanted him to be.

And Tiff didn't even know about Marina.

His mouth opened, but he had no idea what to say.

"N'more shouting," Leo mumbled from the couch. Nate looked over to find his friend wrapping himself around the long back cushion like an infant about to fall asleep. "M'fine..."

Nate cleared his throat. "Look—"

"I can't take this right now," Tiff said, holding up one hand, scrubbing her face with the other. She turned away.

"Tiff, I'm—"

"Just leave me alone."

Nate watched helplessly as she strode into her bedroom and shut the door with a quiet but final *click*. Guilt squirmed in his belly, crawled up his ribs. He knew he'd screwed up but couldn't pinpoint exactly when or how. And worse, he had no idea how to apologize.

Nate stared at Leo, already snoring.

Lucky him, he thought, and then caught himself.

No, Leo wasn't lucky. *Nate* was the lucky one, the one with all the advantages. Tiffany had every right to say what she'd said, but where did that leave him? What could Nate do, when *he* was a part of the problem? The world was so huge, so unfair and broken, and he had no right to change it. No ground to stand on.

That shrieking wind of loneliness and meaninglessness was roving toward him like a mythological monster, threatening to swallow him whole.

Why bother...

No, *no*, he wasn't going down that road again, not ever. He'd promised his family. So he whipped out his phone and dove into his own bedroom, scrolling through numbers.

His parents would be asleep. His friends were probably out. And besides, most of them would agree with Tiffany anyway.

That left...

He was clicking on her number before he could think better of it, listening to her phone ring over the approaching snarl of that unnamable *something* in his brain.

When Marina's groggy voice filtered through, Nate felt like a drowning man breathing air.

"Do you have any idea what time it is?"

"I'm sorry, I know, this is bad. I just... it's silly, but..."

"Nate, what's wrong?" Her words this time were fully awake, razor-focused, and Nate could picture her eyes with that almost frightening intensity, fully zeroed in on something that engrossed her.

Did he engross her?

"It's nothing," he said. "A stupid fight. I just didn't... didn't know who else to call."

"Tell me."

He did.

He told Marina about how fun the dancing had been until the drunk jerk ruined it. He told Marina about what Tiffany said and how her words, in some form or another, had haunted him since he'd learned about the world and his place in it. How he tried so hard to make up for what he was, for the legacy he'd been born with, but it was never good enough.

How all his efforts only seemed to make things worse.

"Nate," she said when he finally paused for air. "I know I joke about you wanting to solve the world's problems. But really, you're putting too much pressure on yourself. You can't fix everything."

Nate snorted and was surprised by the size of the lump in his throat. "I can try, can't I?"

"Sure, but it's like trying to win the lottery or become a billionaire. If you set your sights on an impossible goal, you'll only ever be disappointed."

"Who wants to be an evil billionaire anyway?" Nate said, thumping back on his bed and closing his eyes so he could better imagine Marina's face in front of him.

"I don't think billionaires are—never mind, different conversation. Look, it sounds like your friend was way out of line."

"She wasn't," Nate said, needing to defend Tiffany, to make up for the damage he'd caused.

"You were doing what anyone would do for someone they cared about."

"But that's the problem, isn't it?" Nate insisted. "We can't just go on as we always have, just accepting the culturally appropriate modes of behavior as they are. Because the culture itself is what needs to change. We need to be more aware of our actions, so we aren't constantly perpetuating racism and oppression."

Marina huffed. "It seems like a stretch that standing up for a friend is perpetuating racism."

"It is though," Nate said, wanting her, *needing* her to understand. "Because for years white people have tried to *rescue* black people."

"So helping them is bad?" Marina asked, voice skeptical.

Nate shook his head, even though she couldn't see it. "No, acting as if Leo needed my presence and power as a white man to get out of that situation was bad."

"You were defending him. *Against racism.*"

"While reinforcing systemic bias."

"Nate," Marina said reasonably, "everything will be racist or sexist or biased if you look at it through a certain lens. But sometimes you can just be helping a friend. Sometimes you can just be acting like a *human being*. It's your intentions that matter, not the minutiae of every little interaction."

"That's a cop out," he said. "I'm still responsible for the harm I inflict on people."

Her sigh was one of affectionate irritation. "You'll drive yourself insane with that level of micromanaging. You're not a mind reader, Nate."

"But I have to listen to criticism. So I can learn to do better."

"Fine, if you're *determined* to see what you did as bad, I suppose you can learn from it. But either way, beating yourself up isn't productive. You did your best, Nate. That's all anyone can ever do. None of us are perfect."

Nate hooked an elbow over his eyes and groaned again, wishing she didn't make so much fucking sense, knowing somewhere, deep in the back of his brain, that it was dangerous she did.

"How do you learn to do that?" he asked after a long minute, hating how small and childish his voice sounded.

She laughed. "Let things go?"

"Yeah."

"I guess by accepting that the world is a bit unfair and a bit messy—"

"Understatement of the goddamn millennium right there."

"Shh, I'm answering your question." He could hear the smile in her voice. "Nate, I think you need to forgive yourself for the things you can't control. Your skin color, your heritage. Those aren't your fault. It's what you *do* that matters."

"That's not true," Nate said, rolling into his elbow. "That's like the Republicans using hard work as justification for inequality."

"Well, I mean it kind of is—"

"Don't even."

"Ok," Marina said, chuckling. "Another one for later." She paused, and he clung to the comforting sound of her inhale. "For what it's worth, I don't think you're racist or sexist or whatever else you feel guilty about. I think you're pretty great."

Something seemed to be pressing against the inside of Nate's ribcage, like a balloon was inflating in his chest. "Really?"

"Are you fishing for compliments now?"

"Absolutely. Did I tell you I was a ham?"

"You mentioned it." She laughed. "Once or twice."

"So you were saying how great I am?"

"And now I'm saying we should go to bed."

Nate huffed, but he was grinning. "It's a Saturday night!"

"I have church in the morning."

"*Pfff*, your choice, not mine."

Nate was smiling at the ceiling, wishing Marina was here beside him, a solid comfort for a decidedly un-solid night. Before he knew it, his mind was drifting into fantasies of her body pressed against his, her wide lips on his skin, her fingers in his hair as she whispered his name...

"You gonna be ok?" Marina asked, interrupting his train of thought.

"Oh, yeah, totally," he said, voice breaking on the last word. He cleared his throat. "I'm good. Just need to do a bit of self-flagellation for being an Anglo-Saxon piece of shit."

"Nate!"

"Kidding," he said. "But don't be alarmed if I have some scars on my back next time I see you."

"And you call me a religious nut."

"Because you are."

"Good*night*."

"Sweet dreams."

Marina chuckled. "You too."

And hung up.

Nate dropped his phone on the pillow beside him, eyes tracing the detail of his ceiling, increasingly aware that he was in some very deep shit. Marina's face was an eclipse in his mind, the mystery of her body a black hole in his thoughts. He knew from experience what this was, how strong his infatuation had become, and worse because it was so much more than just physical. Sure, he wanted to kiss her, do all kinds of dirty things to her. But he also wanted to talk to her again. See her face across the table and relish in the joy of making her laugh. Shock her with some radical argument and watch how she responded. Hearing her perspective on the evening—so different from Tiffany's—had been a balm like no other. Her perspective had eased the guilt.

Should he be worried about that?

Absolutely, said old-Nate, the part of him that had been steadily shrinking since their first night at the party. *You're not supposed to feel* less *guilty. You're not supposed to let her change your mind. That's the reason she's dangerous!*

But, he argued with himself, *what's life without a little danger?*

So begins the slippery slope.

Fuck.

Nate rolled over and pressed his face into the pillow.

At least he wasn't upset about Tiff anymore.

Chapter 28

Marina couldn't stop thinking about sex.

Was this what she'd missed out on in high school? Was puberty hitting her late? Or maybe libido was one of those things that built up energy the longer you ignored it, like volcanos or carbonation. She'd always thought of herself as a rational, reasonable kind of romantic. When her friends were *falling* for guys or *obsessing* over a new crush, she'd offered advice and comfort and secretly decided that would never be her.

She'd been wrong.

"What the hell are they even marching for?" Ben was complaining on the couch as Marina pretended to be working on her advanced biomedical engineering coursework. "Women have the right to kill babies. They're equal under the law. What more do they want?"

"Maybe it's fun to protest stuff?" Jordan offered as Marina's thoughts returned, like a snapped rubber band, to Nate's neck, his strong jawline, the way his hair seemed to change colors depending on the light.

The way he looked at her like there was nothing else in the world.

"It's just a spectacle," Ben grumbled, glasses reflecting his iPhone's screen. "There's no *purpose* to it, other than to show how much everyone kowtows to their whims. It's like those awful pride parades, where they prance half-naked through the streets and then yell at *you* for looking at them weird." He shook his head. "Total bullshit."

Marina imagined what Nate's chest would look like, the strong, wiry lines of his body tracing down...

"Marina, are you ok?"

She jerked up to find Jordan staring at her, head cocked.

"Yeah, sorry, just a bit tired," Marina said, praying that no one could see the flush she could feel creeping up her neck. "What were we talking about?"

"The Women's March," Ben answered, tossing his phone aside on the couch. "Or *rally against dystopian governments and transphobic racism* as that deviant is calling it on Twitter."

"Ben..." Jordan said in a warning voice.

"Sorry, that *queer*."

"I'm not sure that's better," Marina said, sharing Jordan's weary expression.

"It's what she calls herself," Ben pointed out, shoving to his feet and wandering into the kitchen. "And anyway, I already wrote a post about how stupid all this is."

"Did you?" Marina asked distractedly as her phone buzzed.

"Of course. Transgender rights are contradictory to her supposed feminism, so it was easy to point out the absurdity."

"Hmmm," Marina said noncommittally, checking the screen.

It was a text from Nate.

<How are you?> he asked as Ben rummaged through the fridge.

<Distracted> Marina answered before she could think better of it.

<Same. You have infected me, oh siren>

194

He's one to talk, Marina thought as Ben and Jordan continued to chat over her head.

<So what's the cure?> she typed out, feeling distinctly like a base jumper about to make a dangerous, potentially fatal leap.

<How she taunts me!>

<You know you love it>

He sent back a wink with, <I love a lot of things that are bad for me>

<Like underage drinking?>

<I am a 22-year-old from Wyoming, thank you very much>

Marina sent back a rolling-eyes emoji.

<When can I see you again?> he answered.

It was mind-boggling that an overused line she'd heard her friends moon over a thousand times could have such a dizzying effect on her.

<Dinner tomorrow?> she asked.

<Aw darn, I have a meeting for this thing…>

<Would this thing be the upcoming march?>

<Maaaaybe>

Marina pursed her lips but was surprised to find that she was still smiling. She typed out, <Well, don't let me step on your gown>

<Hah! You religious picketers couldn't step on my gown if you TRIED>

<Let me guess, you'll be organizing the pride parade too?>

<Hell yeah. It's tons of fun. You should try it>

<No thanks, I don't take pleasure in proclaiming my sexuality to the world>

<You can proclaim it to me if you want…>

Marina swallowed. Hard. <Tempting>

<Fuck it> Nate sent back <They don't need my toxic male ass. Let's get dinner>

Marina found herself grinning. <You sure? I don't want to invalidate your existence or anything.>

<You can invalidate me anytime, baby>

<Urg, don't call me baby>

"Marina?"

She shook herself, blinking away the blue light of her cellphone. Jordan was watching her, frowning. It seemed that, in the few seconds Marina had been immersed in texting Nate, the conversation about the protest had ended. The living room had fallen quiet, and Jordan's bedroom door was closed. Ben was nowhere to be seen.

What had happened?

"Sorry, family stuff," Marina said, ignoring her shame at the lie.

"Is it though?" Jordan asked and Marina finally noticed just how upset Jordan looked.

"Hey, you ok?" Marina asked, placing her phone facedown on the cushion beside her and leaning in.

Jordan's eyes were too bright, not quite teary but close. "It's fine." She scrubbed at her face, as if she could rub the emotions off it. "I'm just worried about Ben. He's digging himself a hole I don't know he can crawl out of. And you're hardly even here anymore, what with your new boyfriend."

"Sorry," Marina said, ducking.

"Look…" Jordan swallowed. "Not to be pushy or anything, but I'm worried about you too. Marina, this guy, this *thing*? It's not like you. You can see that, right?"

"It's nothing," Marina said automatically. "We're just hanging out."

And calling each other late at night to talk about deep personal fears. And thinking about each other in ways that are decidedly not *platonic*.

"It's no big deal," Marina finished lamely.

Jordan rolled her eyes. "As if *that's* not the oldest excuse in the book. Look, I know you. And I feel like this is a waste of your time. How can you have a future with him? How will you raise your kids?"

"We're hardly there yet," Marina said, swallowing.

"Then where is this going?"

It might have been easy to dismiss what Jordan was saying if she hadn't been wondering the very same thing herself, if a shrill voice in the back of her brain wasn't whispering *what are you doing?* over and over and over.

But she wasn't ready to listen just yet.

"I'll deal with it," she said, smiling to offset the dismissal. "Do you want me to help with Ben?"

Jordan shrugged. "You know how he is. There's no stopping him. I'm just... you know."

"Yeah," Marina said, looking at Jordan's bedroom door.

Despite the fact that Ben was one of her two very best friends, Marina knew full well that Ben could be a bit... strident. She'd made a point of *not* reading the Red Nation blog, afraid of the very things on Jordan's face. There was a huge difference between agreeing with the point and agreeing with the delivery.

And besides, she had enough on her mind.

"It'll be ok," Marina said, not sure if she was talking about Nate or Ben. "Don't worry. We'll figure it out. Everything will be fine."

Jordan's cheeks pulled up, but it couldn't quite be called a smile.

Chapter 29

For the life of him, Nate couldn't understand why he was so giddy, so *happy* after arguing with Marina for another full dinner. They'd talked about welfare and school discipline and the balance between providing for people and not bankrupting the country and *how was it* that Marina could make horrible Republican philosophies seem palatable, maybe even logical in a twisted sort of way? And how she quirked her mouth before she spoke, the distant look she got as she formulated a counterargument...

Nate laughed to himself as he unlocked their front door.

He was, as Leo would say, a goner.

"Honey, I'm home," Nate called, tossing his keys on the table and flinging his coat over a chair. He rolled his neck, still chuckling as he reached for a water glass.

The instinct struck him first, a quiet, persistent hum of wrongness.

He froze.

The apartment was silent, but that was normal. Tiff and Leo were busy people. Maybe they were still at the planning event Nate had bowed out of. Maybe they'd had dates or lingered at the library to get some homework done.

But a soft, hiccupping sound was coming from down the hall.

From Tiffany's room.

Nate drifted toward it, straining his neck to peer through the crack in her door, holding his breath.

Tiffany was there, sitting on the end of her bed and facing away from him. Her spine was a sad, bowed curve, like some huge hand was pressing down, crushing her with all its might. From the cradle of her hands on her knees, Nate could see the white glow of a cellphone, illuminating the messy wisps of hair that had escaped her topknot.

She was shaking.

"Hey," Nate said before he could stop himself. He knocked on the door, pushing it open as he did. "Hey, what's wrong?"

Tiff lurched, spun around.

"Nothing," she said quickly, tossing her phone aside and wiping her arm over her face. "I'm fine. Where the fuck were you tonight? You can't just send a last-minute text and not show up."

Because he knew it was coming, Nate could see the armor snapping into place, the fury surging in to fill the cracks she didn't want him to see. But he didn't rise to it. Instead, he sat next to her, bumping her shoulder.

"What's up, Tiff?" Nate asked in a low, calm voice that he hoped conveyed the worry he and Leo had silently shared since she'd come home from Christmas break with a brand-new chip on her shoulder. "What's going on?"

For a moment, he thought she wasn't going to answer. Her lips were pressed together tight enough to bleach the color out of them, a pale slash of defiance.

And then she broke.

"It's m-my sister," Tiffany said, unable to hold back sobs. "S-she just got engaged to this religious a-a-asshole who thinks I'm an a-aberration. He's got her convinced she needs to s-save my s-soul."

"No way," Nate exhaled, as involuntary as the clenching of

his fists.

Tiff laughed, a small, sad sound. "Yeah. And m-my parents are refusing to p-pick sides." She took a deep, shuddering breath. "I always knew they were unconformable with it, but not..." She paused, looked at her phone. "Alison used to be my best friend. I used to tell her everything."

Nate watched helplessly as her chin quivered, as the spitfire Tiffany threatened to collapse.

Fuck this, he thought, throwing an arm around her and pulling her tight against his side.

"I'm sorry," he said, rubbing her back and letting her fold into his shoulder. "That sucks so much. He sounds like a total dick, the absolute worst of the worst. You have every right to be upset."

"Things weren't p-perfect," Tiffany stuttered, voice muffled. "But it was g-good. And now... he's ruining e-e-everything."

Nate clenched his jaw, shook his head. "What a dick."

Tiffany's body was vibrating like a plucked guitar string, her words coming faster now. Angrier. "My parents think just because he's famous or some shit that they need to cater to him. He's given *speeches* so that means he m-must be *smart*."

Nate scoffed. "Have they *seen* our president?"

He was gratified by another shriveled laugh. "Apparently not." Then, with a jerky inhale, she continued, "It just... hurts."

He squeezed. "I know."

Tiffany sniffed into his T-shirt. "Do you?"

Nate glanced down at the top of her head. "What?"

She pulled back, eyes red and puffy but no longer overflowing. Her expression was one of affectionate exasperation, still hurting but not too much to call him out. "I love you, Nate. You know that. But how can you pretend to understand any of this? Your parents practically threw a party when you came out. Your rights aren't being threatened by the current administration. You can choose to participate in marches and protests when it suits your schedule or when it's fun."

Nate shifted awkwardly, glad the room was dark enough to hide the red flush on his healing cheeks.

Tiffany went on. "Maybe what I said the other night was unfair. You are queer. I respect that. But do you even realize how lucky you are, that you have a fifty-fifty chance of being in a straight-appearing relationship?"

Nate lifted his eyebrows.

"Ok," Tiff laughed, for real this time. "Maybe thirty-seventy."

"That's more like it," Nate said, forcing himself to grin, to hide the very real shame that was writhing in his lungs.

She returned her gaze to her hands, as if remembering the phone that had been there moments before. "I just don't think you understand what it feels like to truly be... invisible."

Shoving aside his own selfish feelings of inadequacy and remorse, Nate squeezed her shoulder tighter. "Tiffany Freeman, you are many things, but you are most certainly *not* invisible. In fact, you might be the least invisible person on this campus, maybe in all of Boston."

She snorted. "Tell that to my sister's *fiancé*. Did you know he gave a speech at Harvard last semester?"

Nate made a noise of outrage. "I hope they booed him out of town."

"Nope. The administration hired security because they're gutless colonial apologists."

"Well, you'll show them with this march, won't you?"

She straightened. "I sure will."

Nate was relieved when she smiled at him. It was still strained, but he could tell he'd helped in some small way. *Not* that it made up for him being a shitty ally and an even shittier friend, but maybe it was a start.

"So," Tiffany said, snatching a tissue and dabbing it under her eyes. "Tell me about this mystery person you're seeing."

"Huh?"

Her smile transformed into a smirk. "We all know you, Nate. Only one thing turns you into such a raging space cadet."

Nate ruffled his hair with a grimace. "Well, two things," he pointed out.

Tiffany rolled her eyes and gave him a good-natured punch in the arm. "Give me something. I'm dying here."

"Well…" Nate said, treading carefully. "They're Hispanic."

"Nice. What are they studying?"

"Biomechanical engineering."

"Another nerd then?"

"What else?"

Tiffany watched him from the corner of her eye, at once patient and prodding. "And you like them?"

Nate stared at her dark wall, wishing he could tell her everything. He wanted to describe how the light played in Marina's hair, how smart she was, how ruthlessly challenging. He wanted to pick apart all the tiny details of his date until they were both dizzy, the way he always did with his roommates.

But the timing was all tangled up. How could he possibly explain that Marina wasn't *that* kind of conservative, not like Tiff's future brother-in-law? Especially when Marina was friends with the kind of people who were. And worse, that the very novelty of his feelings toward Marina might confirm Tiffany's worst suspicions about him…

Nate sighed.

"Yeah," he said at last, knowing the word was woefully

inadequate for what he truly felt. "I do."

She stared at him, waiting for more.

Nate shrugged ineffectually. "You're right. I've never been so… distracted by someone before."

"Even Garett?"

Nate moaned. "You had to bring *him* up, didn't you?"

"C'mon, that was hilarious," she said with a grin.

"In *retrospect*."

"Ah, to be young and in love and locked outside in your underwear."

"It was *freezing*," Nate said with a shiver, reliving the humiliation of shouting up at Garrett's window for his pants.

"I think that was kind of the point."

"Yeah, well, this is different."

"I assume you mean your new flame is less dramatic?"

"Totally," Nate said, imagining someone trying to describe Marina as *dramatic*. If anything, *he* was the attention-seeker of their…

Could he call it a relationship yet?

Did he want to?

He fell back onto her bed with a theatrical flourish. "I'm hopeless."

"You are," Tiffany agreed, pushing to her feet. "But I'm glad you're happy."

"That's one word for it."

He sat up to find Tiffany retrieving her phone, the tears gone but the ache still there.

Maybe it always would be.

"Well, it won't come between us again," Nate said decisively, meaning it. "I won't forget what's at stake."

"Yeah." She cocked one hip and planted her fist on it. "I'm

not spending hours fighting that Red Nation troll for shits and giggles, you know."

"We all appreciate your noble sacrifice," he said, leaping to his feet and bowing to her.

She laughed. "Oh, shut up."

Chapter 30

It was their usual arrangement, Marina in her armchair, Jordan's legs in Ben's lap, all of them typing away. It should have been like any other Wednesday night, calm and quiet and focused.

But Marina couldn't *focus*.

She could barely think straight.

<Help meeeeeee> she typed out, continuing the hour-long conversation she'd been having with Alvaro instead of studying.

Alvaro had been the one to reach out first, sending a string of <I'm bored> messages that reminded her of the silent evenings in their rural ranch home in the mountains. Poor Alvaro was looking for jobs, figuring his life out after a handful of community college classes. Consequently, he'd been turning to Marina often over the last few months for advice, stories from the big city, or just to exchange a few funny memes.

But tonight, Marina hadn't been able to hold back. Her brain was too cluttered with thoughts, too overwhelmed with one pounding, insistent question.

Was she going to sleep with Nate?

So, even though it was totally TMI and more than a little weird, she'd asked Alvaro a simple question that had exploded into a frantic conversation.

<Hey, when you slept with Christina... what was it like?>

Now, after Alvaro's pestering insistence, Marina had finally admitted that she was dating someone.

<Don't you DARE say anything to M&P> she wrote.

He responded quickly, <Of course I won't, idiota. Now tellmetellmetellme>

<Urg, you're a pestilence>

<All the best brothers are. Besides, I'm bored>

<You said that. What do you want to know?>

<EVERYTHING>

Marina looked to the ceiling for comfort, typing out, <Double urg>

<Name?>

<Nate>

<How dull>

<YOU>

<But you want to have the sexy time?>

Marina gritted her teeth. <I am regretting all my life decisions to this point>

<Look, Papi knows about me and Chris. The rents are cool with it>

<I know. I still think you shouldn't TELL THEM>

He sent back a rolling-eyes emoji.

<Duh. Poor papi might have a stroke at the idea of his little girl doing the nasty>

<I loathe you>

He responded with a broken heart.

Marina sent back, <I just want to know... did you regret it? You know... spiritually?>

Those three horrible dots blinked for longer than she was comfortable with.

Finally, his answer appeared. <In some ways it's sad that she

and I didn't work out, since it would have been nice to have that connection with just one person. But no, I don't regret it. Because it meant something, and that's what matters>

She stared at the message, longer than anything her brother had sent in months. It was a sign of the closeness of their relationship not only that they were *having* this conversation, but also that Alvaro, who could barely get through dinner without Mami throwing something at him, was taking it seriously.

Her fingers rested silently on the keyboard as Alvaro composed another message.

<You gonna do it?>

Marina closed her eyes as she typed, <I don't knowwwww>

<Look, if you like this hijo and it's more than just a fling, I say go for it. HAVE THE SEX>

Marina laughed. <I thought I'm supposed to be the bad influence sibling>

<DO ITTTTT>

<I just want you to know that we officially have unhealthy boundaries>

<Nonsense, we're family. There are no boundaries with family>

<I think 90 percent of psychologists would disagree>

<Well, we all know those hacks are almost always wrong>

<Don't you start>

<VACCINES CAUSE AUTISM MARINA>

<I'm silencing this conversation>

<Lol, love you. Enjoy the sex>

Marina shut her computer with a *snap*, unable to hold back the smile spreading over her face. Alvaro was insane, but she loved him for it. And she couldn't deny how much she *wanted* to follow his advice. She'd never felt so alive, so electric. It had to be a good thing, right? Surely, God would approve of something that made her so joyful, wouldn't He?

Screw it, she thought, yanking out her phone and ignoring the irony.

<U up?> she wrote out and pressed send before she could talk herself out of it.

He responded almost immediately. <It's 9pm and I'm not in kindergarten, so... yeah?>

And then, <Also, are you booty calling me???>

Marina felt scandalous sitting across from her two best friends, totally oblivious of the choice she was about to make. The cliff she was about to dive off. She clutched her phone like a lifeline, fingers hovering over keys. Was she really about to do this? Was she ready?

Hell yes.

She responded, <Is it working?>

<At your service, m'lady. But really, we gotta work on your pickup lines.>

<I mean, if you're complaining...>

<Nonono, not complaining>

And then, when she didn't respond, <Marina?>

She grinned at the phone, drunk on something no bar could sell. <Can I come over?>

<Absofuckinglutely>

<Be there in 20?>

<Want me to get you an Uber?>

She grinned. <Impatient much?>

<You misspelled suave as shit>

<I'll walk, thanks>

<If I die of excitement before you get here, it's your fault>

Marina coughed to hide the laugh. She set her computer aside carefully, gingerly, as if her every movement might betray her.

"I just remembered," she said, pushing to her feet as nonchalantly as if she was going to the bathroom. "I have to grab something for a project tomorrow."

Jordan glanced up. "Now? Marina, everything's closed."

"There's a corner store in Central that sells it."

"What do you need?" Ben asked looking at her while his fingers continued to type. "I probably have it."

"Oh, no it's a thing for this thing I have to build. It's no big deal. I need the walk anyway."

Jordan squinted as Marina pulled on her boots, her coat, her gloves. Marina tried to keep her head averted. Would the intention be written on her face? Would someone who's been in a relationship as long as Jordan know lust just by looking at her?

"I'll be back soon," Marina called, waving airily.

"Walk safe," Ben called back, totally oblivious.

Marina could feel Jordan's eyes on her as she strode to the door and ducked out. But she didn't care. She was a kid who'd already jumped off the high dive, a base jumper in flight. This was *happening* and there was no part of her that wanted to turn back and return to her homework and her room and her normal humdrum life.

She thought of Nate's lips, their kiss in the snow, his *eyes*, and Marina had never been so ready for anything in her entire life.

Plunging into the cold night, she pulled up her hood and made her way toward Nate's apartment.

Chapter 31

Unfortunately, Nate had a very big problem.

His roommates were home.

"Shit, shit, shit," he muttered, pacing back and forth at the base of his bed, jerking his fingers through his hair. He'd been so overcome with enthusiasm at Marina's message that he hadn't paused to think about the two people — one person in particular — sitting out in the living room who would *very much not appreciate* Marina coming over. A Catholic, a conservative, a woman? No way, especially not after their conversation a few nights ago. He'd promised to make introductions eventually, but not now.

Not like *this*.

And, even more pressing, their raised-eyebrow surprise or even overt disapproval was sure to ruin what should be, by all rights, a super-special-romantic-moment. Her first time? He had a responsibility to make that perfect. It was selfish, *wrong* that he hadn't... what? Gotten a hotel room? Asked her to wait for a better time?

Wouldn't that be mansplaining?

But it was too late to worry about that now. Marina was on her way and Nate had to do something quick or else spoil the most exhilarating thing that had happened to him in years.

Opening his door with a nonchalance he hoped wasn't as fake

as it felt, Nate stretched with a noisy *aahhhh*.

Neither of them looked at him.

"Um, hey, you guys wanna go get some… pizza?" he said.

"No thanks," Tiffany said without so much as a glance up from her laptop.

"I mean, I feel like we should get out of the house, right?" Nate said, brain whirring. "It's dark and all, and you know what they say about being cooped up."

Leo lifted one eyebrow. "Cooped up?" he asked in that deep bass rumble.

Nate waved airily. "Yeah, right? Like, shouldn't we all get some fresh air?"

"Fresh air that's ten degrees and windy?"

"It's bracing."

"And the snow?"

"Good for the calves."

Nate had the distinct impression that his friend, the genius physics major, was not falling for his bullshit.

But Tiffany cocked her head, tapping her nose. "There is that meeting at the library about whether or not drag queen story time should be continued," she said, eyebrows pulling together. "I sort of wanted to show up. In solidarity, you know? But then it was so cold…"

Thank all my queer-ass ancestors! Nate thought, mentally pumping his fist.

"That's right," he said quickly. "We should *totally* go and show our support. A little cold shouldn't stand in the way of social good."

Tiffany was nodding thoughtfully, glancing at the clock. "Well, let me finish this post for the Digest—"

"No, we can't be late!" Nate said, trying to ignore the furious

214

blush, pretending they couldn't see it. "That would be disrespectful to the cross-dressing community."

"They're drag queens, not cross-dressers Nate," Tiffany said in her *get your terminology right* voice.

"Right, yeah, but they need our support ASAP, Tiff. We gotta *go*."

Leo hadn't moved. His gaze had leveled on Nate, as if he could see right through these pathetic excuses. But Nate didn't care. Marina was just a short walk away, fifteen minutes at most, and whatever consequences came from lying to his friends was a problem for *future* Nate.

Present Nate was only thinking about one thing.

Or rather, one person.

"Come on Tiff, I think Nate has a bee in his bonnet about something."

Tiffany pursed her lips, but she wasn't about to let anyone one-up her on politically charged issues. So she put her computer on the coffee table, pushed to her feet, and began to fish around the carpet for her shoes.

Nate had never realized how *slow* his friends were getting out the door. He had his coat buttoned, shoes laced, gloves and hat on before Leo had even *found* his boots. Nate waited by the doorway, doing his best not to rock back and forth on his heels, as Leo carefully arranged his scarf.

"You alright there, man?"

"Fine, just fine," Nate said, for once wishing his friend wasn't so languorously graceful.

"I think I have everything," Tiff said, patting her pockets.

"You do, let's go," Nate cut in, steering the two of them toward the door.

His heart was hammering frantically as he followed them

down the stairs. What if Marina was outside? What if she was already on their street? What would he do? He could walk by her; pretend he didn't see her. That seemed shitty, but the secrecy wasn't just for him, was it? It was for her sake as well, to avoid the awkward conversations, the glares, the strained friendships.

Although she *had* introduced him to *her* friend...

Nate shoved the thought aside as they strolled out into the cold and began to make their way toward the Cambridge Public Library. *Not the right time.*

When they'd rounded the corner, Nate slapped his forehead. "Aw, shit, I forgot my phone."

Leo's expression, when he looked over his shoulder, was smug.

"Dammit, Nate, you were the one rushing us," Tiffany growled, her pale nose already bright red.

"You guys go on. I'll catch up," he said with a casual wave. "No worries."

"No worries my ass," Tiff muttered.

"Have fun!" Leo called.

Nate ignored him, hurrying back to their apartment.

His hands shook as he jammed his key into the lock. *Just the cold*, he told himself as he flung the door open and all but flew up the stairs, limbs loose and clumsy. Why was he so jittery? He'd done this before. Was it because she hadn't?

Was it because he loved her?

Nope, do not *think about that. Clean the room.*

For five minutes Nate was a whirling dervish of tidying energy, throwing all his clothes—clean and dirty—into the laundry bin, straightening books, shoving crumpled papers and bits of trash into any drawer they could fit into. He straightened his bedsheets and arranged his pillows and opened a window to try and air out that somewhat-dank smell he'd never noticed before, *how had he not noticed that before*? And, just when he was tossing his dirty snow boots out into the hallway, the doorbell rang.

Nate froze.

Swallowed.

Here we go, he thought, pressing the button to unlock the front door and stepping onto the landing.

Every time he saw her, she seemed more beautiful. Tonight, her skin glowed bronze under the lemony hall light, her hair like obsidian in the sun. She looked up at him beneath gorgeously thick lashes, blushing, nervous, smiling.

"Hey," she said when she reached him.

"Hey," he said, horrified by the crack in his voice.

For a long moment they both stood there. Nate found himself wondering if her body was pounding with the same heady adrenaline as his. Should he ask if she was sure? Offer her wine or dinner or tell her it was ok to wait? This was *her* moment, not his, and he was desperate to give her the agency she wanted while also making absolutely sure he wasn't putting pressure on her or injecting his own narrative into the experience she was attempting to create, and he wished that he could read her thoughts and figure out what she wanted because it would absolutely fucking kill him if he fucked it up now...

Marina bit her lip.

Looked down.

"Look," Nate said, deflating a little. "It's fine if—"

And then, without warning, she grabbed his face, jammed her lips against his, and shoved him into the apartment, dragging him toward the open door of his bedroom.

Chapter 32

To Marina's surprise, she didn't feel all that different. Sure, there was a strange vulnerability to lying naked, covered only by sheets, beside a boy she'd just met a few weeks ago. And she was a bit sore *down there*. But the act itself had been... nice? Not earth-shattering the way they made it look in the movies, but not horrible either. Nate had been slow and thoughtful, checking in with her often enough that she'd almost told him to just *shut up and get on with it*. But in the end, she'd been grateful for the extra attention. She imagined it could have been much less pleasant without it.

"What are you thinking?" Nate asked, propped up on one elbow beside her, his rainbow hair catching the glow of the streetlamp.

She smiled crookedly at him. "I'm wondering how I'm supposed to feel."

He trailed one finger down her shoulder. "Awestruck? Mind-blown? Saturated in a haze of bliss?"

She laughed. "Quite sure of yourself, aren't you?"

Nate grinned back. "I mean, I have done this before."

Marina's smile faded and she returned her gaze to the ceiling. "Sorry, that was—"

"Nate," she interrupted him, unable to stop herself. "I've tried a lot of new things here."

His eyebrows drew together in question.

Marina took a deep breath, forcing herself not to wonder why he'd stopped stroking her arm.

Finally, she said, "I think it's your turn to try something new."

Nate's grin returned, now playful and impish. "You know me, always up for new experiences. Try anything once, that's my motto."

She didn't answer right away, chewing on her bottom lip hard enough to hurt. This had been on her mind ever since the drive back from their ski trip, but she'd held off. A part of her—a huge, loud part—was dreading his response. Because there was something she wanted, something she hadn't realized was important until he'd admitted he would wait for her. Something she needed to know and couldn't hold back any longer.

She reached for the cross around her neck, one of several she'd owned in her life, the representation of the most important part of herself.

And took it off.

Holding it out to him, she asked, "What about faith?"

Nate's eyes widened. "*Huh?*"

"Look," Marina clarified quickly, rolling onto her side so she could face him, "I'm not expecting you to convert or anything. But you got me to ski and have sex and maybe even consider smoking weed." Nate snorted, but Marina plunged on. "I'm grateful. You've helped me see life through a new lens. But this is my world, my foundation. I go to church because I want to, and it would mean a lot to me if you... thought about it."

"No offense," Nate said carefully, picking at his threadbare sheets, "but what is there to think about? A big man in the sky who made the universe? Some dude rising from his grave?"

"You still think believing in God is stupid?"

"I mean, I wouldn't put it *that* way," Nate said, focusing on his fingers.

Marina rolled back into the pillows. "I did too, actually." From the corner of her eye, she saw his head jerk up in surprise. "I was an atheist most of my teens. I thought God was a fable that people invented to feel better about the world and control the masses." She lolled her head in his direction. "Needless to say, my parents weren't pleased."

"So why give up on all that delightful cynicism?" he asked.

Marina focused on the details of the ceiling, the swirling whorls and bumps of the industrial paint. "My brother challenged me to think about it. Like, really think about it, not just spout internet memes about the great spaghetti monster and rag on the absurdity of biblical stories. As you know, I've never been one to turn up a dare, so I began to research *reasons for God*, expecting them to be totally ridiculous. And you know what?" She smiled wryly. "They weren't."

"Yeah? How so?"

"Well, take creation for example. Maybe it's crazy to think about an intelligent entity creating the universe out of nothing. But isn't it just as crazy to think about the universe coming from nothing spontaneously? Isn't that just a different kind of virgin birth? I mean, maybe there was a universe before the Big Bang, but for everything to go from nothing, no time, no space, to *something* is pretty fantastical, don't you think?"

Nate was frowning, the half-light giving his face a sharp, angular beauty that Marina could have stared at for hours. "But what if there was something before the Big Bang? What if it was everything that existed before compressing into that pinpoint dot and then exploding again? A never-ending cycle?"

Marina propped her head up, mirroring his posture. "It still had to start somewhere, right? Whether endless or finite, the idea that all of this came from nothing, just exists for no reason, seems to me just as wild as believing that it exists for a reason. And, of course, you also have to grapple with the extreme unlikeliness of life. When I began to do the research, I discovered that the fact that we exist at all is so statistically improbable it's basically impossible. If the Big Bang had been slightly stronger, or slightly weaker, we wouldn't have happened. If matter had formed in a slightly different way, we wouldn't have happened. Even with randomness and the size of the universe, *even* if the Big Bang is a recurring event, it's so incredibly weird and unlikely that we exist as we do. Therefore, without any logical alternative, an intelligent creator makes sense, wouldn't you say?"

"I dunno. There is a *lot* of universe out there. And what if we live in a multiverse? We could totally just be the lucky one-in-ten-trillion planet suited for life."

She shrugged. "Even so, at best the odds are there for the development of single-celled organisms. But evolution? Biological complexity? *Consciousness?* Not so much."

Nate lifted an eyebrow. "The multiverse could be a pretty big place."

Marina looked at the cross in her hand, warmed by the skin of her chest. She chewed on her lip, wanting to give up, go back, let this go. But there was no stopping now. She was already deeper than she'd intended to go, and Nate was *listening*.

She took a breath. "And then there's the matter of Jesus."

"Oh, come on," Nate said, tucking a stray hair behind her ear in a heartbreakingly tender gesture. "You can't tell me you believe a guy rose from the dead. It's just a story."

"But what if it's not?" Marina turned the cross over, tracing the little *made in China* on the back. "Hundreds of people claim to have seen him after he died and was buried, and the creeds were written only a handful of years after the event, five or six at most."

She looked back up, trying to pick apart the details of his expression. "That's not long enough for a myth to form, much less for people to be willing to die for it."

"People die for things all the time," Nate said.

"Yes, for legends. Myths. Something distant enough to become real. But people don't die for lies. Look at the Watergate Scandal, or any other government whistleblowers. Most human beings won't sacrifice themselves for something they don't believe. But those early Christians did, very soon after the death of Jesus. They died claiming they'd seen him, shaken his hand, *after* his death. So why would they believe so strongly that Jesus rose from the grave?"

"Mass hallucination?" Nate offered.

"Maybe. But over multiple events and hundreds of people, all with different experiences?"

"What if the whole thing is just a story passed down through the generations, like historical telephone?"

"Except that we do have some records of the time," Marina said, her heart beating frantically. Desperately. Half of her wished she'd never started this conversation, the other half wanted to push harder. "Relatively speaking, it's pretty well known what was happening around the time of Jesus. And there's no evidence to contradict the story of his resurrection."

Nate didn't respond for a long minute, frowning out at his mattress.

"What are you thinking?" Marina asked when she couldn't take the silence anymore.

"I'm thinking that this is some pretty serious pillow talk," he said, laughing.

"All I want is for you to think for yourself," Marina said, holding out the cross. "Like I said, I don't want you to swallow it blindly or pretend. Just… try it on for size."

Marina held her hand steady between them, trying not to wonder if she'd just ruined everything, stomped all over this shiny, delicate thing that had begun to make her life feel like a dream.

But she knew herself.

This was a part of her, had been ever since freshman year at MIT when she'd still been processing her late-night campfire talks with Alvaro and the question her parents kept asking—*have you been going to church?*—and closing the last page of *Surprised by Joy* and falling back on her dorm room bed with her head spinning, no longer able to deny what now seemed like raw, crystalline logic. God had brought her Jordan and Ben, had given her much-needed direction. God had changed her life. And she couldn't hide it, not without hating herself. She didn't need him to agree with her. But she did need to know this wouldn't be a wedge between them.

Nate eyed the little gold chain. "Is it gonna burn me?"

"Only if you put it on the oven," Marina said, holding steady.

"I won't wear it you know."

"That's fine."

Slowly, nervously, he stretched out his fingers and hooked the cross out of her hands. He held it up, examining the way it glittered.

"To think of how many people have been killed for this little symbol."

"Just because Christianity is logical doesn't mean people are," Marina admitted. "And besides, religion doesn't have a monopoly on horrible."

"It sure has a plurality though, in terms of how many wars have been fought for it."

"Nothing has killed more people than the ideas of Karl Marx."

Nate scoffed. "That's because his ideas have never been done right."

"Oh boy, here we go again," Marina said with a chuckle.

He opened his mouth to respond. But just then, there was a slam and a shout.

"NATE, YOU FUCKER!"

Marina yanked up the sheets to cover herself, heart pounding.

"Oh shit," Nate muttered, lunging out of the sheets.

"Is that your roommate?" Marina asked, eyes wild, blood rushing to her face.

"Yeah, I kind of did a bad thing to get them out of the house." He was toppling out of the low bed and digging around for his clothes.

"What are you gonna tell them?" Marina whispered as the thud of angry bootsteps reverberated in from the stairwell.

"No idea," he said, hopping on one leg to pull on his pants. "But unless you want to deal with a very pissed-off Tiffany, I'd hide if I were you."

Marina, feeling dirty for the first time that night, plunged beneath the comforter and curled into as small of a ball as she could, hoping she'd pass for a pile of pillows if anyone glanced in. There was a hammering on the door and Nate called, "One minute!"

"Fuck you, Nate! You blew us off again!"

"Sorry, sorry, I lost track of time!" Finally Nate stopped hopping around and opened the door.

"What the fuck happened to your shirt?"

"I... took a nap."

There was a *click* as Nate closed the door behind him. The voices of his roommates became muffled.

"Not cool, man," said a deep voice that sounded amused rather than angry.

"Sorry, I haven't been myself lately—"

"You're fucking right you haven't. What was tonight all

225

about?"

"It looks like Nate was enjoying some *me* time," said the deep voice.

"Ew, stop it—"

But the girl cut Nate off. "I don't care *what* you do, but next time you drag me away from my *important fucking work*, you'd better have the guts to tell me *why*."

There was a loud stomping, the slam of another door, and then silence.

"Damn," Nate said in a low voice. "She's pissed."

"She's always pissed these days. Being cold doesn't help."

"Well... sorry man."

"Whatever," said the other roommate, voice growing further away. "If you wanted to have the place to yourself, all you had to do was ask."

"I didn't—"

"Just one thing, bro. Make sure you know what you're doing."

Nate didn't come in for a long moment, and Marina wondered what was going through his mind. Did either of them know what they were doing? Did they care? Looking back on the evening—on the past few weeks—the logical side of Marina's brain could hardly believe how foolish they'd been. How reckless and self-centered. But what did it matter when her heart was full and whole and all she wanted was for him to touch her again, kiss her again? Talk to her again...

Finally, Nate came back in, pressing a finger to his lips.

"You can sneak out when they're asleep," he whispered, climbing back into bed with her.

"How scandalous," she hissed back.

"It wouldn't be a secret affair without some skulking around, now would it?"

Marina giggled and Nate stuffed his face into the pillow to muffle his laugh, and she decided she quite liked the sound of that.

Chapter 33

"Something has to be done about that neo-Nazi," Aesha was saying, gesturing with her chopsticks. "His write-up of the Women's March was straight-up misogynist bullshit. *Angry lesbians trying to cover up the fact that they can't get dates?*" she mock-read off her phone. "For fuck's sake, I can't *believe* your professor hasn't kicked him out of class yet."

"I know, right?" Tiffany said, reaching over Nate's arm for a slice of salmon sashimi.

It was their monthly dinner with Tiffany's group of activist friends. Originally called Beers for Queers, it had started as a trivia night where they got together and discussed the various forms of bias and oppression they'd dealt with recently. However, after they'd all memorized pretty much every trivia question the campus pub had to offer, Tiffany had begun to expand their meetings to more exotic locations — India Pavilion, Mongolian BBQ.

And now, Yamato's all-you-can-eat sushi in Copley Square.

Nate chewed on a roll of spicy yellowtail, keeping quiet as he listened to them discuss the problem of Benjamin Sharps. He tried to tell himself it was because he still felt guilty about the stunt he'd pulled the other night. Even though Tiffany appeared to have forgiven him, Nate knew he was on thin ice. But Marina kept invading his thoughts, her calm, reasonable voice asking, *is it really fair to call this kid a Nazi?*

So he sat back and listened, which was what she wanted him to do anyways.

"Maybe we should get someone to hack his blog," Eric offered from Leo's other side. "Take everything down."

"But that doesn't send a *message*," Tiffany said, gripping her beer like a battleaxe. "We need to show everyone what a twisted sack of shit he is."

"We could prank him," said Mimi from the end of the table, pink hair arranged in a stylish half-bun today.

Tiff didn't answer, gnawing thoughtfully on the end of her chopsticks.

"You could just let it go," Leo said, selecting a piece of octopus. "I mean, who cares if a bunch of idiots read this kid's blog. They're probably all trolls anyway."

Tiffany swung around. "And let him keep recruiting for his shitty dystopian vision? Let him spread his hatred and violence unchecked?"

"Seems to me like he's bothering you a lot more than you're bothering him."

Nate winced. He hadn't told Leo about what she'd confessed to him—it didn't seem like his story to share. But he could feel Tiff's anger even across the table, her cornered-animal outrage as the taint of bad ideas threatened to overwhelm yet another part of her life.

"Besides," Leo continued, oblivious to the thousand-yard death stare pointed in his direction. "It would be nice if we could talk about something else sometimes."

"Like what, *Leo*?" Tiff said through a clenched jaw. "The children dying on the border? The climate going past the point of no return? The president turning us into one of the most hated nations in the world? The black and brown bodies being murdered in the streets, gunned down by our state-funded police system? That kind of thing?"

Leo shrugged. "Or, you know, the weather?"

He winked at Nate, who quickly ducked his head to avoid attention.

"I prefer to do something productive with my time on this planet," Tiff said archly.

"Me too," Mimi chimed in, tipping her plum wine. "We just need to find a way to…"

Nate gave Leo a sideways smile. "Nice try."

Leo shook his head. "Don't know why I bothered. She's in a mood."

"The world's been in a mood since 2016."

"At least you've got a good distraction, eh?"

Nate started, suddenly very aware of Tiffany and her entourage all around him, debating various ways to confront the guy in her class.

"I don't know what you—"

"Don't insult my intelligence."

Nate felt his cheeks heat up. He grabbed his beer to hide it. "Ok, fine."

"I do have a question though." Leo smirked. "Do the Catholics spend as much time on their knees in the bedroom as they do in church?"

Nate snorted into his drink.

"What are you two whispering about?" Eric said in a lofty voice, leaning around Leo to look at Nate.

Both of them returned to their plates, Nate red, Leo grinning.

As the conversation swirled on, Nate sank into a contemplative silence. Why did he feel so… guilty? Like he was a kid trying to hide dirty magazines under his bed. With Tiffany on one hand planning war, and Marina on the other asking him to consider

God, Nate felt like his brain was being hooked in two directions, like he was tearing open some fault line that had been built into him since the day he was born. He knew he had to fight his maleness, his biases, his disgusting privilege. It was a daily struggle for him to rebuild his belief system, restructure his instincts into something better, something *right*. But here he was, falling for someone who challenged him to do quite the opposite.

How long could he keep this up?

"I'm gonna find a way to stand up to the bastard," Tiffany was saying now with the air of a soldier about to march. "Force him to say those awful things to my *face*. We'll see how brave he is without the shield of his computer between us."

"Careful, Tiff, he might be dangerous," Aesha said, brows furrowing.

Tiff chomped down on a slice of roll with gruesome determination. "I'll show him who's dangerous at tomorrow's hockey game."

"God help him," Leo drawled, exchanging a knowing look with Nate.

God help us all, Nate found himself thinking, desperately fighting the urge to fish out his phone and warn Marina what was coming.

Chapter 34

So this is what being in love feels like? Marina thought as Nate filed into the rink with his teammates. It felt like a wrinkle had just been ironed out of the world, like the sun had come out from behind thick clouds. Everything else was muzzy and blurred except that shock of unnatural hair, that pale face, those dimples.

She smiled at him covertly, quietly.

He didn't return it.

"Oh it's *her*," Ben said when he saw who they were playing, strapping on his shin guards.

"I told you," Jordan said quietly from the stands.

"I forgot," he grumbled.

Marina was watching the back of Nate's head, the gentle flutter of his hair. When had the color stopped bothering her?

"Well, it just means I get to kick her ass online *and* in person," Ben was saying.

"Wait," Marina said with a jerk, her joy sublimating into something sour and unpleasant. "That's the person you're fighting with? The one who keeps commenting on your blog?"

"Yeah," Ben said, velcroing his hockey pants. "Why?"

"No reason," she said quickly, turning to her own gear to avoid looking at Jordan.

Why hadn't Nate told her? Was it his responsibility to do so?

Maybe he hadn't realized or he'd wanted to protect her, but the lie of omission felt like a betrayal. Like an omen.

She shook her head, lacing up her skates.

Don't be silly, it's between Ben and her. It doesn't affect us. Nothing to be upset about.

Somehow, she couldn't quite convince herself.

Marina finally lifted her gaze to find Jordan's face pinched in worry as Ben snapped the mask of his helmet shut. "Oh, please be careful. She looks pretty mad."

Marina glanced over. Jordan was not wrong. The blonde player looked ready to bite someone's head off.

"Whelp," Marina said with forced amusement, pulling on her team jersey. "One way to find out…"

Before she knew it, she was gliding onto the ice, one eye on Nate as he finished strapping on his own equipment. He still hadn't looked at her and she couldn't help but wonder what was going through his mind. Was he acting aloof for her sake? To prolong the secrecy of their romance?

Or was he avoiding her because of Ben?

When he stepped through the gate, she knocked a puck toward him right away and went to meet it, doing her best to make it look natural, casual.

"What's going on?" she whispered as she passed by.

She barely caught the edge of his agonized expression.

And then the game started.

Marina was quick to take the puck and pass it to Greta, a girl from her bible study. Greta wove, ducked, passed it back. They were flying up the rink.

Without warning, a body slammed into Marina, painfully hard.

She gasped as Nate's friend, Tiffany, stole the puck and

chased it up the rink.

"Woah, foul much?" Greta said as they watched her score.

But the referee had apparently missed it, so the next play continued as if nothing had happened.

Except that Marina now knew why Nate looked so worried.

"You ok?" he called, skating past Marina in a blur.

She nodded, but the puck was changing hands, too fast, swept to one side by Ben.

Marina caught the edge of Ben's savage grin.

Oh no.

"Ben!" she cried out, plunging after him, pumping both arms.

Ben and Tiffany were converging in the middle, her small body flying at his larger one. He rolled out of the way, keeping possession of the puck. She dug an elbow into his ribs.

"Ben, don't!"

He shoved her down.

The whistle blew.

"FOUL!"

But the ref was too slow, because Tiffany was already on her feet, shouting at Ben.

"You Nazi racist piece of fucking shit!"

He folded his arms. "Didn't your mother ever tell you to watch your mouth?"

The teams were gathering around them, oblivious of the exasperated referee trying to shove through.

"I don't get paid for this," the young woman was muttering.

Tiffany was right up in Ben's face. "My mother was too busy teaching me about fairness and equality, you *pig*."

"Oh, so you were raised by idiots?"

"Fuck you!"

"No thank you."

Ben was grinning, Tiffany swelling like a balloon. Marina did her best to reach them, thrusting through the teammates shouting for them to *back off, calm down*. From the corner of her eye, she could see Nate trying to do the same.

"Ben," Marina cried out, "stop—"

Without warning, Tiffany drew back and punched Ben right in the face.

He went down with a surprised *oof*.

Everyone fell deathly silent.

"That's... that's a foul?" the ref said in a confused voice, gaping at the scene, completely out of their element. Everyone was. Marina felt vaguely like something was rushing at them, too fast, too dangerous, a freight train out of control.

Ben reached up to touch the blood slowly leaking out of one nostril.

When he saw the red on the tips of his fingers, he smiled. "Oh, you've done it now."

Marina twisted, her gaze shifting to Nate's friend. In the intervening seconds, Tiffany had turned a worrisome shade of maroon, her face so twisted that it transformed her usually pretty features into something grotesque.

"This isn't over," she spat before stalking off the rink.

"No it is not," Ben said, watching her go.

"I guess that means the game is done?" Greta asked as Tiffany's teammates followed, rushing after her with expressions ranging from worried to gleeful.

Nate hesitated, his eyes meeting Marina's.

"I think so," Marina said, trying to silently ask what neither of them could say in person, not now.

Are you ok?

Are we?

"What are you gonna do, man?" one of Ben's friends asked, helping him to his feet.

"Oh, I'm taking her *down*," he said, dabbing at his nose. "Even MIT can't ignore outright assault."

Marina bit her lip, saying nothing.

Ben was right. Of course he was right. Tiffany was way out of line. But he'd provoked her, had *been* provoking her all semester. Just this morning, she'd browsed through Red Nation's newest pieces, skimming articles defending gun ownership of any kind, dismissing the March for our Lives, condemning the "baby-killers in Congress," and claiming that the poor only stayed that way because they were lazy and anyone in this country could pull themselves up by their bootstraps if they worked hard enough.

Privately, she thought he was being a bit unreasonable.

She imagined Tiffany thought far worse.

Why didn't Nate tell me?

Jordan was waiting for them by the gate, breathless and urgent as they stepped off the ice.

"Oh, Ben, are you ok?" she asked, patting Ben's face and making sure the nose wasn't broken. "She really got you. Does it hurt?"

"I'm fine," he said. "Just fine."

Marina pursed her lips.

Was she imagining it, or was he really saying he was *glad*?

Chapter 35

I am the luckiest guy in the world, Nate thought as he watched Marina examine the art on his walls, utterly resplendent in nothing but one of his T-shirts and her underwear. She'd snuck over again, this time when Tiffany and Leo were out on their own accord; him on a date, her researching something at the library. And so Nate lounged, relaxed, propped up on pillows with his hands behind his head, wishing this moment could stretch on for the rest of his life.

"Your cousin did all these?" Marina asked in an awestruck voice as she wandered from one beautiful landscape to the next.

"Yeah, he's kind of a prodigy."

"I can't imagine," she whispered, trailing her long fingers over the elegant frame of Nate's favorite, a rural scene of horses riding over a hilltop, wild and free. "It must be wonderful to have such artistic talent."

"You're artistic."

She laughed. "Afraid I never got past stick figures."

"But you're a good writer. You got that internship in Cali, right?"

He didn't tell her that he'd read—and loved—her work.

"I haven't applied yet," she said, quieter, suddenly more subdued.

"Will you?"

She shrugged and fell silent, stepping up to the next painting, effectively cutting off the conversation.

He wondered why she was so defensive about it. Was she scared of the risk? Were her parents less than accepting of a non-traditional career track? Science journalism was hardly *radical* by any means, but he supposed it wasn't as stable or predictable as engineering. And Marina was nothing if not practical.

He'd have to work on that.

"What are you thinking?" he asked, watching the muscles in her legs ripple as she rolled up on her tiptoes to examine the brushstrokes.

"It's so nice that you have these." She offered him a shy smile over one shoulder. "It must be like living in a gallery."

"Everyone decorates their room."

"Yeah, but most people our age just do posters of bands and movies. Not real *paintings*." She tilted her head to appreciate a glorious seascape.

Nate squirmed. He'd never thought of his own decorations, but through Marina's eyes he realized it was just another entitlement. And worse because he didn't even notice it. He was like an old British king, taking for granted the luxury all around him. It was surprising that Tiff had never pointed it out.

He bit back a sigh.

More stuff to work on.

"So," Marina interrupted his thoughts, turning toward him with a steely, determined expression. "Why didn't you tell me about your roommate?"

Nate froze.

Uh oh.

"What about her?" he said, attempting nonchalance.

"That she's the one starting a war with Ben?"

240

Nate bristled, dropping his hands to his sides. "She didn't *start* anything. He was the one who began posting all that crap."

"No one forced her to read it."

"He's making the classroom into an unsafe environment."

"By stating his opinions?"

"His opinions are atrocious."

Marina planted her hands on her hips, eyes dangerous. "Oh are they now?"

He flushed but didn't back down. "Come on, you have to admit he's kind of a dick."

"I'm sorry, but I believe she's the one who *hit him*."

Nate folded his arms over his chest, narrowing his eyes. "He triggered her."

"That's not an excuse for violence."

"She was responding to violent language!"

Marina's mouth fell open. "That's not the same thing."

"Sure it is. Hate speech can hurt people."

"Hurt people's *feelings*. Besides, since when is what Ben doing hate speech?"

Nate begins to tick off his fingers. "He wants to deny the existence of trans and gay people. He proposes taking away women's rights to their own bodies. He's actively belittling the experiences of the poor and mentally ill. He expresses clear misogyny and white supremacy on a daily basis."

Marina rolled her eyes. "All that is such an exaggeration. And besides, you think your friend is such a saint?"

"She's trying to be."

"So is Ben."

"Yeah," Nate said with a snort. "Right."

Marina released a breath, gaze sliding from him to the bedside table, where her cross glittered in the pale lamplight. Nate wondered

241

what was going through her head. Did she know he hadn't touched it, hadn't even really thought about it except to worry that Tiff or Leo might catch a glimpse of what she'd left behind? A part of him understood how scary it must have been for her to ask, how important that question was to someone with her background. Or at least he could hazard an educated guess. But the rest of him couldn't imagine shouldering another shadow of his ancestry, another historical burden. It was too much to even *begin* to wrap his brain around.

Deflating a little, she slid back into bed and folded her legs beneath her.

"The thing you have to understand about Ben," Marina said at last, eyebrows knitting together, "is that he's incredibly frustrated. He has a good heart, really. But he's angry at the world for rejecting, or at least discouraging, the skill he's most proud of."

"Which is what, exactly?" Nate said, lifting an arm so she could lean against him. Marina accepted the peace offering, nestling into his side. His gaze drifted to her fingers on his bare chest, tracing the line of his sternum.

Finally, she spoke. "He grew up the youngest of five siblings in a really smart family. All of his older brothers and sisters are lawyers or doctors. One's running for senate, I think. And, of course, they're really conservative."

"I never would have guessed," Nate said with thick sarcasm.

Marina looked up, lashes silvery in the dim light. "Well, imagine trying to hold your own in that household. Everyone constantly challenging, constantly one-upping one another. He got really, really good at debate, at seeing the holes in any argument and taking pleasure in deconstructing it. But that's not what people want right now. In his view, there's more public interest in being kind-hearted than being factually correct or logical. It drives him crazy." Her eyes drilled into him, focused, dizzying. "And beyond that, I think he wants to be seen."

"Everyone wants to be seen."

"Exactly," she said, leaning in with more intensity. "The social structures that affect his life doesn't see people like him, not really. These current trends for diversity and safety and religious freedom and inclusive entertainment? They're not for us. Not for Catholics and certainly not for straight, white, conservative guys." She looked at her hands. "He wants to be met on a battleground of reason and facts and instead he gets dismissed for things he has no control over. Things he can't change about himself, even if he wanted to."

I know how that feels, Nate found himself thinking before tamping it down. That was *exactly* the kind of dangerous, contagious thing Tiff was worried about. It was vitally important that what Nate had with Marina didn't threaten who he wanted to be. He didn't want to have to make that choice.

Because he wasn't sure what he'd choose.

He focused on her as she kept talking.

"I think Ben was bullied as a kid although he never talks about it. And maybe he was overshadowed a bit by his siblings. Nowadays, I think he feels overshadowed by a system determined to misjudge him and shut down his voice, so he shouts louder. He wants to be evaluated for his merits and his mind. To have the chance to earn his place in society." Marina looked up, almost cautiously. "We all do."

Nate grinned, stroking one hand over the erotic slope of her hips. "I see your merits."

She cocked her head. "Maybe. But I don't think it exactly bothers you that I'm Hispanic, does it?"

"You're a conservative. That negates any positive points you get for ethnicity."

"But see, there are positive points, right? Don't you think

that's unfair?"

"The minorities in this country were oppressed for hundreds of years. It's only *fair* that we make up for it."

"Except that I'm not oppressed now. You didn't oppress my people. Ben didn't oppress anyone, at least not intentionally. So why should he be punished for something he didn't do?"

"Because it's justice."

"Or it's payback," Marina said softly. "Fueled by people like Tiffany."

"Hey now—"

"Nothing against your roommate," Marina said, holding up her hands. "I do understand why she's mad at Ben. I just don't think her horse is all that much higher than his. Do you really think everything she does is for other people? Or to make the world better? Don't you think there's some part of her, even if it's just a little bit, that enjoys the attention and power?"

Nate adjusted his hips, leaning on one hand. "No, I don't think so. Tiffany is obsessed with defending the weak."

"Or taking down the strong."

"What's the difference?"

Marina's smile was enigmatic and eerie and made Nate feel like there was so much more to life than he'd ever thought. "Quite a lot."

Nate shrugged, trying to keep his spiraling, chaotic thoughts from showing on his face. "I've seen what Tiffany's been through and I can tell you, she's legit. She really cares about making the world a better place, and look," he lifted one hand to stop her protest, "maybe her methods aren't always the best, but her heart's in the right place."

"So is Ben's."

"Right, because online rants about how the pride parade

symbolizes the decay of our society are totally kind-hearted."

She pushed him lightly. "When we first met, you had some pretty stupid ideas about conservatives."

"And you had some pretty stupid ideas about queer people." He leaned in, brushing his lips against hers, desperate for them *not* to be talking about this anymore. "Now you're in bed with one."

"You weren't the person to change my mind there," she said, a little breathlessly.

"I think I helped." He trailed kisses down her neck, over her shoulder.

Her inhale hitched. "Well one thing's for sure. Neither of them can do what we do."

"What exactly do we do?" he said, pulling up his T-shirt to grab hold of her waist.

"Discuss ideas."

"Is that all?"

Marina grinned down at him, half-laughing. "We already—"

Nate didn't let her finish. He pulled her onto him, silenced her protests with his mouth, his tongue, his hands kneading the flesh of her thighs. He longed to be dizzy with her again, intoxicated by the delicious isolation of their little world where his guilt didn't have to be all-consuming and her outrage softened and everything could be solved with the soft reassurance of skin on skin. He didn't want to face his own weakness or the fact that she was the cause of it. He didn't want to deal with the slow erosion of his ideas. No, her mouth and her face and her hair and her smell left no room for it, so he allowed the sensation to crowd out his worries until his mind was as blank and blissful as fresh snow.

Finally he drew back, smirking. "You were saying?"

"You changed the subject," she accused in a dazed voice.

"Do you want me to stop?"

Her kiss back was answer enough.

Chapter 36

Walking home from Nate's apartment, Marina worried. Something was off between them, something she'd noticed for the first time after that last hockey game. They were still discussing, still talking, still debating. But there was a distance in Nate's eyes, a guarded defensiveness that was setting off alarm bells in her brain. Was it because of Ben and what was going on? Because of the cross she'd given him and her pushing about religion?

Or something else?

A small, bleak voice in the back of her mind whispered, *you knew it was too good to be true. Even that first night, you knew it would end badly. You expected this.*

She shook it away.

It was fine. She and Nate were strong, they'd figure it out. They'd *communicate*. So what if their friends were feuding? It had nothing to do with them. It would blow over, like all of Ben's political spats.

And yet, she hadn't asked about Alvaro.

Marina bit her lip, exposing her teeth to the cold.

Alvaro had written last night saying that he'd booked a flight and was coming up for the weekend. He'd sworn up and down that he hadn't told Marina's parents the true reason—they thought he was planning to look at schools. But Marina knew. Alvaro wanted to gawk at the guy with tie-dye hair and all the wrong beliefs who had somehow managed to defrost his "ice-queen sister." Marina would have been insulted if she hadn't been so thrilled by the idea of Nate defrosting her.

So why hadn't she asked Nate if he'd be willing to meet her brother?

Was she afraid?

That was silly; it would be fine. Nate would be as polite as she'd been with his parents. But this was different. This was *Alvaro*, her best friend, her *brother*. She'd always been closer to him than to stalwart, strait-laced, hyper-faithful Nick. It had been Alvaro's idea to steal wine from their basement and get drunk in the fields outside town. It had been Alvaro who had whispered to Marina about what making out had been like the first time (disappointing) and the second (mind-blowing) and the third (kinda gross). It was Alvaro who had helped her hash out her faith, let her give voice to the questions her parents and Nick only dismissed with a shrug, shown her it was ok to believe thoughtfully, intelligently.

What would she do if Nate and Alvaro hated each other?

How could she move forward from that?

Marina scuffed her boot against the ice, ignoring the itch of worry in the back of her mind. She was changing. She knew she was. There were piles of homework in her room she hadn't even thought about, not to mention all the volunteer work she'd been slacking on. And Nate had her rethinking a lot of things she'd previously written off as "figured out": poverty, climate change, lifestyle acceptance.

Ben.

But she was in love.

That made everything ok, didn't it?

Sighing, Marina trudged up the stairs, bracing herself for the unfolding blog-wars drama and whatever new issue Ben would be on today. For once, she didn't actually want to talk about politics. She had enough to keep her thoughts occupied, much closer to home.

Marina unlocked the door and opened her mouth to call a customary hello.

But the noise of an argument made her stop.

"It wasn't a big deal," Ben was saying loudly, almost shouting. "I just told her to back off."

Marina froze in the act of unbuttoning her coat. She'd never heard Ben's voice like this, tight, defensive and... scared.

Jordan shouted back, "You don't understand, she's posting things online. It's starting to gain steam. She claims she has a video!"

"That's impossible because I didn't *say that.*"

Marina entered the living room, boots still on, to find Ben and Jordan on opposite sides of the coffee table. Ben had his arms folded, eyes squinted, feet apart. Jordan looked close to tears. His laptop was open between them, and even from that distance, Marina could see the telltale blue bar across the top, decorated with a cheerfully animated bird.

Twitter.

"What's going on?" she asked, dropping her bag.

Ben didn't look at her. Jordan was staring at the laptop. The air between them was thick and worried and ominous.

Something was very wrong.

An instinct began to creep up on Marina like an incoming storm. She glanced from one to the other to the scrolling newsfeed.

"Ben," she said at last. "What did you do?"

Chapter 37

"He told me to kill myself!" Tiffany sobbed, stumbling inside.

"*What?*"

Nate surged to his feet and scrambled into the kitchen. But Leo, who had been busy making tea, beat him to it. He wrapped his long frame around Tiffany's body like a brace, stroking her back.

"Tiff," Nate said, hovering uselessly behind her, "What happened?"

She only buried her face in Leo's shirt.

Nate looked to his friend for answers.

"I don't know," Leo said, voice low and angry. "All I know is that the guy from her journalism class published some pro-life piece, saying that abortions are evil and women who get them should be ashamed of themselves."

Nate inhaled sharply, looking at the back of Tiffany's head. Everyone on campus—or at least everyone who read the Dyke Digest—knew how firmly Tiff believed in legal abortion, how she donated all her spare money to Planned Parenthood, how she viewed the right to choose as a necessary manifestation of female empowerment and independence.

How she'd had one herself.

But what most people didn't know, what had taken her years and a *lot* of alcohol to admit to her two roommates, was that her abortion had been because of an unwanted sexual encounter in the fraternities her first year. She'd been drunk and the guy had been pushy, and things had gone much further than a young and naïve Tiffany wanted. She hadn't had the courage to report it — a decision that she admitted would torture her for the rest of her life — and the faceless asshole had disappeared into the dark. But Tiffany had been left with more than just emotional scars. She'd had to make that decision alone and shaking. Walk through those blue doors and admit she was pregnant and didn't want to be.

For someone to call that decision evil...

Nate patted Tiff's back as Leo went on.

"Obviously, she couldn't stay silent about that. She texted me that she was going to confront him in the quad, coming out of the student center."

"I tried to tell him to take the article down," she said, voice muffled in Leo's chest. "That it was harmful and t-triggering."

Nate grimaced, wondering if she'd been so polite.

Tiff lifted her head, face blotchy. "He y-yelled that I'd assaulted *him*, said *he* was the victim here." Leo scoffed. "And then," she hiccupped, "he told me I should kill myself!"

"No!" Leo said.

"Yes," Tiff said, sniffing. "He said no one would care if I died. That I was a blight on society and my own f-f-family doesn't even w-want me." She dissolved into fresh sobs.

"What a fucking asshole," Leo growled.

But Nate found, to his surprise, that he didn't share their immediate, knee-jerk rage. He was staring down at the tips of his shoes, his face carved in a frown. Ben was Marina's friend, and Marina wouldn't have ever stooped to something so personal and pointed. And sure, Ben was worse, but they shared ideas. They spent time together. She'd defended him as a friend and a person.

Could he really be that horrible?

And more than that, how could Ben know, with such awful precision, about Tiff's family issues?

There must be some mistake…

"Nate?"

He looked up to find both Tiff and Leo watching him, tears still beading in her eyes.

Nate coughed. "Are you, er, sure?" he asked carefully. "That he actually said… that?"

Tiffany's eyes flew wide. "You don't believe me?"

"Of course I do, it's just—"

"You're taking *his* side?"

"No, never, I just—"

"That kid is a monster! He's a misogynist and a Nazi who wants to put women in their place! You've seen that girlfriend of his, who never talks. I'll bet he tells her to shut up too!"

"Tiff," Nate said, trying to calm her down. "I didn't mean that, I'm just worried that maybe you—"

"I didn't fucking *misunderstand*!" she screamed, voice ripping through three octaves. "How dare you take his side on this? What he said, the way he looked at me…" she trailed off, looking around the room with a mixture of rage and pain. She stalked into the living room, tugging at her hair.

"What an asshole," Leo said again, shaking his head and looking right at Nate, as if he knew what his roommate was thinking, as if he wasn't just referring to Ben.

Nate's mouth fell open. "I didn't… I don't…"

Leo left him to join Tiff in the living room and pulled her back into a hug.

Nate stayed where he was, numb.

Shocked at himself.

Disgusted.

Did I really just say *that?*

The guilt returned, crashing over him with all the pent-up energy Marina had kept at bay. Because god fucking dammit, Tiffany was *right*. Friend of Marina's or not, that kid had to be dealt with. Ben's ideas were corrosive, contagious. Even Nate himself had been infected by them. How could he possibly doubt someone's lived experience like this? How could he even *think* about questioning a woman's accusation? This, right here, was everything he'd tried to purge from himself, everything he'd slowly dismantled over years of careful thinking.

It had all come rushing back because of one thing.

Marina.

Nate wanted to shout in rage, to break something.

To cry.

He'd become the very thing he hated the most: a defender of the patriarchy, a supporter of the vile power structures that elevated him and kept people like Tiff and Leo down. No one should be able to go around saying things like that to women, especially a woman with Tiffany's history. And what had Nate been doing all this time, as she fought Red Nation's vile influence, as she dealt with her family shit? Giggling in the bedroom? Laughing as Marina rolled her eyes at Tiffany's beliefs?

Shame curled up his spine.

When had he stopped standing up for what was *right*?

When had he turned into such a dick?

He took an unsteady breath and looked up, meeting Leo's eyes. "I'm sorry, Tiff. I'm so sorry."

Leo frowned, not offering anything. And Nate had never felt so lonely, so small. Everything was ruined, and he wanted to fix it, wanted to prove to them that he wasn't what he had become.

But how?

Clearing his throat, he asked, "Tiff, what can I do to help?"

Tiffany pulled away from Leo to glare at him. There was a horrible skepticism in her eyes, but Nate could see the determination there too. The blazing defiance that had drawn them to her, that kept her standing when the whole universe wanted to knock her to her knees. And he decided right then and there that he'd do anything, *anything* to atone for what he'd done. What he *was*.

"What can *we* do?" Leo amended, folding his arms and flicking a cold look at Nate.

Tiff's jaw clenched, hard enough to make a muscle in her cheek tic.

"I have to go to the school," she said with a deep, hitching breath. "It's my responsibility to stop him. I'll tell the administration what he said; they can't ignore something like that." She rubbed her face, lips quivering. "But what if they don't believe me, especially after his stupid claim that I attacked him first? I can't..." The way her voice trailed off made Nate feel even worse.

A thought occurred to him, as quick and electric as a shock of static.

"What if we say we saw it," Nate said, almost to himself.

Tiff's eyes widened.

Leo looked thoughtful. "Yeah," he said, tapping his chin. "We can be your witnesses. We'll support your story."

Nate kept silent, letting his idea spin to life. *This is the right thing to do, isn't it?* he thought as Tiffany glanced between them. *This is a proper use of my privilege. Those in power don't believe women, but they'll believe me. This is what it means to be an ally, using my voice to make sure others are heard.*

Or, came that persistent whine from the back of his head, *is it just that night at the club all over again?*

But to his relief, Tiffany was nodding, slowly at first, then gaining steam. "Of course. They can't ignore it if both of you claim you saw what happened."

"That he told you to kill yourself?" Nate asked, trying to convince himself that he was just clarifying, just making sure he understood what she wanted him to say.

"Yes." She began to pace, still scrubbing away tears. "You can say you were close by, having lunch at the student center or something. You overheard him yelling at me but didn't get there in time to stop it. I'll lodge a formal complaint tomorrow, through the same office he did." She stopped, punching her fist into her open palm. "If there's any justice on this campus, they'll expel his ass so quick, his bigot head will spin."

Leo was nodding too, expression tightening into hard lines. And Nate tried to follow suit, to rally the expected outrage and excitement at taking down someone so clearly deserving of it.

But all he could think about was Marina.

Would this be it for them?

He didn't want that. The idea of ending things, of never seeing her again, was worse than anything he could think of. But he couldn't go back to just listening to her, just laughing when she said something immoral or disgusting. Maybe that had been his issue in the first place, that he hadn't fought her ideas on the spot. Hadn't rejected them in his mind. He'd let her words take root and they'd grown into strangler vines that made him doubt Tiffany, doubt *everything*. Nate had been the one to argue that some facts were dangerous. Some arguments spread like wildfire.

And now he'd been burned.

The world wouldn't change if people like him let bad things slide. He *knew* that. And Nate—rich, white, straight-appearing Nate—had to use the power society had given him to support the marginalized. He had to stand for the right things. He'd never be able to forgive himself if he didn't.

We'll figure this out, he told himself. *She'll understand. She'll accept that things need to be different between us. She'll see that I have to do this.*

Nate's fists clenched in his pocket, and he felt the prickle of the cross she'd given him digging in, almost painfully.

"Let's do it," he said aloud, but neither of his friends heard him because they were already sitting down and composing the email that would set the ball in motion.

Chapter 38

Marina was tapping her foot as she waited for Nate in the coffee shop, but it wasn't impatience with him.

It was worry for Ben.

The school had written yesterday morning, demanding that he take down his "harmful and threatening" articles. They'd already scheduled a hearing next week with the dean to discuss the "incident" in front of the student center. Predictably, Ben had refused to close his blog, instead sharing the email on Twitter, Facebook, and Reddit with his own additional commentary about how the MIT administration had ignored an outright bodily assault by the very same angry leftist. He argued that the school was trying to silence *his* freedom of expression to preserve *her* safe space. That she'd been the one to verbally attack *him* in the quad.

His posts all went viral.

Now, less than a day later, conservative media outlets were picking up on the pro-life blogger fighting the oppression of a liberal-leaning college. YouTube stars were calling it the "Battle of the Brainiacs." The local news was suddenly flooded with quick, piecemeal stories about the clash happening on campus. Ben seemed almost giddy at the attention, the validation, the *fight*. He was writing at a ferocious rate now, putting up post after post about censorship, free speech, the war on religion, the power of liberals in the social institutions of America.

But to Marina, it didn't feel like a virtuous battle.

It felt like a mess.

What will he think about it? she wondered as Nate burst through the door. *Do I want to know?*

He hurried over to her, shaking off snow and flushed from the cold. "Sorry I'm late."

"I'm getting used to it," she said, forcing a grin.

He shrugged off his coat, hanging it on the back of his chair with his helmet.

"You *biked* in this?" she asked incredulously as he slid into the seat across from her.

"Of course. I bike in all weather."

"That's terrifying."

"It's actually great when it snows. Less people on the road." Finally removing his hat and ruffling the rainbow, he looked up at her. "So, what was it you wanted to talk about?"

Marina swallowed, fiddling with her phone. Was it normal for him to cut right to the chase like that? Had there always been that indifference in his eyes, the careful detachment? Was this a terrible time to introduce him to arguably the most important person in her life?

Too late now.

"Well… my brother's in town this weekend," she said to her hands, not quite brave enough to look at him. "And I was wondering…" She swallowed and glanced up, "if you might want to meet him?"

Nate cocked his head. "Of course! You dealt with my parents, right? It's only fair."

She bit her lip.

"What?" Nate asked as the waitress came over. "Does he have

two heads or something?"

Why aren't you smiling at me like you used to?

But she couldn't ask that, because things weren't *wrong*, exactly. Just subtly different in a way she couldn't put her finger on. And how does one talk about something that can't even be verbalized?

Marina was quiet as Nate ordered his coffee—mocha latte with extra sugar and whipped cream. In her mind, Alvaro was already here, waiting for Nate to go to the bathroom before saying something about Marina's boyfriend ordering a *bitch drink*. He'd mean it as a joke, just some friendly jockeying between men.

But maybe Nate wouldn't respond with the lighthearted humor she thought he would.

"What?" he asked, grinning back at her as the waitress left. His cheeks were flushed from the cold, his eyes bright and intelligent, and Marina wanted to freeze that moment, ignore everything rolling on outside this warm little coffee shop until it all went away.

She swallowed again. "Well… you're not going to agree on much."

"You didn't agree with my parents."

Marina winced. "That's different."

"Why?"

She forced herself to meet his gaze, to ignore the whine of worry. "Your parents didn't campaign for the current president."

It was almost comical, to watch Nate's mouth fall open in shock. "Your brother did *what*?"

Marina shrugged. "I told you my family's pretty conservative."

Nate accepted his coffee, shaking his head. "There's a difference between conservative and campaigning for the literal equivalent of Voldemort. Your parents are immigrants!"

Marina straightened, relishing the familiar outrage because at least it was better than nothing. "What does that have anything to do with it?"

"He wants to build a *wall*."

"My parents love that, actually."

Nate's coffee froze on the way to his lips. "Explain."

"My parents," Marina said, "are *legal* immigrants. They did all the paperwork, pay all their taxes, and are grateful to this country for sheltering us. But the people sneaking in illegally give my family a bad name. With every caravan that marches on our border or person who makes a run for the fences, our nation's perspective on immigration shifts, and not in a good way. You have to acknowledge that there are people who live here for decades without paying their share, who flout the law and disrespect the process. They're trying to skip the line. It makes US citizens angry, which fuels more anti-immigration sentiment, and eventually makes the lives of *legal* immigrants harder. So yes, in their view a wall would be a great idea."

Nate put his coffee back down with a *clink*, frowning. "Even though it wouldn't actually change anything? Even though the cartels and human smuggling will still happen?"

"It sends a message."

"A five-billion-dollar message."

"Which is nothing compared to the rising costs of our leaky system," Marina pointed out, wrapping her hands around her cooling tea. "There's a humanitarian argument for the wall too. Think of all the people putting themselves in danger, trekking over dangerous terrain or swimming the Rio Grande to try and reach our border. Do you think they'd still do that with a wall? Or if the immigration laws were reformed to close the asylum loophole?"

"Yes, because they're *refugees*," Nate said, leaning back, away from her. "They're fleeing gang violence and risking rape and murder for the slim promise of something better. It's heartless to turn them away when they get here."

Marina bit the inside of her cheek, almost painfully. "I know it's sad, but the unfortunate truth is that we can't save everyone. The US can't afford to solve the world's problems. We have enough of our own, what with homelessness and the opioid crisis."

"These people are coming from *terrible* situations."

"True, but if we lower the standards so that anyone who's suffering can qualify, then what? Everyone in the world would want to come here."

"Then let them!" Nate said, his expression a little darker than usual.

"Are you telling me you support open borders?" Marina asked, sipping her chamomile.

Nate's mouth was a thin line, his smile long gone. "We are so privileged—"

"There's that word again," Marina said, but Nate kept going as if she hadn't spoken.

"—to live in this country. As far as I can tell, it's just raw luck that put me on this side of the border and those migrants on the other. How can I possibly claim that I have any more right to the wealth of this nation than they do? My people didn't own it and killed ninety percent of the ones who rightfully did. Most of our ancestors are immigrants!"

"*Legal* immigrants," Marina said.

Nate's eyebrows furrowed. "You can hardly call Columbus a legal immigrant."

Marina tilted her head in concession.

"Anyway," Nate continued, sipping the foam off his cocoa-dusted confection. "To me, it seems wrong to hoard our resources as if they belong to us. Because they don't. We live on stolen land, benefiting from an economy built on slave labor, and enforcing borders that were drawn by a bunch of rich white dudes acting in their own best interest."

"Even if all that's true, which is a whole different conversation," Marina said, pulling at the string on her teabag, "it doesn't change the logistical issues of the world we live in *now*. Open borders would be a catastrophe. Why bother having a nation if you don't draw the lines somewhere. What would happen if we couldn't keep out criminals or terrorists?"

"It's racist to associate terrorists with immigrants."

"And it's stupid not to think of them at all. They do exist, Nate. There are bad people out there."

"Yeah, on Wall Street."

"More importantly," she went on over him, "how can you argue for tons of free stuff *and* open borders? It would bankrupt us."

"If we restructure the tax system, we could pay for it."

Marina shook her head. "Not a chance."

"There's a lot of money tied up in the top one percent."

"Yeah, and it's *their* money."

"No individual needs a billion dollars."

"It doesn't matter, they earned it. Besides, how will you stop the rich from leaving the country and taking their money with them?"

"We'll create a penalty for trying to leave."

"That doesn't sound authoritarian at all," Marina said sarcastically.

"Everyone needs to pay their share."

"And the billionaires already do. They pay tons of money."

"Not if they can help it."

"But higher tax rates will only encourage more people to avoid the IRS. Besides, Amazon and Google have made this country incredibly rich. Why would you chase them away?"

"They've made *some people* in this country incredibly rich."

"Over half of US citizens have smartphones."

Nate glowered. "Having an iPhone doesn't make someone rich."

"Maybe not, but it does make their life easier and more luxurious."

"*Eating* is luxurious. *Rent* is luxurious."

"That's a strawman argument," Marina said, heart pounding for all the wrong reasons. *Why did this, for the first time, feel like a real fight?* "Jeff Bezos isn't stopping anyone from paying their rent."

"He's hoarding a huge amount of capital."

Marina folded her arms. "Just because it's a big pile doesn't mean anyone else is entitled to it."

"Think about how much good it could do."

"Yeah. If Bezos chooses to do good with it. It's *his*."

"Not in my ideal world."

She pursed her lips. "Your ideal world is terrifying."

Nate straightened, mirroring her posture, and for a moment they glared at each other over the battle line of the table. Neither blinked. Neither moved. And Marina found herself wishing they could go back, return to his bedroom and his artwork and the nights when these same conversations had seemed romantic and not infuriating.

Finally, Nate smiled. It almost looked sincere. "Your brother's going to love me, isn't he?"

"You'll be BFFs by the end of the weekend," she said, loosening her arms.

"Maybe I'll convince him to dye his hair."

She snorted. "God help you."

"Won you over, didn't I?"

Marina found herself blinking back tears.

But did I win you?

She lifted the huge, round mug to hide her expression.

"So," she said when she'd composed herself enough to continue. "What night should I tell him—"

Suddenly, the table under Marina's elbows was buzzing, vibrating violently from a steady stream of texts. She flipped her phone over to see it cluttered with new messages, more arriving even as she watched. It was their group thread, usually used to coordinate meals and bible studies.

She skimmed the most recent message from Ben.

<I swear to GOD she's lying, Jordan>

Marina looked up to see Nate also checking his phone, his smile dimming.

"What is it?" she asked.

"Nothing," he said, tucking it away.

It took Marina a moment to clear her throat. "I thought we were supposed to talk about things."

Nate didn't grin, didn't make some coy joke about political differences like he would have a week ago. He looked somber, worried, and worst of all, evasive.

"What's going on?" Marina said, unlocking her phone to read three more messages from Jordan as they came in.

<It's up to three million views>

<I think you should come over>

<Someone just doxed your address>

"I don't think…" Nate started, but he didn't seem to know where to go from there. He coughed, glancing around the quiet coffee shop, as if the end of his sentence could be found in the mumbling patrons or the noisy traffic outside.

Marina was scrolling through the messages, looking for where it had started.

There was a link to a video posted on Twitter.

She glanced up at Nate, who still wasn't looking at her.

Then pressed play.

It was Nate's friend, the blonde girl who'd punched Ben. She was sobbing, face a mess of smeared mascara and blotchy flush. Marina couldn't hear what she was saying with her phone volume turned down, but she could read the title of the post.

HE TOLD ME TO KILL MYSELF.

"What the...?"

Marina looked up to find Nate staring at her, eyes unreadable, mouth tight.

"Did you know about this?" Marina asked, showing him the screen. The fact that he didn't even glance at it answered her question. "That can't be right. Ben would never..."

"Look, I don't want it to get between us," Nate said, leaning back. "But she's my friend."

"And he's mine."

"Well maybe you need some better ones."

"Nate," Marina said, unable to keep the shock and hurt out of her voice.

His posture didn't change. "I'm sorry, but how do you know he wouldn't say something like that? He doesn't strike me as the kind of person to hide his opinions."

"He's not. But he doesn't believe *anyone* should kill themselves." Marina frowned at her phone, struggling to make sense of it. "He's *Catholic*."

"Catholics can still hurt people," Nate said, his voice colder than Marina had ever heard it.

Things were shifting nauseatingly fast, making her head spin. But maybe everything had shifted already, without her noticing. Was this what had come between them and made him change his mind

267

about her, without ever giving her a chance to explain?

Nate went on, "Your church does stuff like this all the time. Just look at the pedophile cases lately."

Her eyes sliced up. "Are you comparing Ben to a *pedophile*?"

"I'm just saying maybe you're giving him too much credit."

"And maybe you're jumping to conclusions. What if your friend misheard him?"

Or lied.

"I believe women." Nate said, folding his arms. "Always."

Marina was flooded with the sudden impression of the restaurant closing in on her, the walls tightening, the heat becoming oppressively thick. She shoved to her feet, grabbing her coat.

"I gotta go," she said. "I... I need to make sure they're ok."

When she glanced across the table, she wanted desperately to believe that Nate looked as sad and lost as she felt. But that couldn't be right; she was just projecting. After all *he* was used to this. He'd done all this — dating, sex, *love* — more times than she wanted to think about. Of course he could disengage when he felt it coming to its inevitable, horrible conclusion. Of course it didn't hurt him the way it hurt her.

He'd changed her life so much it was hardly recognizable anymore.

But why should that mean she'd done the same for him?

She blinked frantically, stuffing her arms into the sleeves of her pea coat as fast as she could. She had to get out of there. She had to *think*.

Nate touched her arm, making her stop.

"I'm still down to meet your brother," he said softly. "If you want."

Marina didn't know how to respond to that, so she just nodded. Was there something she could offer, something to leave like a tip on the table that would *fix this*?

Nothing came to mind.

So, pulling on her hat and praying silently, desperately, that this wasn't what she thought it was, Marina hurried out into the cold to help her friends.

Chapter 39

Nate couldn't deny that things had become awkward. Maybe worse than that. Even as he biked to India Pavilion to meet Marina and her brother, squinting against the bitter March wind, half of him wondered if it might be better to turn around. Claim illness or injury. Deal with the fallout later. He and Marina had been texting all week, but despite the jokes and banter, he knew there was a new wall between them. An elephant in every conversation that neither of them acknowledged.

The messy and escalating stalemate between their friends.

Both Tiffany's video and that stupid Red Nation blog had gone supernova in the last few days, and the effects were becoming harder and harder to ignore. There were now packs of news crews and activists roving campus, gathering quotes like projectiles to be launched at the other side. Twice, Tiffany had been stopped outside their Ethics class to give tearful testimonies of the experience that led her to post such an emotional plea online. Nate was sure Marina's life was similarly impacted, as the school weighed her friend's future in the balance.

And yet they hadn't talked about it.

To be fair, they hadn't really talked about anything. At least not anything of substance. Was it his fault? He was certainly keeping her at arm's length now, trying to put up walls around his mind.

Around his heart. And if Nate was being honest with himself, he hated it with all his being. He missed the giddy, wonderful freedom of diving into a taboo conversation and feeling like it would be ok, knowing she wouldn't judge him or dismiss him or call him names. But that euphoric carelessness had stemmed from the belief that the intellectual space between her mind and his had been safe. Romantic even. Just a bit of harmless fun.

He'd been wrong.

All those nights debating the validity of horrendous ideas had poisoned Nate, made him question what shouldn't be questioned. What he'd laughingly called open dialogue was really just normalizing hate and violence. They couldn't go back to that.

So where did it leave them?

The question made him feel as fragile as the ice beneath his wheels.

Nate pulled up in front of the restaurant and bent over to lock his bike. He paused in front of the door, glared up at the elegant script of the restaurant's name over the front window.

Shaking his head, he shoved the clutter in his brain aside.

He'd deal with it later.

Plunging into the aromatic heat, Nate yanked off his hat and looked up to find Marina standing next to a man, shorter and younger than himself. Dark eyebrows pulled together and even darker eyes darted up to the top of Nate's head.

Here we go.

"Nate," Marina said, and he could see the nervousness in her smile. "This is Alvaro."

"Nice to meet you," Nate said, accepting Marina's brother's hand and trying not to wince at the grip.

"So you're the mystery boyfriend," Alvaro said as they were seated in a booth by the window.

Nate swallowed. "I guess."

"Can't say I ever expected Marina to bring home a city boy."

"Not a fan of cities?" Nate said, snapping his napkin out to put on his lap.

Alvaro shrugged. "It's fun for a visit, but I'd want more space for my trucks." He chuckled, looking to his sister. "Ma's been on my case though. She keeps trying to talk me into being a *brilliant computer engineer like my daughter*." He put on a high, falsetto voice to imitate his mother.

Marina rolled her eyes. "*Aye*, she knows that's not my major."

"She's just proud to have a genius in the family." Alvaro winked at Nate. "Marina's the only one of us to go to college."

"So far," Marina said pointedly.

"And be in debt forever?" Alvaro snorted. "No thanks, not for me. Did you hear Nick just bought his third house?"

"What does Nick do?" Nate asked with what he hoped was a warm smile.

"Plumber." Alvaro shook his head. "The jerk likes to rub it in all our faces. Keeps inviting me to manage his *rental property* or help his *business*."

"Well, it is a job," Marina said slyly, reading the specials.

"A shit job," Alvaro said. "Sometimes literally."

Nate forced a laugh. "So are you tempted to become a plumber?"

Alvaro's gaze slanted up to him, a little less friendly. "I'm more into mechanical stuff."

"Like cars?"

"Diesel engines. I hear you can make a pretty penny in the oil fields."

"Rough work," Nate said.

"I'm used to that," Alvaro said, dropping a quick glance to

273

Nate's clean, uncalloused hands.

A family was seated next to them and began to wrestle their noisy, kicking toddler into a high seat. Nate found himself clenching his jaw against the high-pitch shrieks, tapping his thumb on his knee under the table in an attempt to calm down.

"Do you worry that people might move away from oil soon?" he asked, trying his best to sound polite. "In favor of greener energy sources."

"No," Alvaro said as Marina hid behind her menu. "World ain't changing that fast."

"I mean, it better. For all our sakes."

Alvaro rolled his eyes. "They've been calling doomsday on the climate for years. Hasn't happened yet."

"That doesn't mean it won't."

"Far as I can tell, the pointy-headed scientists just want to cause a stir. That's what happens when they run out of *real* problems to solve."

Nate's openmouthed shock was interrupted by the smiling, pretty waitress who swung in to take their order.

"Mari, I can't pronounce half of these," Alvaro complained, laughing as he pointed his meal out to the Indian woman. "Is this one spicy? I don't like spicy."

Nate tried to catch Marina's eye, but she was watching her brother, her whole body as tense as a bowstring.

"Oh unclench," Alvaro said with a grin after their server had bustled off. He bumped his elbow into Marina's side. "Stop acting like I'm a bomb about to go off in the restaurant. I'm country, not dumb." He took the napkin and dabbed at his face in a facsimile of elegance.

"Sorry," Marina said, smiling at Nate.

Nate couldn't quite return it.

"So, are you a genius too?" Alvaro asked, seemingly oblivious to the mounting tension at the table.

Nate curled his mouth up. "Hardly. I'm studying Urban Planning and Development."

He chose not to mention his second major. Right now, that felt like flirting with calamity.

Alvaro cocked his head. "You mean like buildings?"

"Not the actual buildings," Nate said. "That's architecture. I'm studying the *structure* of the city. Where low-income housing should go, the equity of the layout, potential solutions to income distribution and environmental issues. That kind of thing."

"Huh. Didn't think people studied that."

"People study all kinds of things," Nate said.

Alvaro nodded sagely. "Yeah, I heard about this new thing in college. Gay studies?"

"Queer theory," Nate corrected, not quite able to keep the growl out of his voice. "They're trying to make it a major here at MIT."

"Why? What's the point?"

Marina flinched. Nate leaned forward, elbows on the table. "There are lots of important things to study in the LGBTQA community."

Alvaro smirked. "Might as well just recite the whole alphabet at this point, eh?"

"We strive to be inclusive."

"*We?*"

"Yes."

Alvaro pursed his lips. "Interesting."

"How are Mami and Papi?" Marina interrupted, not looking up from her drink.

Alvaro kept his eyes on Nate for a heartbeat longer than was comfortable before turning to his sister. "They're fine. Dad just got a new semiautomatic he's all excited about."

"You mean a gun?" Nate clarified, putting down his cocktail with a *clink*.

Marina seemed on the verge of tears, but Nate didn't look at her. He kept his gaze on Alvaro, who turned toward him with the glint of danger in his expression.

"Yeah," he said, drawing out the end of the word. "And?"

Nate straightened. "You do realize that there are protests going on all over the country, right? After the Parkland shooting where seventeen people were killed?"

Marina's eyes went wide, Alvaro's narrowed, and Nate knew he'd pushed too far but he couldn't help it. Everything was broken and messy and ruined *already*. What was the point of hiding anymore when he and Marina were up in flames? When they *should* be up in flames? He *should* have done this ages ago, should have pushed back on the encroaching line of her opinions before they got anywhere *near* as close as they had. He was standing for something, fighting for a better world.

So why the fuck did it feel so wrong?

"Are you saying my dad's gonna kill seventeen people?" Alvaro answered in a laconic, almost bored voice.

"I'm saying that it's irresponsible for us to allow weapons like that to be available to people who will."

"I'd rather have the ability to defend myself."

"Do you really need a gun to do that?"

"If the criminals have one, then yes."

"Alvaro, maybe he has a point," Marina said, but Nate was talking over her, his eyes fixed on Alvaro's.

"Have you heard of the protest? The March for our Lives? One of my roommates is helping organize the one in Cambridge."

"You mean how the media is trying to guilt-trip everyone using a bunch of crying kids? Bit hypocritical coming from the party that kills babies, don't you think?"

"They lost their *friends*," Nate said, deliberately ignoring the last part.

"And I'm very sorry for them. But they aren't politicians."

"Why does it matter who they are?"

"They're kids. They don't know anything."

"They know about the shooter who put all their lives in danger."

Alvaro shrugged. "There are bad people in the world. And I don't trust the government to protect me from all of them."

Nate planted his hands on the table. "Children should not be shot in school."

"I agree. And maybe that day would have ended differently if the teachers had been armed."

Marina opened her mouth, but Nate was already shoving to his feet. He couldn't sit still, couldn't stay in this seat without making things worse. Tiffany's voice was in his head to *correct this backwards motherfucker*. But what would that do to Marina? How much would that hurt her?

Why did he still care?

"Sorry," he said to a horrorstruck Marina. "I think I should go."

"Maybe you should," Alvaro said, ignoring the wounded look his sister threw at him. But Nate didn't stick around to hear Marina's response because he was already swinging his coat around his shoulders, plunging back outside to his bike that he knew was in full view of their table. His shoulders hunched as he clicked open the U-lock, trying to pretend they weren't watching him, and it was like his body was being pulled in by some kind of dreadful gravity, a hideous black hole of regret and confusion that shouldn't exist, shouldn't be so fucking overwhelming. But it was. Frantically, he jammed his helmet on, leapt onto the saddle, and pedaled away.

What had he done?

Did he really have to push Alvaro so far? Was it really important to get into a fight about something none of them had any control over? But what else was there? Nate believed in justice, believed in *change*, and how was anything going to change if people didn't speak out against the terrible, awful, hateful ideas out there? Alvaro was *wrong*, but he was Marina's brother, Marina who was wrong too, but more eloquent about it. More confusing. She was able to defend her opinions with reason and humor and warmth, and maybe that's why they were so sticky. Why they'd dug under his skin like so many splinters and lodged there, weakening him, making him *doubt*.

He wanted to apologize so badly it hurt.

But he couldn't.

Now what?

Nate had known doomed relationships. Hell, he'd been in enough of them to be the crowned king of unrequited, irresponsible, stupid love. But this was different. There was no thrill in understanding this was bound to fall apart—was perhaps already in tatters. There was only pain, only the confusing, tugging, roiling panic that something beautiful was going to end and there was nothing either of them could do about it.

Nate blinked away frozen tears and pedaled as fast as he could, as if he could outrun himself.

Chapter 40

Somehow, Marina made it through the rest of dinner without crying. She'd even held it together, barely, when Alvaro texted her his own kind of apology after she dropped him off at his Airbnb.

I'm sorry I pissed off your friend. I hope his snowflake feelings aren't too hurt.

But now, in the silence of her bedroom, Marina couldn't help but feel that Nate hadn't been a snowflake. Quite the opposite. He'd stood up for something he believed in, and perhaps he could have been more polite about it, but really had Marina been any better at the brunch with his parents? Had she *let things go* then?

And maybe this was supposed to happen. God's will and all that. Because, no matter how much she wanted to deny it, Nate was a bad influence on her life. He'd made her shirk her homework, her charity, her friendships. He'd seeded ideas in her head about rebellion and irresponsible lifestyles and casual sex.

He'd made her lie to her *priest*.

Marina slumped in her desk chair, computer open in front of her. But her email homepage blurred. The black script of unread messages seemed like its own kind of onslaught, bold and aggressive. She was sunk too deep in her own bewilderment to concentrate, trying to pinpoint the exact moment things had gone wrong, when it had tipped them into *this*.

"I love him."

She said the words to herself slowly, softly, weighing them. And oh, how she wished they weren't true. She wanted so badly to pretend that she never wanted to see Nate's stupid rainbow hair ever again, especially after tonight.

But she couldn't.

Thou shalt not lie, she thought wryly to herself.

At least, not anymore.

She stared blankly at her laptop.

What now?

The front door opened with a sad, creaking sound, accompanied by footsteps. Longing for a distraction from her own dark thoughts, Marina shoved to her feet, feeling ninety years old as she opened her door and stepped out to greet Ben and Jordan.

Right away, she could tell from their expressions that this wasn't going to be the escape she was hoping for.

"What happened?" Marina asked as Ben plopped himself bonelessly on the couch.

Jordan looked up. She'd been crying.

"The dean called him to a hearing at school this week," Jordan said in a quiet voice, breath hitching slightly. "They're considering expulsion."

"*What?*" Marina breathed, leaning against her doorframe.

Ben didn't respond, just glared at his knees. So Jordan continued.

"They have a list of witnesses to the alleged 'assault,'" Jordan said, making air quotes.

"I didn't say it," Ben muttered, shaking his head. "All I said was for her to get away from me. She was yelling at me, so I yelled back. But I didn't tell her to commit suicide." He looked up. "You know I'd never..."

Marina opened her mouth to comfort, to protest on his behalf, but when Jordan turned back to her, the words died in her throat. Because her best friend's eyes were filled with a soft, sad accusation.

"What?" Marina asked.

"One of the witnesses," Jordan said, not blinking, "is Nathan Campbell."

Marina collapsed into the nearest armchair.

"That's not possible," she whispered, but even as she said the words, she knew that it was.

Nate, who stood for *justice* and thought religion was a great big fantasy.

Nate, who casually called her friends white supremacists and racists.

Nate, who *believed all women*.

Why was she even surprised?

"I..." Marina said, fumbling for words.

"Do you know him?" Ben asked numbly, looking up.

Marina's heart broke for Ben. For Jordan. For all of them. But especially for her own foolish, naïve, *stupid* self. She'd been so blinded by the very things she'd sworn never to get caught up in that she'd missed the reality under her very nose. *These* were her friends. *These* were the people she should have been helping, defending, all along.

Because despite being sad, angry, disappointed, scared, Jordan had kept her secret. Jordan had been honest with her.

But Nate hadn't.

Over and over, he'd been less than forthright. He'd left out key details, hidden important things.

Like this.

Marina bit her lip hard enough to chase away the tears. She looked at Jordan, trying to convey with her eyes what she couldn't say aloud without crying.

I'll do better. I swear I will.

Ben shook his head, as if disagreeing with himself. He looked as lost and hopeless as Marina had ever seen him.

"I'm screwed. She's manipulating the school to side with her, and they will. Of course they will. Everyone always does…"

"No," Marina said, doing her best to sound strong and convincing. She shoved to her feet, desperate to feel empowered again. "*No.* They won't expel you, not for this. They'll hear your side of the story, Ben. They have to. The whole country is watching, and more people every day are talking about this story. We'll find a way to get people on your side. We'll fix this."

Ben didn't respond. He remained slumped in the couch, looking at his hands as if they were too small and frail to stand against a world that hated everything he was.

Chapter 41

I'm here to support oppressed minorities and marginalized people everywhere. I'm here to fight the patriarchy.

I'm here for Tiff.

But despite Nate's pumping fist and loud, affirming voice, everything felt hollow, like someone had carved out the marrow of the world. Tiffany shouted from her egg-crate podium in front of the MIT dome and the crowd roiled around him, but all of it was muted. Bleached. He tried not to wonder if it was because of Marina and the strange, radio silence that had fallen over their message thread, or if it was because she'd cracked some core, foundational part of him so badly that he was having trouble finding his footing again.

Either way, he didn't like it.

"This school needs to deal with its long history of sexism and racism!" Tiffany called, the Sunday morning sun making her hair look like gold.

"Yes!" the crowd called back.

"MIT has always favored men, believed men, put men first! It's time for the white-centric, male-centric, heteronormative model of engineering to *change*!"

"Preach it!" Leo thundered beside Nate.

"This is about more than just me, more than just the rights of women to control their own lives and bodies. This is about *our future!*"

Nate lifted the sign he'd made that day in their apartment, scrawling on poster board with permanent marker as Tiffany rallied all the people she could find. Tiff's whole community was there, along with a good chunk of students Nate had never seen before. Stragglers had trickled in too, drawn by the noise or the Twitter hashtag or maybe just dragged here by their friends.

And, of course, the media.

Little by little, the crowd on Mass Ave had expanded until the bright square in front of the dome was packed, blocking the crosswalk, everyone nodding along with the petite blonde shouting into a megaphone. And Nate forced himself to nod along with them, arrange his features into the proper expressions even as the frustration built in his chest. His thoughts were suffocating, heavy, almost too much to bear.

Unfortunately, they weren't the right kind.

He *should* have been drinking in the heady fumes of revolution, raging at the unfairness, filled with the urge to set things *right*. He *should* be posting supportive, hot-take comments on his social media, condemning Ben and everyone associated with him, pointing out the wrong-think of the other side.

But he wasn't.

Instead, he felt arrogant, entitled, gross. He'd *lied*, and, even if it was for a cause, the choice was eating at him. He kept wondering if maybe he didn't have all the answers, if maybe none of them did. How could he be sure he'd done the right thing? But every time his mind wandered down that road of *what if this is all a mistake*, he shook himself, disgusted by his own disgust. This, his doubt, was *exactly* what Tiffany was trying to purge from campus. No wonder she fought so hard. Ben couldn't be allowed to spread this *thing* that had made Nate question everything he was, everything he fought for.

Right?

A rumble was rising from the gathered protestors, echoing against the granite facade of the building. The police cars around them waited silently, lights flashing, standing guard. Were they keeping the protestors in or keeping the world out? Or was that the same thing? What if the walls were created by both sides, supported by both parties? Because if they weren't, then maybe they'd come tumbling down.

Would that be such a bad thing?

Nate focused on the words, on the chant Tiffany was leading.

"Hey hey, ho ho, this Nazi asshole's got to go. Hey hey, ho ho, this Nazi asshole's got to go."

Nate swayed. Everything was gaining steam, rising to a frenzy, and he felt like driftwood in the ocean, being ripped away from shore.

"Dude, you ok?"

Nate blinked up to find Leo staring at him, head cocked, eyebrows pulled together.

He swallowed. Blinked again. "Don't you think..." Nate said in a low voice, ducking to avoid one of Leo's nonbinary friends who was enthusiastically waving their hands in the air, "that maybe there's a more... productive way to do this?"

Leo's frown deepened.

"No," he said. "We've done the peaceful sit-ins and boycotts before. The civil rights movement tried to do things quietly and slowly, and it didn't work. We still live in a racist, sexist, homophobic country that's getting worse by the day."

"But what if there was a better way to respond? You know, more... friendly?"

"We're fighting their bigotry, Nate, not having *tea*," Leo said, the lines of worry on his forehead deepening. "We're trying to turn this ship toward a better future and stop everything from dissolving into an even worse hellscape than the one we currently have." Leo bent closer. "You sure you're ok?"

"I'm..."

But Nate's voice trailed off as the chanting morphed into jeers and catcalls, sharp voices diving like gulls.

"Just got out of your KKK meeting?" Tiffany shouted into the megaphone to general agreement. "Heading to your Proud Boys assembly?"

Leo straightened, stretching his neck to see over the bobbing heads.

"What? What is it?" Nate said, jumping up and down to try and see.

"Nothing," Leo said, his tone making it perfectly clear that it was not *nothing*.

"Fuck this," Nate grumbled, elbowing through the crowd.

"Wait!" Leo called after him, but Nate was already pinching himself through the narrow opening between bodies, sliding sideways toward the crosswalk button. After a few harrowing seconds of claustrophobic breathlessness, he burst into the open, pinwheeling his arms to stay upright.

And then he saw them.

Marina, Jordan, and Ben, fighting through a dense knot of reporters waiting outside the MIT Chapel. They looked frazzled and frantic, eyes wide as influencers and journalists shoved microphones in their faces, spun cameras toward them. The protestors swarmed.

Nate couldn't help but think of hyenas.

"Marina..." Nate breathed, but she didn't see him. Her eyes were tracking over the angry faces, shouting voices, all of it so brutally directed at her and her friends.

"Go back to your Aryan conclave!" Tiffany yelled even as

Nate tried to gather his wits enough to do… what? Call to her? Stop the chanting? Get her out of there? She looked so small and frightened and confused.

A strange instinct surged through him, almost a *compulsion* to protect her. It was, no doubt, the vapors of toxic masculinity clouding his head; the lingering effects of Marina's charm making him doubt what was, by all accounts, a fair and just reckoning.

At that moment, he didn't give a single shit.

Nate couldn't stand it anymore.

"Marina," he said again, louder this time, elbowing forward. "MARINA!"

Chapter 42

"Jordan!" Marina cried out, trying to find her friend.

But the snowy lawn in front of the Chapel was a riot of news crews and protestors and *rage*. Jordan had ducked into the crowd to catch Ben before he could say anything he'd regret, and bodies had pushed in to fill the space she left, shoving phones and cameras closer. Now they were both gone, swallowed by the chaos, and Marina found herself drifting in a sea of anonymous, unfriendly faces.

Alone.

She took a deep breath, trying to hold back the terror, the choking claustrophobia.

It had been a week since she'd last seen Nate. They hadn't spoken since the dinner with Alvaro, and Marina guessed that meant they'd broken up, if she could even call it that. Had they been dating? Sure, they'd met family members and talked about the future, but what did that mean? What were labels to a couple as strange as them? And worse, Marina couldn't talk to anyone about it because Jordan was the only on campus who knew and, unfortunately for all of them, Jordan had bigger things to worry about than Marina's confused love life.

Ben's voice rose above the din.

"I am a man of God," he said loudly, aggressively. "I would

never tell anyone to harm themselves, even someone who attacked me first."

"Then what exactly did you say to Tiffany Freeman?"

Marina burst through a tight knot of young, hungry-looking reporters to find Ben cornered against the brick wall, face flushed, eyes flashing. Jordan was hunched beside him, looking distinctly like a spooked deer.

Gritting her teeth, Marina stepped in front of her friends, blinking in the bright assault of a camera flash.

"Show's over," she said, waving one hand. "Go back to your internet holes."

"Are you involved in the case?" cut in a woman with bright eyes and an angular, hawkish face.

"It isn't a *case*," Marina said, herding Jordan and Ben out of the semicircle.

"The school is investigating—"

"Privately," Marina interrupted as they reached the sidewalk.

"How do you feel about becoming a turning point in conservative politics?"

"Like you want this to be a turning point in conservative politics."

"Are you aware of the harm your friend's comments have caused? The trauma his articles have created in the feminist and queer communities?"

Marina shoved Jordan gently toward the student center before swinging around to face the young woman. "Harm? Trauma? Please, it was an *alleged* comment—"

"Witnessed by her friends."

"Who could have misheard."

"Are you doubting the accuracy of their statements as well as that of Ms. Freeman?"

Marina took another breath, keenly aware of the phones, the cameras, the churning virtual waters ready to surge forward and crush her. Behind the reporter, someone waved a sign that read: *All men are liars. Believe women first.*

"Look," she said in what she prayed was a reasonable tone. "Whatever happened, it was a personal conflict between two people. The school will sort it out, hopefully without bias. Whoever feels *harmed* by this needs to base their life worth on more than a misunderstanding between people they don't know on a college campus they wouldn't care about any other day."

"So you deny that he did anything wrong?"

Marina found her lips pursing, her eyes prickling with frustrated tears. She believed that Ben hadn't said what Tiffany accused him of. She understood the depth of his faith, the stubbornness of his commitment to it, and therefore knew with absolute certainty that Ben would never, ever tell someone to commit a mortal sin. But could she claim that he hadn't done *anything*? That his blog hadn't been purposefully incendiary? That he'd left no room for dialogue or friendly debate? That, cornered and frustrated and bristling for a fight, Ben probably *had* said something dismissive, mean-spirited, or even downright cruel?

And maybe there should be repercussions for Ben's actions, a reprimand that didn't ruin the rest of his life. Maybe speech could be free and open, but people like her also had a personal responsibility to keep their friends in check. Maybe Marina herself was at fault just as much as Ben or Tiffany for letting this spiral so far out of anyone's control.

Or was that just Nate's voice in her head, making life more complicated than it needed to be?

"I think you should go find some real news," Marina said at last.

The volume rose again, swooping, slicing, demanding. She tried to elbow through to the student center, but people were everywhere, blocking her in. She wanted to scream.

She wanted to cry.

"Marina!"

A hand grabbed her arm. She swung around, fists clenched. But it wasn't a journalist or protestor.

It was Nate.

"Come on!" he shouted, tugging her forward, not into the student center but toward the overhang of the gym. The voices followed, feet pounding after them. And a part of her just wanted to give up, let them *have* her if that's what they wanted. But Nate was determined, and Marina allowed him to lead the way, dragging her along like they were a pair of runaways.

They plunged into the fitness center, sprinted by the hockey rink.

"In here," he panted, pulling her through a side door she'd never noticed before.

They surged inside, shoved it shut behind them, and collapsed against it, panting over the thundering of feet. The noise level rose and then fell away, leaving them in silence.

"Thanks," Marina gasped, her chest heaving.

"It looked like you needed some help," he said and then winced.

Marina straightened her coat with what she hoped was a prim and lofty sniff. "I had everything under control."

Nate ducked his head. "I know."

She reeled, not knowing what to say. Just a week ago, he would have made some joke about white supremacists and the media not getting along. And she would have pointed out that his definition of white supremacist was an awfully large umbrella, not to mention an unkind generalization about the people in her life. They would have dissected the various reasons students were blocking the crosswalk on a Sunday morning and whether the protestors had the right to disrupt people's lives. The conversation would have lasted hours, filled with illegal drinks and outraged smiles and maybe a few stolen kisses.

But here, now, neither of them spoke.

"I…" Marina said, and then trailed off. She coughed. "I should make sure Ben and Jordan are ok."

"Yeah, sorry," he said, with no indication what he was apologizing for. "I should be… getting back."

To protest my existence? To shout insults at my friends?

Marina swallowed the words. What was the point? Things were wrecked enough between them without her making it worse. But despite all her fury, all her fear, she couldn't ignore the awareness of how close he was, the lingering heat his fingers had left around her wrist, how his face was *right there*. And what if the vast, howling, overwhelming hole in her chest could be solved as easily as leaning in and pressing her mouth to his…

She adjusted her backpack.

"See you later then?" she said, cringing at the inadequacy of those words. She turned to go.

"Hey," he called, stopping her. "I, um, read your article. In the National Geographic."

She looked over one shoulder to find him watching her, eyes molten with something she couldn't name and didn't want to.

"It was really good," he went on. "I know you're scared to go to California, but you should think about it." He shrugged, shoving his hands into his pockets. "You'd be a great journalist."

A deep, horrible sadness welled in Marina, almost suffocating in its intensity. She wanted to be angry with him for invading her privacy and having the nerve to try and advise her about a future that he'd chosen to extract himself from. But wasn't this just a reminder of their differences, God showing her how hopeless they'd always been? Nate had made the irrational tempting, the reckless justifiable.

He'd made her world feel like a dream.

But it wasn't.

Nate's mouth twitched when she didn't answer. "Be careful out there, ok?"

His gentle sincerity almost made her fall apart right there.

"You too," she said, hoping he couldn't hear the break in her voice.

Using her hip to open the door, she kept her eyes straight ahead, her feet moving mechanically forward. She would *not* mourn Nate, would *not* think about how gray and lifeless she felt without him, would *not* let him make her doubt her plans and her life and her *everything. He'd* been the one to draw the battle lines. *He* was the one who hadn't called. And besides, she was better off without him. No more sneaking into bars. No more procrastinating assignments. No more wild, stupid fantasies that made no sense. She'd get over it, eventually, like everyone did. Ben wouldn't be expelled, and the world would move on, and everything would be *fine.*

The tears freezing on her cheeks didn't mean a damn thing.

Chapter 43

"What. The. *Fuck*."

Nate slung his bag onto the couch with a little more force than he'd intended, stalking into the kitchen, ignoring Tiff. She followed him, Leo trailing behind.

"For fuck's *sake*," she exploded. "Nate, what is going *on* with you?"

He hunched his shoulders as he filled the kettle. "Nothing, would you just leave it alone?"

"You *helped* her? You went forward and *grabbed her hand*?" From the corner of his eye, Nate saw Tiffany turn to Leo. "Am I missing something?"

Leo didn't answer, just watched with his arms folded, his lips pursed.

Nate gritted his teeth as he turned to face them, leaning against the counter in what he hoped was a casual, laid-back posture. "Tiff, they were cornered. It looked like a scary situation, and I didn't want anyone to get hurt."

Tiffany's mouth fell open in disbelief. She looked at Nate as if she didn't recognize him anymore. "You didn't want anyone to get *hurt*? What about when that jerk-off was writing all those articles? What about when he was spreading his violence? What about that, Nate? Where were you for *that*?"

Nate's pulse was roaring in his ears. "This was more than just words. It looked like real trouble."

"More than just *words*?" she repeated. "Listen to yourself, Nate. Words *matter*. Ideas *matter*. Those people are more dangerous than anyone who was out with us today."

"That's not true," Nate said before he could stop himself.

Tiff recoiled. "Excuse me?"

He took a breath, trying unsuccessfully to calm himself down. "A mob is a mob, Tiff. Just because they agree with you doesn't mean they're not dangerous."

"I can't believe I'm hearing this."

"Listen, you know I support you. But don't you think you're taking this a bit far?"

"I'm doing what has to be done!"

"No," Nate said, shoving off the counter. "You're doing what you *want*. You were the one who started calling him names on his blog. You escalated *on purpose*. You *hit him*. You're not a fucking saint, Tiffany, so stop pretending to be one."

For a long moment, no one spoke. Mouth open, eyes wide, she gaped at Nate with an expression of utter, blindsided shock.

But Leo didn't look the least bit surprised.

"This is about that girl, isn't it?" he said at last.

Tiffany's head whipped to the side. "What girl?"

"The one he was seeing." Leo's frown darkened. "The Catholic one he swooped in to rescue."

Tiff swiveled back to Nate.

"Explain please," she said, voice shaking.

"I don't have to justify my dating life to you two," Nate snapped, feeling ganged up on and surrounded. *Was this how Marina felt today? Is this how Ben feels all the time?*

"But you do have to justify what you're saying now," Leo

said. "She changed you, man. Got under your skin."

"No she didn't."

"Then what's—"

He couldn't take it anymore.

"Why is it so crazy that I wouldn't agree with every single goddamned thing you say and do and feel?" Nate said, throwing his arms out. "Why is that so hard to understand? Maybe I think he was wrong *and* that you didn't deal with it very well. Maybe I can believe you and also wonder if it's our right to judge. And maybe, just maybe, it's possible to think differently and not be some literal incarnation of evil!"

The kettle clicked behind him, indicating that the water had boiled. His friends watched him as if he was a rabid animal. Tiff was shaking her head.

"I can't believe it," she said, scowling. "I thought you were better than this."

"Well sorry I couldn't live up to your insanely high standards," Nate spat, pouring himself tea. "Maybe someday you'll find one fucking person who can. But for now, I have some homework to do."

Grabbing his mug and stalking into his bedroom, Nate kicked the door shut behind him. The paintings clattered, reminding him of Marina, which made his mood, if possible, even worse. He grabbed his laptop and hurled it on the bed, spilling some tea on the floor. Anger pulsed through him, alive, raw, not quite drowning out the fear.

What had he done?

What was he *doing*?

A part of him, the part that he'd fed and nurtured all these years, wanted to go back out there and beg forgiveness. He could explain that it was Marina's fault. That she *had* changed him in ways that he hadn't quite sought out and destroyed yet. But the very idea of apologizing sent another wave of anger crashing over him. They were responsible too. Let them suffer; let them deal with their own part in this whole goddamn catastrophe. They deserved to be called out, *everyone* deserved to be called out and *should be*.

Nate's gaze snagged on the gold cross, thrown haphazardly on his desk.

Well, he thought viciously. *What would* you *do?*

It didn't have an answer.

Two slams told him Tiffany and Leo had gone into their own rooms, cutting off his chance to turn things around now, maybe ever. And suddenly, Nate was more alone than he'd been in a long, long time.

Fuck, he thought, clutching his mug for dear life, standing in the middle of his room with no idea of what to do next.

Fuck.

Chapter 44

How does one do homework at a time like this? Marina thought, slumped over her desk and staring blankly at the same sentence she'd been "reading" for the past hour. Four other tabs were open on her browser, each one to a different news site covering the "Blog Wars."

CNN, The New York Times, and Buzzfeed were all firmly behind Tiffany. One journalist had dug up a bunch of old information about Ben's life; the time he'd dressed up as a Confederate Soldier in high school; a picture of him with a "known white supremacist" politician in Texas; a leaked email chain between his scouting buddies where one of them had used a racial slur. Reading those articles, Marina could understand the hate mail and death threats. Ben looked like the worst kind of monster, an embodiment of everything the radical left insisted was haunting this country.

But then there were the articles in Fox, Quillette, and The Daily Wire, pointing out that Tiffany had struck first on the hockey rink and had a muddled history of her own. Several long think-pieces had appeared, describing the way Tiffany shut down a local coffee shop in her hometown for displaying art that "celebrated colonialism." How she'd gone after people online—professors, news anchors, radio hosts, celebrities—at the slightest provocation. How her language often became downright vitriolic, exaggerating the supposed "damage" to the point of meaninglessness. These news sources referred to Ben as an Eagle Scout and energetic intellectual, perhaps a bit too raucous in his language but well-researched and brave. To them, he was a bastion of free speech, a man of strong principles setting himself against the tide of cultural erosion.

A hero.

The effect was dizzying.

It was as if two worlds existed, side-by-side, spheres that did not touch. And which one was real? Was Ben a disgusting bigot? A bannerman of American ideals? Or just some normal guy who got in over his head?

Marina buttressed her head in her hands, trying to hold the paradoxes together.

And, most of all, trying not to think about Nate.

Her phone buzzed.

It was embarrassing how quickly she flipped it over and unlocked the screen.

Please be him. Please don't *be him.*

It wasn't him.

<Hi Marina, it's Austin. I hope you don't mind that Jordan gave me your number. I hear that things are really bad over there and I was wondering if I could take you out to dinner tomorrow, get your mind off things? We're all rooting for Ben!>

Marina read the text several times before its meaning sunk in. Austin was… asking her out? Did that even happen in this strange twisted Wonderland they'd all fallen into?

Apparently so.

Her fingers hovered over the keys, but she didn't know how to instruct them. What should she say? She was absolutely, totally sure that whatever had been between her and Nate was over now, shredded by the campus drama and their own inexorable differences.

But the pain of that, of his absence, was so absolute that the idea of seeing someone else hadn't even crossed her mind. Without consciously deciding to, she'd seen this ending as just that. An ending. Permanent. Unchanging. Her status in life, now and forever.

Did it have to be?

After all, people moved on from breakups all the time. There were so many movies and songs and books about it. This was no different, just another part of the human experience. She'd find someone new, someone great, and forget Nate ever existed. He'd be a story she told her kids someday; a scandalous tale of how *adventurous* mom had been in college.

Maybe the man in that theoretical future could be Austin?

<Yes please!> Marina texted back, each letter like a pulled tooth. <I do need a night off. Where do you want to go?>

She pressed send before she could think better of it.

Best way to get over someone is to find someone new, she told herself firmly, placing her phone down and waiting for Austin's response. *Life will go on. Everything will be just fine.*

Her phone buzzed again, but this time it was ringing.

"Hi Mami," Marina answered, making an unsuccessful attempt at upbeat.

"*Marina*, why are you on the news?"

"Oh, that," she said, rubbing the bridge of her nose. "It's just the thing with Ben, nothing to worry about."

"Are you safe, *mi hija*? Do you need anything?"

"No, I'm fine thanks. We're dealing with it." Did she sound as tired as she felt? "It's just... a lot."

There was a worried pause on the other end of the line. "Honey, is everything ok? You don't sound good."

"Don't I?" Marina asked, staring at the ceiling.

"And you're not telling me everything. A *madre* knows when

301

her children are lying to her."

"Oh?"

"Alvaro is not as subtle as he thinks he is."

Marina chuckled. "Yeah, I know."

"What happened when he was there? Are you two fighting?"

Marina chewed on the inside of her cheek. Why not tell her? After all, it was over now. They'd never meet Nate, never see that rascal smile or those sky-blue eyes. They'd never have their chance to hate him and all the ways he changed her.

Besides, she was tired of lying.

She sighed. "He met a friend of mine."

"Oooh," her mother said in a delighted voice. "A *boy*friend?"

"Sort of," Marina said, a lump forming in her throat. She coughed. "But it's over now. He's not in the picture anymore."

"Oh, *mi amor*, what happened?"

Marina couldn't see. The ceiling was blurring, wavering like a mirage. She swallowed hard but couldn't dislodge whatever had grown there, stuck there.

"It's fine," she said, lip trembling.

For a long, saturated moment, neither of them spoke. Marina could hear the TV in the background, her father calling for something over the steady churn of the Kitchen Aid and washing machine.

She wondered if it was possible to die of homesickness.

At last, her mother asked, "Does this have anything to do with what's going on? The issue with your friend?"

And then, unable to stop herself, Marina burst into tears.

Chapter 45

Nate was very, very drunk.

"Can I get you another one?" asked the guy he'd been dancing with, winking suggestively.

"Yes!" Nate shouted over the pounding of the music, now dense and thick in his bones.

Bodies gyrated around him in a dizzying haze, and he tried to enjoy it like he always did. There was release, even freedom, in the sheer untethered bliss of being so intoxicated that he couldn't feel guilty or confused or enraged by the injustice in the world. In this sweaty, swirling miasma he wasn't his labels; white, wealthy, half-straight, *liar*. He was just Nate, just a collection of cells and neurons experiencing this moment. This place. This state of blurry euphoria.

But Tiffany's face kept leaking into his buzz, her disgust following him like a rancid smell.

I thought you were better than this.

"Here!" the guy shouted, shoving a plastic cup into Nate's hand. Nate shot it back in one swallow without even noticing what it was. The guy smirked. "You're in for a good night, eh?"

"Come here," Nate said, grabbing the man's hips and pulling him close. The music shifted into something haunting and delirious, the bass so deep it was almost physical. Nate and this stranger were dancing, grinding, their bodies rubbing up and down one another. He felt hands slip under his shirt and into his belt, curving over the hard line of his hip bones. He retaliated by grabbing the closest face and jamming himself into it, mouth moving, lips parting, all of it mechanical and rote. He was a programmed thing, a machine, socially conditioned to behave this way, going through the expected motions. His bright hair, his rainbow T-shirt, his tight jeans. All of it an image, all of it a projection to send the right assortment of messages.

Smoke signals in the dark.

Was this person before him a projection too? Not a human but a ghost playing at being one? Or did this man know himself, understand the fucking maze of his own mind in a way Nate never would?

Was he anything like Marina?

Nate pulled away suddenly, stumblingly.

"I gotta go," he muttered, reeling back.

"Hey, don't—"

But Nate was already shoving through the crowd, too rough, panic climbing up him like a swarm of insects. Oh god, why did he have to think about Marina right now? Why did he have to think about anything at all? There should be a way to turn his brain off for *one night*, a switch that would let him be the untroubled party-animal he'd always been. Nate would give anything, *anything* to go back to a time before Marina, when he'd been so *sure* of everything. Life had been a simple story, good versus evil, the right standing against the wrong.

And then she'd come along and *ruined it*.

Nate surged outside without his coat—where had he left it? He gulped air like a drowning man, clutching the wall. His breath misted, and he was reminded of that first night walking home with her, when he'd invited her upstairs and she hadn't come. What if she had? What if they'd just fucked and gotten it over with? Maybe then she wouldn't have burrowed so deep into his brain, taken him over so completely.

But she *had* slept with him, had come to him willingly, generously. Had overcome her nervousness to be with him. Had maybe even begun to fall for him.

Why?

He didn't deserve her. He didn't deserve Tiff or Leo either. He was a broken piece of a broken machine and the best thing he could do for the world was to stop trying to fix it because he only made everything worse.

Leaning against the club facade, Nate tried to make the world stop spinning.

And then he saw them.

Across the street, walking away from the Central Square T-stop, two figures with linked arms. One was tall, broad, vaguely familiar.

The other was Marina.

He'd recognize her anywhere, the long legs, the black hair, the way she ducked her head when she laughed. He pushed off the wall, blinking frantically to try and clear the image so that her hand wouldn't be on another person's elbow. Because he had to be imagining it. He *had* to be.

She stumbled a bit on the ice and the big dumb idiot caught her, wrapping a too-thick arm around her shoulders, saying something in a too-deep voice.

They disappeared around the corner.

"No," Nate croaked, pushing off the wall. "Stop."

The world was tilting too much for him to follow. Did he even want to? What could he say?

Hey, sorry your friend is an asshole and I'm a disaster and we

305

can't be together because that would mean being implicit in all the things I've hated my whole life, but please don't go out with someone else because I can't stand the idea of another man's hands on you, even though that's grossly misogynist of me.

Yeah, that would go over *great*.

"Hey, you left in a hurry."

It was the guy he'd been dancing with, watching Nate from the club's entrance the way a cat watches a toy. Nate stared at him, vaguely aware of the cold turning his arms into gooseflesh. This stranger was exactly Nate's type. Tall, wiry, confident, *gay*. Nate knew he could go back inside and dance and drink and fuck this guy's brains out. He'd done it before. He knew he could numb himself with more booze and more sex and believe that none of it meant anything, like always.

The guy's smile flickered. "Are you gonna puke or something?"

Without another word, Nate pushed off the wall and stumbled into the darkness.

Chapter 46

Sitting across from Austin at The Smoke Shop, Marina wished she'd turned him down. She was too hollow. Too distracted. She felt like something pale and slimy pulled from a cave and put under a spotlight and every part of her strained with the desire, the *need*, to crawl into bed and never come out again.

But that wasn't fair to either of them.

So she smiled and leaned in. "Jordan tells me you were an Eagle Scout?"

He shrugged, humble. "All my brothers were. I guess it kind of runs in the family. I would have been a disappointment if I hadn't been one too."

"What are your brothers doing now?" Marina asked, stirring with her black cherry.

"One's in the military, about to be sent to South Korea for a language program. The other is training to be a stonemason."

Marina smiled, thinking of Nick. "That must be cool."

"Oh yeah, it's a surprisingly lucrative industry. He's gonna do just fine."

Austin chuckled, and Marina forced herself to echo the sound.

"What about you?" he asked, tilting his head. "Any siblings?"

Doing her best to focus on the moment, on his face, Marina told him about Nick and Alvaro and her life in Roanoke. She told him about her childhood roaming the forests, about how her parents tried to make her join the Brownies but that she was too much of a troublemaker for it to stick.

"I always had a bit of an issue with authority," she admitted.

"Seems like you grew out of it," he said, toasting with his Old Fashioned.

Marina didn't answer, sitting back to let the waiter slide a few appetizers between them. Chicken wings coated in brown sugar and spicy sausage with a cheese spread. She knew the food looked delicious in a clinical, detached sort of way, but she couldn't quite convince herself she was hungry.

"So, how are you holding up with this whole Twitter thing?" Austin said carefully, glancing up to gage her reaction.

Marina sighed, staring into her drink, not sure if she was angry or relieved that he'd brought it up first. "It's kind of eclipsed everything."

"I'm sorry. Sounds like some real bullshit."

"I suppose."

"No, it's ridiculous," he said, slicing open the sausage. "Everyone's so keen on believing *her*, but when Ben tells his side of the story it's all lies, lies, lies. There's no space for reasonable doubt, no waiting for the verdict." He shook his head. "This whole movement has gone too far."

"What movement?"

Austin looked up. "What's it called, Me Too?"

Marina pursed her lips. "Maybe. But I get where it's coming from," she said, selecting a chicken wing. "For a long time, it was hard for women to be heard, especially when they were up against someone in power. Just look at all the Hollywood stuff coming out, about having to sleep with someone to get a role."

Austin shrugged. "But that was the understood way of things.

I'm not saying it was right, and of course there were jerks who took advantage. But the world was different back then. We can't judge everyone by modern-day standards."

Marina's lips curled, quite against her will, as she remembered saying almost the same thing to Nate not so long ago.

People are always ignoring the context.

"Something funny?" Austin asked.

"No, sorry." She straightened her features. "I agree with you. But still, I understand. Women have been frustrated for a long time. And maybe the pendulum has swung too far at this point, but I imagine it had to, so we can find a place of balance."

"You think *this* is balance?"

Marina examined her chicken wing, trying to build up the desire to eat it. "No. But I do think the girl accusing Ben really does believe what she's saying. She has her own reasons."

Reasons Nate could probably explain.

She took a bite, chewed, swallowed, barely tasting the flavors.

"You're a lot more forgiving than I'd be in your situation," Austin said, smearing cheese on a cracker.

"Don't get me wrong, I'm angry. But don't you think it's more productive to try and understand rather than just dismiss her story as an exaggeration?"

"What is there to understand?"

Marina looked at her half-eaten chicken wing.

What was *there to understand?*

Only the way Nate would laugh when she said something he found offensive. Only the flush of pleasure she got when he'd argue with her, punch a hole in her reasoning and fill it with his own.

Only the way she kept wishing that Austin would do the same.

"To tell you the truth," he was saying even as Marina pulled out of her thoughts with considerable effort, "I'm excited to leave

309

Boston behind. Move back South among other like-minded people. Can you *imagine* trying to raise kids in this environment? With the schools pumping their heads full of leftist agendas and anti-religious rhetoric?" He shook his head. "No thank you."

Marina's mouth twitched, but she couldn't quite manage a smile. "Yeah."

"What about you? What are you gonna do after graduation?"

"I'm not sure," she admitted, wiping her fingers. "I worked with a study group in the Media Lab last summer that could lead to a government job, if I keep going back."

"That sounds amazing. Why wouldn't you go back?"

She shrugged. "I guess I'm tempted to try something new."

She found herself thinking of that application to the science journalism internship, still on her desk.

Why hadn't she thrown it away?

Austin frowned. "I guess that's fair. But I feel like it's dangerous to spend your life chasing novelty. Too many young people nowadays just float along, looking for *experiences*. It's like they're hoping a future will fall into their laps."

Marina nodded as the waiter took their empty trays. "A lot of millennials do seem to struggle for direction."

"I think it's because our generation was raised to believe we could have everything we wanted. That life would be fair. Remember what they used to tell us in kindergarten? About us all being special and unique and destined for greatness? I mean, it must have had an impact, right? We weren't trained to believe in hard work and sacrifice, the struggle to do meaningful things." Austin finished his drink. "I count myself lucky. My parents harped on the fact that nothing would come easy. They used to tell me I wasn't entitled to anything I didn't earn."

Marina nodded, thinking of Papi's lectures. "Same."

"I can't imagine what life would be like if my family hadn't done that. If they'd told me I was perfect just the way I was."

"Me neither," Marina said.

"And then think about how hard it must be, to realize it was all a lie. To leave school and find out the world is *un*fair and *un*just and there's only so much we can do to fix it. I can't imagine how much that would screw a person up."

"I can," Marina said without thinking, and then bit her lip.

Don't bring up Nate right now, she said sternly to herself. *Don't ruin this too.*

But Austin only smiled, toasting. "Maybe you're right to have sympathy for them."

She lifted her glass, hooking her mouth up to mirror his expression. "And you're right that we were lucky to avoid it."

Austin clinked his empty cocktail against hers. Then they both pulled back to make space for the generous tray of barbecue meats the waiter slid between them, steaming and savory and, to Marina, entirely unappetizing.

"You ok?" Austin asked, picking up his fork. "You seem pretty quiet tonight."

"Oh, yeah sorry. I'm fine. Just distracted by everything, you know?"

But the truth was that she was quiet because she didn't have anything to say. She mostly agreed with Austin, pretty much shared his views. And, as Marina dug into their meal with artificial enthusiasm, she didn't understand why that felt so entirely unsatisfying.

Chapter 47

Nate had never looked at the MIT Chapel before.

Sure, he'd walked by it, made jokes about the awful things that must happen inside, chased after Marina on this very lawn. But he'd never really *seen* the rounded brick design, the accessibility walkup, the glass doors. It was all so innocent, a facade of industriousness, that the building could have been anything. A lecture hall or an office.

But it wasn't.

It was a church.

Nate swayed, colder than he could ever remember being in his life and hardly caring. He deserved this discomfort.

He deserved everything.

His palm was open in front of him. Staring at it, he examined Marina's cross. The gold looked almost silver in the streetlights, harmless, maybe even pretty. *Dangerous.* He wanted to throw it into the snow, make it disappear forever. But no, this cross mattered to her. He needed to give it back. Because at least he could do this one small good thing, fix this tiny bit of chaos. He might be a broken asshole and a liar, but he wasn't a thief. He wasn't going to keep what was hers.

That's why he was here.

Right.

Nate would leave the necklace with someone, the first person he found. Then he'd never have to talk to Marina again. He could cut off contact and finally screw his head on straight.

At least, as straight as it had ever been.

He huffed a halfhearted laugh at his own joke.

See? He was getting better already.

Staggering forward, Nate made his way up the ramp, toward the entrance. A brief flicker of thought popped into his brain—*what if it's locked?* But the door opened. He stumbled inside, the warmth an almost painful relief.

Wonder if I'll burst into flames.

He turned, zigzagging down the hall to the closed chapel. Using the weight of his whole body, he yanked open one door, stumbled a bit.

And stopped.

Huh, he thought, taking another clumsy step into the wide, elegant space. His eyes tracked over plain wooden chairs, an elevated dais, a beautiful waterfall of glittering shards suspended behind the altar. Glass? Foil? Bits of snow? He had no idea, but whatever the decoration was made of, it was captivating. There were no crosses, no signs of what this place was for. Just polished marble and a sparkling road, leading up...

He grabbed a chair to keep himself from falling over, jerking his gaze back to the ground with a shake of his head.

Evil, he reminded himself sternly. *All of this is evil. Beautiful things can still be wrong.*

Like Marina.

"I have to admit," came a voice from behind him, "I wasn't expecting anyone to come in here so late."

Nate whipped around to find a man sitting to his left, short and handsome and wearing one of those black outfits with the white collar.

Priest, his mind supplied helpfully.

"Sorry," Nate muttered, doing his best to stand straight and still. "I'm just… looking for someone."

"Anyone in particular?"

"Do you know Marina Salinas?" Nate blurted, holding out the cross. "I need someone to give this to her."

"Sure," the priest said, accepting the gold chain. "But why don't you give it to her yourself?"

"I can't."

"Why not?"

"It's… complicated." Nate blinked, trying to steady himself. A strange emotion was rising in him, like anger but heavier, more problematic. It was as if Marina's cross had been a tether that had been suddenly sliced, something he hadn't even realized was holding him together until he'd given it away.

He took a tottering step forward. "Hey, do you really believe all this?" He gestured vaguely around him.

"I do," the priest said calmly.

"You shouldn't," Nate said, unable to stop himself. "It's not real. None of it is."

To Nate's surprise, the priest only smiled, folding his wrists over the chair in front of him and leaning forward, as if to welcome Nate's drunken antagonism. "Ah, but that depends on what you mean by real. When you get down to the philosophy of it, pretty much nothing can be confirmed except for the fact that you exist. After all, *life* is what you carry around in your head, is it not? The world you live in is created by your perceptions and emotions and your interpretation of them. In a very physical way, we create our own reality."

"No," Nate said, shaking his head and alarmed at how the world continued to move after he stopped. "No, we are created by our

315

surroundings. We're all products of the system we were raised in."

"I think that's surrendering too much agency, son. Human beings are remarkably powerful. And the God we follow is even more so. He would never leave us so helpless."

"If He's so great, then why does bad stuff happen, huh?" Nate said, grabbing onto a chair with nerveless fingers, knuckles white. "Why do good people get hurt and bad people win?" He scoffed, glaring at the beautiful cascade of cut glass. "This world is ugly and horrible and none of us can do *shit*."

Nate shoved off the chair, making for the exit. He was done having this unsettling conversation with a man who seemed altogether too sure of himself. He was *leaving*.

"I used to be a drug addict."

Nate froze in the act of opening the door. The priest continued, his voice light and conversational.

"My parents were dirt poor. They used to say they fell on hard times, but then Dad would spend his paycheck on booze, and Mom would disappear into herself and let him. My siblings and I had to more or less raise ourselves." The words were wrapping around Nate, holding him there like iron chains. "I spent two years in juvie and eventually ended up on the streets. I blamed my parents, my siblings, the system, the world. Like so many people, I felt stuck."

Nate turned slowly. But the priest wasn't looking at him. He was looking at the cool light filtering in from the roof, an easy, relaxed smile on his face.

"One night, I was hungry. I hadn't eaten in days and was more strung out than a laundry line. I followed some signs for a free meal and ended up in a church basement where they were handing out soup. There were all these happy people, laughing and joking and offering their time for nothing. I imagine I was pretty rude to them, angry as I was." He smiled ruefully. "But they welcomed me in. Told

316

me about God. And one man, an older gentleman, clapped me on the shoulder and told me everything that had happened was my responsibility. That I was the one framing my life, and it was up to me to change the narrative."

"The *fuck*?" Nate said, squinting.

"I was mad at first too. But then it clicked for me. I don't know why, but I realized in that moment that if the past was in my hands then so was my future." His eyes shifted to Nate. "Suddenly, I had tremendous power."

"Because of God?"

"Because of *choices*," he said. "Choices, my friend, are the true power in this world. It was a choice to believe that God is good and looks after me. It was a choice to shoulder the burden of my own existence and take ownership of my life. That decision pulled me up and brought me here, where I can help other people do the same. It gave me the peace I needed to do better."

Nate scowled at the man, eyes narrow, gaze blurry. "You're wrong," he said. "We can't choose the things that happen to us."

"Perhaps not. But as the saying goes, we can control how we react to them." His expression was soft and calm. "Isn't that tremendous?"

Without consciously making the decision to move, Nate plopped down into the chair he'd been gripping.

Choices.

He was crap at those. Of course he was, when his upbringing and surroundings had infected him with all the wrong ideas and instincts. He wanted to fix things, but that was only because of his male privilege. He wanted to get the world back on track, but that was just his whiteness and colonialism talking. He was a bundle of mistakes and paradoxes and really, what did he understand? Nate couldn't be sure about anything. He was a mess! He didn't know right from wrong anymore, couldn't possibly make any real decisions when everything was so fucking *relative*.

But that's not true, is it? came a small, unfriendly voice from the back of his head. *You know it's wrong to lie.*

Nate stared at his hands, feeling laughably helpless.

"So you're not trying to convert me?" he asked at last.

"Oh, I'm always trying to spread God's word. But maybe that's not what you need right now."

Nate looked up, feeling strangely childlike under the warm heat of this man's smile.

"And what do I need right now?"

"To feel empowered, I think." The priest cocked his head. "And to know you're not alone."

Nate snorted. "We're all alone."

"Only if you choose to see it that way."

"So you're admitting that God is just a story then? A lie you tell yourself?"

The priest chuckled, but it wasn't a derisive sound. It was friendly, almost encouraging, despite Nate's insolence. "Tell me something in this world that isn't a story. Science, economy, politics. It's all an elaborate lens through which we attempt to understand the incomprehensible. We're all in Plato's Cave, trying to figure out the shadows."

Nate struggled to remember what he knew about Plato's Cave. Something about a fire and shapes on the wall, but what did it *mean...*?

Before he could sort through his thoughts, the priest stood and came over to him, putting a hand on his shoulder. The gesture was so tender, so completely without agenda, that Nate fought the urge to fold in on himself.

"You ok, son?"

"I'm fine," he said, convincing no one.

"Let me call you an Uber."

Nate tilted back, almost toppling off the seat. "You do that sort of thing?"

"You're thinking of the Amish," the priest said with a smile, pulling out a cracked smartphone. "God never specified about the internet."

"No kidding," Nate exhaled. "So... you'll give that to Marina?"

The priest's expression was inscrutable.

"I can," he said, and then crouched down. "But may I offer you some free advice?"

Nate huffed. "I don't think I can stop you."

"Whatever it is that brought you in here tonight, it's yours to handle. It's not out of your control, however much it feels that way."

Nate was shaking his head, unable to stop, the world spinning around him.

"It's your decision," the priest said, dangling the cross in front of Nate's knees. It glittered like the decorations behind the altar. "But I think you should talk to Marina yourself. After all, honesty is the best policy."

Nate glared at the necklace. "Your God say that?"

He smiled. "Only if our Lord was speaking through Benjamin Franklin."

For a long moment, neither of them moved. The cross spun lazily, invitingly, and Nate wanted so badly to ignore it, shove to his feet and *leave*.

But, for reasons he couldn't quite comprehend, at least not at that moment, Nate reached out an unstable hand and snatched the cross out of the air.

"Good choice." The priest smiled down at him in a way that

made Nate feel at once validated and deeply disturbed. "Now let's get you home."

Chapter 48

Marina was waiting outside the hearing room, her arm around Jordan's shoulders, wondering what was going on inside. What was the dean saying to Ben and Tiffany? What would the school do?

What was she hoping for?

Obviously, she didn't want one of her best friends to be expelled. But maybe this would be a wake-up call for Ben. Maybe this could be a lesson for everyone involved, to be a little kinder, a little less extreme. She'd watched Tiffany stride into the conference room, head held high, dark rings under her eyes. And Nate's tall friend from hockey was sitting on a bench down the corridor, jiggling his foot, waiting just as impatiently as they were. Marina couldn't help but wonder what it must be like for them, to see their lives as such a battleground. When every day is a war between good and evil, a struggle for the soul of the world, how can anyone enjoy their life? How could one breathe under that kind of pressure?

Had that pressure driven Nate away?

Marina sighed, tilting her head so that it rested on top of Jordan's. "You ok?"

"Yeah," Jordan whispered in that frighteningly small voice. She'd lost weight since this whole ordeal began, and Marina knew she was having trouble sleeping. Jordan wasn't a confrontational person—it was the reason she and Ben worked so well together. Yin and yang. But seeing her face on the news, plastered all over the internet with the caption "Republican Blogger's Silent Girlfriend" had been harder on her than any of them had expected. Marina bristled at the unfairness of it. Jordan wasn't *silent*, she was *quiet*. Just because she didn't post angry tirades online did *not* mean she didn't have her own opinions or that she never countered Ben with soft-spoken but equally powerful views.

Marina squeezed.

"How was your date with Austin last night?" Jordan asked.

Marina wondered if she should lie, if it would make Jordan feel better that she'd paired her friend with someone *awesome* or *fun* or *swoony*. But Marina couldn't bring herself to do it. She was tired of hiding. If she was going to live honestly, speak truthfully, then she had to start somewhere.

"It was… fine."

Jordan snorted. "That great, huh?"

"He's nice and all," Marina admitted. "But I don't think he's right for me." She paused. "In fact, I'm not sure what's right for me."

"What do you mean?"

Marina chewed on her lip before answering. "I think I'm going to apply for that internship at Stanford."

Jordan straightened, forcing Marina to lift her head.

"What about the Media Lab? What about the government program you were so excited about?"

"Excited is a strong word."

"But you had it all figured out." Jordan's eyes were huge and pleading, as if desperate to hold onto this last island of stability. "Your plan made so much sense."

Curling up one side of her mouth, Marina twined her hand into Jordan's small fingers. "I've recently come to understand that life is about more than making sense. Some things are worth it, even if they're risky." *Even if they go down in flames.*

It took a few moments for Jordan to answer.

"I'm sorry," she said at last, turning to stare out the window.

"For what?"

Jordan blinked a few times, and Marina imagined she was trying to organize her now-perpetually scattered thoughts.

"For what happened between you and that Nate guy. I knew you were excited about him, although I never understood why. And it seems like things went wrong in a bad way. I hope it wasn't because of... all this."

Marina forced herself to smile, forced herself to keep the pain out of her expression. "Jordan, he *definitely* wasn't right for me."

"But you seemed so happy, sneaking off to his house and everything."

Marina coughed in surprise. "What?"

A little of the old Jordan glimmered through as she smirked. "I'm not stupid, you know."

"I never said—"

"And the stairs squeak."

"Oh," Marina said, blushing furiously. "I thought..."

Jordan shrugged. "I was glad for you, even if I didn't show it very well. He just seemed so unlike you." She paused, lip quivering. "But that shouldn't have meant anything. It shouldn't be a big deal, if you disagree or choose different ways to express yourself. Relationships are compromises and you have to learn to take the best and worst of the person you fall in love with."

Marina wasn't sure they were talking about Nate anymore.

"Some compromises are bigger than others," she whispered.

Jordan shook her head. "If it's real, I don't think it matters." She blew out a breath, leaning back against the bench and glancing at the closed door, behind which her boyfriend's future was being decided, maybe hers with it. "Love is a smoke made with the fume of sighs."

"What's that from?"

Jordan shrugged. "Some English textbook." She grinned, almost managing to hide how much it cost her. "How am I supposed to know? I'm the math nerd, remember?"

Marina returned the smile, trying to think of something comforting to say. A conversation that would make the interminable wait go faster.

She was interrupted by the heavy slap of footsteps echoing down the long hallway.

They both turned.

It was Nate, flushed and out of breath and looking distinctly worse for wear. His hair was rumpled, his skin the color of milk, his jacket buttoned up wrong.

Marina jumped to her feet. "Nate, what are you—?"

"Where's the thing?" Nate panted as his friend shoved upright.

"What?" Marina asked.

"*Nate?*" the other boy rumbled in surprise.

Nate waved a frantic hand. "The trial or whatever! Did I miss it?"

"No, it's in there, but—"

Nate blew past her, smacking a hand against the heavy wooden door.

"I don't think anyone's supposed to—"

"Nate, what the—" his friend called.

He ignored both of them, bursting into the small conference room where the dean of students sat with Ben and Tiffany. Marina exchanged a quick, shocked look with Jordan before following him inside, the other student close on their heels.

"What is the *meaning* of this?" the dean snapped at Nate with a scandalized glint of her glasses.

"Nate, Leo?" Tiffany said with a frown, looking between them. Her expression was hard and furious, as impenetrable as a brick wall. "What's going on?"

Nate was breathing, steadying himself, and Marina felt as if the whole world hinged on that inhale, that exhale, the expression in those beautiful blue eyes.

"I lied," he said at last, dropping the words like stones into still water.

There was a beat of silence.

After a moment, the dean lifted one eyebrow and said, "Excuse me?"

"Nate, what the fuck?" Tiffany said, surging to her feet.

"I didn't actually see what happened," Nate said, his confession coming fast now, as if he'd broken a dam and couldn't hold the water back. "I didn't see anything, wasn't even there. It was my idea to say we were witnesses, and I'm so, so sorry. I just wanted to be a good person, and it seemed like the right thing to do at the time because..." he took another deep breath. "Because I believe Tiffany." He turned to her, earnest, painful. "I really do. I *believe* her, and I think it happened just like she said it did. Which is why I wanted to help. She should be supported." He blew out. "But I also believe in due process. I interfered with it, and I couldn't live with that anymore."

Marina glanced at Tiffany, and her heart fisted at the raw pain in the other girl's eyes.

"*We?*" The dean adjusted her glasses, sharp gaze cutting between Nate and his two friends. "Are you telling me that both of these witness statements are falsified?"

Nate winced, lifting one hand to his temple as if he was fighting off a headache. He glanced at Leo.

"Not cool, dude," Leo said, folding his arms.

The dean turned to Tiffany, her frown carved deep. "Is this true?"

Tiffany, Marina thought, looked ready to collapse. The stony expression she'd been wearing when they all burst in was gone and her eyes were rapidly brimming, overflowing. She shook all over.

"How could you?" Tiffany asked Nate, not answering the dean. "I f-fight for my existence every day, struggle to be seen by this *asshole*, by the school, by my own fucking *sister*. You know that. But you...you..." her voice broke, trailed off in a wild storm of hitching gasps.

"I'm sorry, Tiff," Nate said, holding out his hands. "I know how this looks, but I couldn't go through with it. That was the only thing I knew for certain anymore." He hung his head. "I'm so sorry."

"Well." The dean was scanning the room like a hunting lioness. Marina wasn't sure which of them was the wounded gazelle. "This certainly changes—"

"I'm sorry too."

All of them swung around to find Ben standing, shoulders hunched a little, looking like every word cost him.

"Ben?" Jordan whispered, but Marina touched her friend's arm, holding her back. It suddenly felt very important for none of them to speak, for none of them to so much as breathe.

Ben glanced up. "I didn't think you were actually upset."

Tiffany hiccupped a sob. *"What?"*

"I thought it was a power-play. Like everything else you... well, that's not important." He gestured helplessly. "You were yelling insults at me, so I just figured that's what we were doing. I didn't mean to make it any more personal than it already was. But I'm sorry if you felt like I really meant...that."

Tiffany scoffed, straightened. "Because you did."

326

Ben straightened too. "I did not!" Then he appeared to catch himself. "But I can see how what I *did* say could have been, er, misinterpreted."

There was another heavy silence, pressing in on all sides.

"Tiff…" Nate began, but the dean was standing, fingers splayed on the hardwood table.

"Things have undeniably changed in the last five seconds." She rounded on Tiffany, a hard sympathy in her eyes that made Marina think of her Catholic school teachers. "Ms. Freeman, do you wish to continue this investigation without witnesses? Especially considering that we have a record of you punching Mr. Sharps in the face, calling him a Nazi in public, and starting a viral campaign against him that has brought significant disorder to this campus?"

Marina watched, wide-eyed, as Tiffany glared first at Ben. Then at Nate.

Then at the dean.

"No," she said at last, and Marina could see the way she pulled the word out of herself, how it stuck in her throat like a fishhook.

The dean nodded curtly, lips pursed.

"Well then, I hope you'll all take this as a lesson in complexity. The adult world isn't written in absolutes, much as you both seem to wish it was. And it would make my already very difficult job easier if you students didn't default to the worst assumptions all the time. I'm sorry you both felt attacked, and I'm especially sorry it escalated to such a degree. But since no one can be sure what happened, I'm afraid this is the end of it."

She rounded on Nate, who shrank back, staring at the toes of his shoes.

"As for you," she said, "falsifying a witness statement is grounds for disciplinary action, even expulsion." Marina's heartbeat was painfully sharp, too fast to be safe. "But I understand you were acting for a friend and frankly, it's not the dumbest thing I've seen an undergraduate do. Sometimes it seems like a miracle that any of you make it to commencement in one piece."

Nate looked up under his eyelashes. Marina held her breath.

The dean snapped her binder shut. "Luckily, I believe in second chances. Can I trust you all to do the same?"

There was an impressive power to the flash of her glasses and the pull of her gray-streaked eyebrows as the dean looked at each of them in turn, lingering on Tiffany. When they'd all nodded, Tiffany only begrudgingly, the dean shoved to her feet.

"Good day, everyone. I hope I do *not* see any of you again."

And then she was gone.

Tiffany was on her feet the moment the gentle *click click click* of the dean's heels disappeared.

"Fuck you, Nate," she said, voice shaking, tears streaming down her face. "You double-crossing, queer-baiting, virtue-signaling, apologist *piece of shit*."

"Hey now," Marina said, lunging forward. But it was Jordan's turn to hold her back, stopping Marina with a quick shake of her head.

"I couldn't live with it, Tiff," Nate said miserably. He sounded so exhausted. "Someone's future was on the line."

"It was your idea," Leo growled.

Nate hung his head. "I know. I thought I had the answers to things, but I didn't. I was wrong."

"It wasn't *wrong*," Tiffany exclaimed, throwing her arms out. "You were on our side. We were saving this campus. We were *fighting hate*!"

"And creating more," Nate answered.

Jordan was in Ben's arms now, holding her boyfriend as if nothing in the world mattered but his body around her, the end of her ordeal. Ben was watching the exchange between Nate and Tiffany over Jordan, brows pulled together, silent for once. Leo stood with his arms folded, shaking his head.

Marina's heart was in her throat.

"You turned your back on me, on *us!*" Tiffany shouted. "You put words in our mouths and reinforced everything that's wrong with the world! You used your privilege to silence us!" Her rage was rapidly eclipsing the tears, giving her back the strength that had seemed as thin as tissue paper moments ago. "*This* is the reason nothing will ever get better. *This* is why I have to keep fighting for my right to live and breathe. People like *you.*" She all but spat the last word.

Nate shrugged, curling in on himself. "Maybe. But I can't control everyone else. I can only control myself."

She sneered. "Sounds like some cowardly bullshit to me."

"Or it sounds like the bravest thing I've heard all day," Marina said, stepping in at last.

Tiffany glanced between them, jaw clenched, shoulders shaking.

Leo wrapped his big hand around Tiffany's shoulder.

"Let's get out of here," he said. "They're not worth our time." Gently, he tugged the small, blonde woman away, leading her out of the room.

Before he left, he looked over his shoulder, right at Nate. "Look who was a white savior after all."

Nate deflated even more, watching his friends go with the expression of an abandoned house pet. Marina opened her mouth, struggling to find the words.

"Whew," Ben muttered. "Glad that's over."

Marina rounded on him, her temper snapping like a flag in the breeze. "No, Ben. No. You don't get to just say sorry and forget it ever happened. Nate's right, you were spreading vitriol just as much as she was."

His mouth fell open. "I was fighting for—"

"Don't you *get it?*" Marina said, unable to hold back her frustration anymore, not now that her friends were no longer in danger. "You sound exactly like her! Fighting! Battling! That doesn't. Solve. *Anything!*"

Ben puffed up. "Look, I don't know what's gotten into you lately—"

"*Common sense*, Ben!" she shouted. "It's common *fucking* sense that people don't listen when you insult them. That people don't like it when you call them names. That volleying slurs and spreading outrage is never going to help!"

He opened his mouth like he was about to respond. But Jordan put a small hand on his chest.

"Guys..." she said in an exhausted voice. "It's over."

Marina took a deep breath, closing her eyes, clenching her fists. "It won't be," she said. "Until we're all honest with each other." She opened her eyes. "And *to be honest*," she said, full of a wild, furious energy, "I'm in love with *him*."

She jabbed her finger over her shoulder.

"Um..."

At Ben's frown, she turned toward the place where Nate had been just a moment ago.

He was gone.

Chapter 49

Nate slumped on a bench in the hallway, rubbing the bridge of his nose. He was hungover enough that even the filtered light deep in the administration building felt like needles in his eyes, mirroring the fracturing ache of his heart.

What the fuck did I just do?

He'd woken up with a single clear directive in his brain: *get to the hearing*. Something had sparked in him last night that he couldn't quite name, triggered by what the priest had said. Maybe it was about choices or honesty or whatever-the-fuck, but Nate had decided in a flurry of getting dressed that he was *done lying*. He couldn't just *pretend* to be a good person anymore, saying and doing things someone else had decided was correct, going through the motions as if empty imitations could make up for the monstrosity of his existence. For the first time, perhaps in his whole life, he wanted to listen to his own gut, his own instincts, even though they were the instincts of someone white and male and grotesquely privileged and screwed up as hell.

So, in a frenzy of still-drunk recklessness, he'd done the only thing that made any fucking sense.

He'd told the truth.

And now he couldn't help but feel overwhelmed by it.

What have I done?

He knew what he'd done. He'd become the very thing he hated, the very thing he used to pay lip service to standing against. When the rubber had hit the road, he was as bad as the rest of them. White savior. Patriarchy. An entitled, arrogant, privileged man standing up for another entitled, arrogant, privileged man.

But what if it was the right thing to do?

Did that make it any better?

He groaned, leaning his head back and hooking an elbow over his eyes. Could he just stay here forever? Just fall asleep and never have to deal with Tiff and Leo and these stupid, heavy *choices* that weren't nearly as great as the priest had made them out to be?

That sounded nice.

A voice cut through his self-pity.

"That was a pretty noble thing you did back there."

Lifting his arm, he opened one eye to find Marina sliding onto the bench next to him, resplendent as always even in the painfully bright glare.

"Was it?" he asked. "I'm not so sure."

She smiled. "It was certainly dramatic."

He covered his face back up. "You know me. The ham."

She was quiet, and Nate found that he didn't want to look at her. He didn't want to see the judgement in her eyes, feel the shame of everything he'd done wrong reflected back on him. But he was already in this shit deep enough.

Might as well keep going.

"I'm sorry," he said, voice muffled by his coat. "I was a dick to you. I was a dick to everyone. I don't even know what to apologize for because it was pretty much all my fault, so yeah, I guess I'm just generally sorry for everything that happened. Ever. To anyone."

"That's a lot to take responsibility for."

"What can I say? I'm growing up."

She didn't answer and he couldn't take the silence anymore. Gathering his courage, trying to convince himself that everything would be fine, he peeked out from under his forearm.

But her expression wasn't condemning.

It was thoughtful.

"I don't think you were a dick," she said slowly, staring at the opposite wall. "I think you were a good person doing your best in a very complicated situation." She smiled, and it was enough to make his head spin. "Besides, I was hardly any better."

"You didn't lie and ostracize all your friends."

She laughed. The sound was so bright, so wonderfully surprising, that Nate felt the low clouds of his hangover lift ever so slightly.

"Wrong on both accounts. I did lie, Nate. I lied about you. About us. I lied to my parents and roommates and even my *priest*." She shook her head, grinning to herself, and Nate was sure he'd never seen anything so beautiful as her downcast eyes and the flash of her white teeth. "I guess I wasn't brave enough to face it."

"Face what?"

She looked up "That maybe I needed to change."

He lifted one eyebrow, an unwilling smile tugging at the corner of his mouth. "Is that so?"

Marina laughed, shoving him. "We all do sometimes." Then she winced. "And I might have ostracized my friends. Just a little."

"Huh?"

She wobbled her head back and forth. "I kind of yelled at Ben for being, well, an asshole. I pointed out that it's not enough to apologize, he has to *learn* from this, or else it's just going to happen again. We'll see how long it takes him to forgive me."

Nate let out a surprised chuckle. "Good for you."

Her smile faded. "But the worst part is that I lied to you." She took a deep breath. "I never told you how I really felt."

Nate straightened, taking the arm off his face so that he could present his whole flawed and ridiculous being to her.

"And how did you really feel?" he asked, voice raspy.

She was blushing, but it wasn't with shame or embarrassment. No, this Marina glowed with a dazzling corona of self-assurance, a confidence Nate was certain he'd never master, not in all his life.

But maybe he could spend his life trying.

"I was... am... crazy about you," she said. Her lashes fluttered in a quick blink and Nate wondered if anyone had ever thought to bottle up beauty as a cure for headaches. "Even after all this. I think... I think I fell in love with you Nate, somewhere along the way. And I think it might just be the best thing that ever happened to me."

Emotion was swelling in Nate's chest, so thick and strong it was almost painful. He found himself grinning, his face splitting open, the fog of nausea vanishing as if it had never existed.

"Despite the hair?" he asked, a chuckle in his voice.

She narrowed her eyes. "Hair isn't permanent."

"It sure isn't. I was thinking of going full purple next."

She laughed and he joined her, and suddenly Nate felt like maybe the world wasn't such a terrible place after all.

He reached into his pocket, pulling out her cross. "I think this is yours."

She stared at it for a moment, the gold reflecting in her eyes.

And then she closed his fingers around it with her own, her hand warm on his.

She squeezed once. "Keep it." Her lips curled up. "You need it more than I do."

"Still trying to convert me?" he asked, leaning in.

Her breath was warm on his cheeks. "Maybe."

"A doomed endeavor."

"Oh well," she whispered.

They lingered there, in that private infinity, and Nate found his thoughts narrowing to the flecks of green in her irises and the brilliant glimmer of her hair and how beautiful she looked mid-laugh. And maybe this was how things were supposed to be, not grand, world-changing gestures but small moments, saturated with meaning, inherently personal; a series of experiences that one savored and learned from, perpetually imperfect but no less important because of it. He'd always felt like life was this enormous weight, a crushing burden that could only be endured.

But right here, right now, it felt like a gift.

"You still owe me chocolate," Nate murmured.

Marina rolled her eyes. "Come here, you."

She grabbed his neck, pulled him forward, and as Nate's lips touched hers and the moment melted into something as soft as butter, he allowed himself to be joyously, ridiculously, wonderfully at peace.

He was grateful. He was happy.

That was enough.

Epilogue

Nate was late, of course, but Marina had a cocktail ready for him when he bustled into Green Street. Sliding into the seat across from her, arms bare and pink from a full Saturday in the late-May sun, he flashed her both a grin and a glimpse of his brand-new Massachusetts driver's license.

"Congratulations, you're no longer breaking the law," Marina said dryly, sipping her Pink Lady.

"And you don't have to look like a fugitive on the run every time we go out together," Nate said, slipping his wallet into his back pocket. "What did you get me?"

Marina offered him her best innocent expression. "A sugar daddy."

"Har har," he said, sampling the drink. "Clearly you don't realize how much government employees make."

"Well, we can starve together."

"Parents still giving you shit?"

"Oh, they're adjusting," she said with an airy wave that Nate could see right through. "And they're not the only ones losing sleep over all this."

"You're gonna be fine. California is fun!"

"For *you*," she said pointedly.

"Exactly. I'm looking forward to my visit."

"Oh dear."

"We'll go to gay bars and smoke weed and eat good Mexican food."

Marina was laughing. "All at once?"

"There are some pretty wild taquerias."

Her smile faded a little, disappearing behind her drink.

Nate leaned forward, wrapping a comforting hand around her wrist. "You're gonna do great."

"I've never been that far away on my own," she said in a rare show of vulnerability. "I won't know anyone."

"You'll meet people."

"How?"

"Well, maybe don't introduce yourself as Marina the Republican," he said with her favorite impish grin. "That might not go over so well."

"Why not? They're always talking about diversity out there."

"Yeah, *ethnic* diversity."

"Which is the least important kind of diversity there is, if you ask me," Marina said, swirling her drink. "It's so much better experience a diversity of *ideas*, so you can decide for yourself what to believe. Look at us!"

Nate leaned back, ruffling his hair, now a subdued turquoise. "But ethnic diversity brings new ideas to the table too. People from different cultures have different life experiences and views on the world. We know how language shapes our experience. Imagine how much the cultural perspectives of typically marginalized people can do the same."

"Ok, but take you and Leo for example. Different ethnicities, but a remarkably similar upbringing, right? Both wealthy suburbanites from Massachusetts. Both queer and liberal, with terrible taste in movies."

"Hey now, careful what you say about Leo. He's just getting

used to you."

"You do have to admit," Marina said, lifting one eyebrow. "You're cut from similar cloth."

"You mean tall, gorgeous, and brilliant?"

"And modest?" she said, running a finger around the rim of her glass.

"Well, he is anyway," Nate admitted, folding his hands behind his head. "Maybe that's why Tiff still talks to him."

Marina's grin flickered. She knew how much it haunted Nate that he'd hurt Tiffany. For Tiff, the betrayal had been so immense, so comprehensive that her hardening against him had been a necessity. As Nate had explained, it wasn't so much the admission of lying but the fact that he'd been the one to put her in such an awkward spot. That he, a white, wealthy man in a straight-appearing relationship who *knew* the demons Tiffany faced, had placed himself in a position of power over her. It would take her a long time to trust him again, if she ever did. And in Nate's opinion, every second of cold shoulder was well-deserved.

To everyone's surprise, however, Tiffany and Ben had reached an almost peaceable armistice, surviving the rest of their class together with only a handful of shouting matches to show for it. Nate now joked that Tiffany had kinder things to say about Ben than she did about him.

"She'll come around," Marina said.

"Eh, probably not. She's pretty stubborn, you know."

"So is Ben."

"Hey, he's kinda fun," Nate said with a laugh. "If you ignore all the gun-toting, pro-life, conservative shit."

Marina's lips quirked up. "He says much the same thing about you."

Nate's eyes glittered. "Well I am quite charming. Besides, he offered to take me shooting sometime."

"You? Shooting?"

"Don't look so surprised. After all, the gays need to learn to defend themselves if the homophobes come knocking."

"I thought you hated guns."

"I do. But if everyone else has one…"

"Now you sound like my brother."

Nate clutched his chest. "The horror."

"He says he's forgiven you." Marina ducked. "He's excited to hang out with us in San Francisco."

"He'll be right at home."

Marina smiled shyly. "You don't mind that he'll be there for part of your visit?"

"Naw, see I've figured it out. I just need to get him plastered and then we'll be the best of friends."

She snorted into her glass. "Oh dear."

"We'll sing bar songs and reminisce on old times and he won't even notice when I steal his MAGA hat and burn it in a trash can."

"Good luck with that," she said, laughing. "I think he sleeps in it."

Nat groaned.

"I did tell him he can't bring it to the west coast though," Marina said. "I don't much like the idea of getting beat up by Antifa."

"I'd protect you."

Marina shot him a skeptical look. "Nate, you'd be marching with them."

"*Pshh*, I'm *so* over that phase," he said, waving one hand. "All that protesting gets exhausting you know. And besides, we both have busy summers coming up."

"Yeah, you might actually have to study for once," Marina said, smirking.

"Excuse me, I am very hardworking." He wobbled his head before admitting, "Just not when it comes to school."

"Well, I'm glad to see you taking your courses more seriously."

"I can't let you beat me to graduation. Gotta catch up."

"Look at you, making *plans*," Marina said, grinning.

He toasted. "You know I'd do anything for you."

"It's still nice to hear you say it."

"Love makes fools of us all."

"The best kind of fools."

Marina was looking up at him through her eyelashes, and Nate decided he'd never seen anything so utterly magnificent in his entire life. He could devote the rest of his days to making her smile like that and consider his time well spent.

"And who knows," he went on, sipping his cocktail, "maybe Alvaro and I can bond about something other than politics."

"But Nate," Marina said in mock-surprise. "What else is there to talk about?"

Acknowledgements

This novel owes a huge debt to the inimitable Rain Dove. Rain's insightful work as a sensitivity reader was critical to Nate's storyline, helping me understand the nuances of the queer community and activist lifestyle. Beyond editing help, Rain has also gone on to do far more for this book than I ever expected, becoming an advocate for Nate and Marina's story and connecting me to lovely audiobook narrators. Thank you Rain for making my best wishes for this book come true. We've come a long way from Vermont, but I'm glad art can still bring us together.

An enormous thank you to Fowler Brown for being an early reader and brainstorming partner for this novel. I don't think you ever expected me to bring something like *this* to our science fiction and fantasy writing group, but you gamely gave *The Stars and Stripes* the same clever treatment you've given all my books. For that—and so much else—I'm grateful. I look forward to the next wacky thing one of us brings in to brainstorm.

Thanks to Christine and Sam, who read versions of this story and helped shape it for the better. Thank you Jenn, for being a hawk-eyed proofreader, insightful editor, and great friend. Thank you Moe, for the shared publishing gripes, emotional support, and entertaining distractions. I don't know what I'd do without our Slack channel!

My heartfelt gratitude to the New York Pitch Conference for teaching me everything I know about publishing (and for being full of awesome people). Without Michael, Paula, and Susan, I would no doubt be years behind where I am now. Thank you all for everything, especially Michael, who is kind enough to let me keep coming back to bother him. I'm glad we're friends.

An infinite, bottomless thank you to my family, for being such an eccentric and opinionated group of humans that no one can ever hold an unchallenged view for long. You taught me to debate, but also to sit back and listen and to never let the bad taste of a fight linger the next morning. There is no way for me to ever earn the incredible privilege of being born into the Woods clan (or stumbling into the Vascik family), but that doesn't mean I won't spend my whole life trying.

Finally, thank you Parker. You're my rock in the storm, the external embodiment of my sanity. Without you, I'm sure I would have long ago devolved into ripping out my hair and posting angry tirades. Thank you for inspiring me to be better, always. Thank you for making me into the person I want to be. And most importantly, thank you for being mine.

May we always have lots to talk about.

Thank you for reading!

I hope you enjoyed *The Stars and Stripes Between Us*.

If you'd like to support the author, please consider leaving a review or sharing the book with your friends.

For more information or news on future books, go to audreyrivero.com or follow the author on Instagram or Facebook @writeraudreyrivero.

Made in the USA
Middletown, DE
06 October 2020